S0-BDL-755

THE RISE AND FALL
of the
TREVOR WHITNEY
Gallery

Lauren Walden Rabb

This is a work of fiction. References to real people, events, establishments, organizations or locales are intended only to provide a sense of authenticity and are used fictitiously.

All rights reserved. No part of this book may be reproduced or transmitted in any form or by any means, electronic or mechanical, including photocopying, recording, or by an information storage and retrieval system without the written permission of the Author or her estate, except where permitted by law.

ISBN: 978-0-9905520-1-7

Copyright ©2014 Lauren Walden Rabb

Cover design: Donna Snyder – www.rsdesign.net

Layout: Julie Rustad – www.JulieOriginals.com

Cover image courtesy of artist Jesse Waugh.
The image is derived from a Martin Johnson Heade painting,
"Hummingbird and Passionflowers" ca.1865-75.
The original is in the collection of the Metropolitan Museum of Art.

Author photography: Bob Snyder

Also by Lauren Walden Rabb:

- Interview with Mrs. Berlinski

- Walking Through Time

This book is dedicated to

Hollis, Carl, Jody, Elizabeth and Kim,

for living it with me.

ONE

"You don't **know** what happened to Trevor Whitney?"

My host, Lewis Trenton, was astounded at my ignorance, and I felt very young indeed.

"No, Sir, I'm afraid I don't."

"Bernie! Bernie! Come in here. Our guest doesn't know what happened to Trevor Whitney."

From the kitchen of their elegant New York apartment, Lewis Trenton's longtime companion, Bernard Steuben, emerged with a tray of tea and scones. He gave me a conspiratorial smile as he set the tray down on the coffee table, turned to his partner and remarked, "Well, Lewis, here's your chance to tell the whole story — someone who actually doesn't know about the incomparable Trevor Whitney."

"Don't make fun, Bernie. If the boy's going to meet him he needs to know. Besides, it's a cautionary tale. No one should go into the art business today without knowing."

The year was nineteen ninety-five. Lewis and Bernard were friends of my mother, who had once been a promising artist in New York City before returning to Charleston, South Carolina to marry. She'd kept in touch with many of her New York friends, and when I came to the city for undergraduate studies in art history at NYU, Lewis and Bernard invited me over to chat about the art world.

I was there when they received a phone call from Trevor Whitney, who apparently was in town and wanted to stop by. When Lewis expressed delight at the opportunity for me to meet this famous art personage, I had to admit I'd never heard of him.

"But if you ever want to have your own gallery," Lewis said, "you must hear the story. Trevor was a Southerner, an outsider — like you. He came here with dreams of becoming one of the greatest art dealers of all time, and he succeeded beyond his wildest dreams. He had a few years of incredible fame and fortune, and then it was all over. Just like a shooting star — from beginning to end the whole thing took less than five years. 'The rise and fall of the Trevor Whitney Gallery.' It was tragic."

"Lewis never got over it," Bernard said, patting his partner affectionately on the shoulder.

"Oh, pooh. I did, too. Anyway, neither did you. That was the most fun we ever had."

"We were involved with the gallery from the beginning," Bernard explained.

"It was wonderful! If you only knew him."

"Well, hopefully he will, Lewis." Bernard looked at his watch. "He should be here in a few hours."

"You'll stay, won't you?" Lewis pleaded.

I nodded and took a scone. Bernard and Lewis continued to exclaim over Trevor Whitney's impending visit.

"What made him so successful?" I ventured to ask.

"Well, Trevor had the best eye of any dealer we've ever known," Bernard said.

"Oh, it was more than that! Trevor was the handsomest, most charming, most generous...."

"And here I thought you were in love with *me*...." Bernard teased.

"Oh, always, Bernie! But I want our young friend to understand. Trevor had something special. And then, of course, there was Charles, and Claire. And I suppose some credit must go to us."

They paused, apparently awash in memories. Then Bernard said, "Lewis, we've got this young man on the edge of his seat, and all we're doing is confusing him. Let's start at the beginning...."

TWO

Trevor Whitney had led a charmed life. Born in 1956 into the wealthy North Carolinian dynasty of Whitney Tobacco fame, he grew up in a town bearing his family name and spent his carefree youth in the woods and fields surrounding the vast plantation home that had belonged to his family for generations. A loving black nanny took care of him, his mother and sisters doted on him, and his father offered stern but sound advice in all details of his young life. Trevor was raised to believe he was king of the hill, and if he was a bit full of himself, no one could really blame him.

At fourteen he was sent up north to school. At Lawrenceville Prep in New Jersey the other boys did a good job of beating out most of his vanity and all of his Southern accent. He was accepted at Princeton, where he studied art history. He then entered Georgetown Law School because it was the sensible thing to do, but he continued to study art history on his own as well.

He became a favorite of the Washington D.C. museum guards, haunting the Corcoran, the National Gallery, and the National Museum of American Art with a law book under his arm. He was fond of the European masters, but even fonder of American art. He once spent an entire afternoon holed up in a little National Gallery anteroom, enthralled by Thomas Cole's *Voyage of Life*. He vetted possible dates by asking whether they were familiar with Frederic Edwin Church's *Niagara*, or had ever seen *Whistler's White Girl* at the Freer. Needless to say, he didn't date much.

Having no desire to actually practice law, after graduation in 1981 Trevor embarked on a tour of Europe. He spent a year visiting all the great museums, further developing his knowledge and eye. During that year he made an impression on many important people. One well-respected British art dealer reminisced about Trevor:

"Everyone fell in love with him. The men appreciated his knowledge and love for art; the women appreciated his pre-Raphaelite good looks. But no one could understand why this rich, handsome young man took up with no particular woman. Oh, to be sure, he was seen with women everywhere, but usually at their invitation. Of course, there were rumors that he was gay, but those of us who are keen knew that he was not. No, the truth about Trevor is as simple as it is astounding: he was just too busy studying art to be bothered with romance."

By the time he returned to the States, Trevor had decided what he would do with his life. He would open a private art gallery in New York City, specializing in American art created in the 19th through early 20th centuries.

This might seem odd after having spent a year in Europe. But in the early 1980s, the field of American art was relatively new. There were only a handful of prominent scholars, and the subject wasn't taught in many art history departments. For generations, art historians had dismissed American art as being derivative of its European counterparts. Yet Trevor's love for this under-plumbed area of art history grew out of his upbringing and personality. He loved 19th century paintings of New England and the vast western landscape because they struck a sympathetic chord with his memories of rural North Carolina. And his love for early 20th century paintings came from an understanding that these works articulated a unique American optimism, and a determination to create a beautiful world from a reality that often wasn't pretty at all. Trevor, himself, was a hopeless optimist.

And it didn't hurt that from a dealer's perspective, the field was exciting. Every day brought new discoveries of paintings and artists and the opportunity to unearth a previously unknown masterpiece.

Trevor's father — who long ago had realized that smoking was harmful and sold Whitney Tobacco to RJ Reynolds — gave to Trevor the son's share of the family fortune and told him "if he wished to be an art dealer he had better succeed at it, for no more family money would be wasted on such a ridiculous endeavor."

Trevor, with all the confidence of youth, answered, "My gallery will not only be successful, it will be one of the greatest art galleries ever."

And so, February of 1983 found Trevor Whitney in New York City with a good name, a vast fortune, a few important contacts, no works of art and no idea how to begin.

But, in the first of many serendipitous moments that made his gallery the small miracle that it was, Trevor was introduced to two people who could provide him with the secret to success: Lewis Trenton and Bernard Steuben.

They met at a cocktail party hosted by Raymond and Margaret Horowitz, art collectors who had a knack for bringing together people who could be of use to each other. They eagerly introduced Trevor to Lewis and Bernard, two longtime collectors and connoisseurs in the field of American art.

Sipping Chardonnay and munching on asparagus puffs, Lewis and Bernard drew Trevor into a corner of the room and listened to his life story. When he'd finished mapping out his dreams, they felt duty-bound to inform him that to break into the art world with any significance was impossible:

"It takes years to gain a reputation," said Bernard.

"No one who's anyone will have anything to do with you. Oh, I don't mean you, personally, I mean you as in someone whom nobody knows," added Lewis convolutedly.

"Of course, your name is good — people will think you're

connected to the Whitney Museum — but you just can't break into the New York art scene that easily," Bernard continued. "People have been doing business the same way for years."

"They don't like newcomers and they detest change," Lewis said.

"And the old guard will do anything to keep you out," Bernard added, but not without a sympathetic pat on Trevor's shoulder.

Trevor just kept looking expectantly at his new friends, and Lewis and Bernard looked helplessly back.

"Unless..." Lewis suddenly said. "Unless! Oh my, it's such a daring idea that it's actually giving me goose bumps." He held out his arm for his two listeners to see.

"You know, there is someone...." Lewis dropped his voice to a whisper. "Bernie, what do you think would happen if Charles Brightman were to agree to help this young man?"

Bernard's eyes grew large with the audacity of the idea, then narrowed again. "It's an intriguing idea, Lewis, but Mr. Whitney here — Trevor, if I may — could never coax Charles out of retirement. The man doesn't need the money, and I hear he's happy as a clam fishing all day off the dock behind his house."

"Who's Charles Brightman?" Trevor asked.

"But he can't be that happy, Bernie, he must miss some of the excitement," Lewis insisted, ignoring the question. "And imagine the possibilities if he would do it! Why, Trevor would have inside information on every name, every player, almost every painting that's ever been on the market. Charles could tell him what brand of scotch Alfred Cummings drinks; why the Seward sisters have never sold off a piece of their collection; which runners get the good paintings; how much any painting sold for ten or even thirty years ago. Don't you see, Bernie? It's his inside ticket to success!"

Bernard turned to Trevor with his first words of encouragement.

6

"It's a long shot...," he said.

"Oh, you must ask him!" Lewis said, then quickly looked around the room for eavesdroppers.

"Who is Charles Brightman?" Trevor repeated.

"Come." Bernard took Trevor's arm, and duplicating Lewis' suspicious glances around the room, told him, "Say goodbye to our hosts and let's retire to our apartment — it's only a few blocks away. If we're really going to do this, we must do it in private. In the art world, even the walls have ears. There's your first tip about the business, young man: trust no one. Even the walls have ears."

A few hours later, after Trevor had left Lewis and Bernard's apartment with his head full of amazing possibilities, Lewis turned to Bernard, poured his partner a glass of evening port and suddenly said: "Why did we do that, Bernie? We don't even know the young man. Perhaps he's an idiot. Or has no eye. Oh, he doesn't seem so, but nonetheless. Why, I might have just wasted the best idea I've ever had."

Bernard shook his head and chuckled. "It was just the idea, Lewis. Just the idea of shaking up the old guard, giving them something to sweat about. If Trevor Whitney can pull this off it will scare the hell out of them!"

Lewis laughed. "You're right. That's why we did it. For the sheer fun of it."

"To the fun of it!" Bernard concurred, and they drank to Trevor's success.

THREE

Charles Brightman sat on his dock, leaning back in his favorite rocker. His right hand casually flicked a brand-new fishing pole against the water in Long Island Sound, and his left hand caressed a large, floppy-eared yellow mongrel named Whistler. But Charles wasn't really paying attention to either activity. He was thinking.

Wasn't he happy in retirement? Why should he go back into that crazy world of art again? What could he possibly have left to gain from it?

Revenge. The word popped into his head unbidden. Immediately Charles laughed at himself. Revenge! That was too harsh a word. It was more... getting a bit of your own back. Showing them that you're powerful, that they had underestimated you.

Maybe he should do it for Sid....

Sid Steinman. Charles had gone to work at the Steinman Gallery when he was only fourteen — during the Depression — when Sid himself was only seventeen. The Steinman Gallery was already twenty years old then, and the very fact that it was still in business attested to its popularity, and to the business acumen of its owner — Sid's father Harry.

Harry Steinman had always sold fine American art, even during the decades when it seemed all the collectors wanted were European masters. Harry had studied painting at the Art Student's League, and through his teachers and former classmates became friendly with all the important American artists of the day. Naturally they came to him for representation when he opened his gallery, and it wasn't long before a few collectors started noticing that Steinman carried important works of art, for a lot less money than European paintings of the same period. During the 1920s, when money flowed like water, Harry built a number of great collections of American art that were the pride of families in New York and New England.

Harry was still alive when Charles came to work for the gallery in 1937, and had managed to keep the business afloat despite all the clients who had lost their shirts after the Great Crash. With admirable forethought, Harry bought back all the paintings he could from clients who desperately needed cash, making the gallery stock-rich and cash-poor for many years. But his reasoning was sound: he earned the kind of gratitude that gets passed down through generations. When prosperity returned after WWII, families remembered they owed their allegiance to the Steinman Gallery, and made their up-and-coming children buy back the families' paintings, and patronize no one else.

The ensuing years saw the Steinman Gallery become one of the country's foremost galleries for traditional American art. As Harry Steinman's most eager employee and Sid Steinman's friend, young Charles Brightman learned the business from the bottom up. He was encouraged to ask questions and was instructed to educate his eye. The Steinmans sent him to museums to study paintings, paid for a drawing and painting class so Charles would gain a feel for technique, and even taught Charles how to do the accounts. Officially, Charles' job description changed from errand boy to art handler to administrative assistant, but unofficially the Steinmans simply treated Charles like a protégé.

Other employees came and went, but Charles stayed. He really had nowhere else to go, but that never occurred to the Steinmans. When Charles married Mary Jones, Sid was his best man. When Sid finally married Gloria Putnam, Charles and Mary were the only guests at the ceremony who were not family.

Sid took over his father's business after the older man's death in 1950. Sid was as good a businessman as his father — with as good an eye — but he also had a special gift. He was one of the most brilliant salesmen the art world has ever seen.

Sid knew which clients he needed to kowtow to, which he needed to bully, which he would have to seduce. Rarely did Sid fail; if he couldn't generate a purchase on his first go around, he could cultivate a relationship for years to make someone a client. He was tenacious, he was patient, and he was smart. But he was always the first to admit that he owed a great part of his success to Charles.

Charles was the means to make it all happen.

Charles had the ability to be invisible to clients, so he overheard conversations that Sid couldn't. He knew, for example, when Sid needed tickets to a sold-out play to magically appear for a client. Or when a New York dowager thought she didn't have the space for one more painting (Sid fixed that by sending Charles to her home to rearrange the furniture). Charles was the silent partner who discovered a client's favorite drink, her favorite perfume, his favorite book.

Like a delicately balanced clock Sid and Charles worked in tandem to master that greatest of all business arts: schmoozing. Sid engaged in lively competition with the other American art dealers, and for years he was the undisputed schmoozing champ. Then, in 1978, Sid became ill and began to lose interest in the game.

For two years Charles kept up appearances. Working behind the scenes, making excuses for Sid's absences, Charles made deals happen completely without him. No one seemed to be any the wiser. Sid's panache outlived his own involvement; if it was the Steinman Gallery, then it was a painting worth buying. No one even questioned Charles' sudden increased presence. Obviously he was just the mouthpiece for Sid.

And then Sid was hospitalized, and the doctors said there was no hope. Charles came by daily with business news, but Sid was beyond caring about the gallery.

He was not, however, beyond caring about Charles.

11

One day, he interrupted Charles' conjectures about the authenticity of a Winslow Homer painting to remark, "You know, Charles, you don't need me. You could run the whole show on your own."

Charles couldn't help smiling. "I have to admit, it's been fun. I always wondered, myself, if I had what it takes to run the gallery. I've been glad to have this opportunity to find out, but I wish it were under different circumstances."

"It should be under different circumstances. By all rights, you should take over the gallery when I go."

Neither one said anything for a moment. They were both thinking about what was unsaid. Charles could never take over the gallery.

Charles was black.

In the early 1980s, the art world was still very conservative, and almost completely white. It was dominated by middle-aged white males who had inherited the businesses from their fathers. The few black art dealers in the field dealt almost exclusively in African-American art. No black dealer owned a major historical American art gallery in New York City.

Charles' foothold in this world had always been tenuous. As an errand boy in the 1930s, he had been considered cute — a little novelty to entertain the rich and patronizing. As an art handler in the 1940s and 50s, it was assumed that Steinman kept him on for physical labor. When Charles didn't go away, even into the 1960s and 1970s, clients chalked it up to the Steinmans' eccentricity. "Loyal, that's what the Steinmans are, and a bit sentimental." Most collectors would have been shocked to learn the extent to which Charles was trusted and respected.

And so, Sid had been unable to leave his gallery to the one person who deserved it, for the clients and contacts would have gone away and the gallery would have gone under. Instead he'd made out his Last

Will and Testament ordering the gallery sold, with a large part of the proceeds left to Charles.

So Charles had retired to City Island a wealthy man, able to spend his days in peace and quiet; able to chaff his wife Mary for continuing to work even though they didn't need the money; able to take long walks with his dog and sit for hours on the dock fishing; able, in fact, to be completely happy and completely, frustratingly, unfulfilled at the same time. Life was, he had to admit, boring.

And then had come the telephone call from a young man named Trevor Whitney.

At first Charles was disinclined even to meet him. What was the point? Why should he leave retirement just to help someone else build up another great gallery with his aid but not his credit?

But then Trevor said something irresistible: "A full partnership."

So Charles Brightman agreed to meet Trevor Whitney for lunch.

Four

Charles arrived first at the restaurant on Madison Avenue, and Trevor arrived only moments later, breathless and excited. He realized who Charles was immediately, and grasped his hand in a buoyant handshake.

The restaurant hostess gushed over Trevor as she led them to a table. Charles could see why. It wasn't just Trevor's classic good looks, but the way he moved. He exuded friendly enthusiasm, like an energetic puppy.

Once they were seated, Trevor plunged into his plan.

"Thank you for meeting me, Charles. I know it's crazy to think you would want to leave retirement, but like I said on the phone, I need someone to show me the ropes. And I'm willing to pay for it. I want you to be a full partner, but you wouldn't have to invest a cent. I have plenty of money — I need your expertise. Your *knowledge* would be your investment."

As Trevor went on about his vision for the gallery, Charles became more and more intrigued. But there was something missing in Trevor's analysis of their future.

"I have to admit it's a very attractive — and flattering — proposition you're making. But I need to be sure you've thought this through," Charles said.

"What do you mean? What have I missed?"

"Well, for example, have you thought about what it might mean to take me for a partner?"

Trevor smiled. "I've been thinking of nothing else! You know *everyone,* Charles. You can teach me a million things it would take years for me to learn."

"That's not what I mean."

"What else, then?"

Charles looked the younger man over, and chose his words

15

carefully. "I make a habit, Trevor, of never taking my suit jacket off in a restaurant. No matter how warm it is. Do you know why?"

Trevor looked at Charles in honest bewilderment.

"Because if I do, and I get up to pay the bill or go use the restroom, someone will undoubtedly address me as the waiter."

"Oh."

"You see, Trevor, Sid and I discussed my taking over the Steinman Gallery when he was dying, but we knew it couldn't work. The other dealers and clients were used to seeing a black man as his employee, but even though they'd known me for years, they never accepted that I had the same knowledge or business skills as Sid. No black person has ever been a partner in a traditional American art gallery in this city."

"Don't you think times are changing?" Trevor asked.

"I've lived here my whole life, and times have certainly changed. But not enough so that the color of my skin won't be an issue. I'm not saying that everyone you'll come in contact with is ignorant. I just want you to understand the facts. When you take a black man on as a partner in this business, you're not just getting his expertise. You're making a statement and breaking a long-held tradition. *That's* the part I want to make sure you've thought through."

Trevor contemplated this for a moment. "Do you think it will hurt business?" he asked.

"You need to be prepared for the fact that it might."

Trevor said firmly. "I wouldn't want to do business with anyone for whom your skin color would be a problem."

Charles laughed. "What if that turned out to be too many people to count?"

Trevor shook his head. "But Charles, this is different. You're coming in as a partner. Everyone knows I don't know anything. So they have to see that it's you who's teaching me."

"Granted, that's part of the appeal. There is definitely an opportunity to make some real progress here. The key is to be... subtle."

"Subtle how?" Trevor asked.

"We can't hit people over the head with it. Take the name on the door, for example. The gallery will have to be 'The Trevor Whitney Gallery,' not 'Whitney and Brightman.' If you throw my name out there you're forcing people to acknowledge something they may not be ready to."

Trevor considered this for a moment before asking, "What else?"

"The way we work with people. You'll have to be the front man. If everyone knows you consult with me before you make any major decisions, that lets them know I'm a partner. But if someone doesn't want to deal with me, they don't have to."

"I see." The more Trevor thought about it, the more he knew Charles was right. And he began to feel guilty about asking him to go back into a world that was so prejudiced. "What I don't get, Charles, even if I'm willing to concede that some of this stuff might be necessary in order for us to succeed, is why you might be willing to do it. Why should you?"

Charles smiled. "I miss the business. I miss the paintings, the thrill of the chase — all of it. But if I'm going to come out of retirement to build a new gallery, it's got to be a success. In a traditional market like American paintings, that means giving the public what they expect — great works of art, great service, exciting shows. No one's going to get rich in American paintings if they make it their battlefield in a personal race war.

"If we break too many molds, we'll make our clients uncomfortable. Uncomfortable clients won't buy from us." Charles leaned over and said conspiratorially, "And we're going to build the best damn gallery this city has ever seen.

"That will be my triumph, my boy," Charles summed up with a flourish. "Success is always the best revenge."

Trevor was unable to contain his excitement. "So you'll do it?"

"Maybe. I need to know something about you, first. Let's take a walk."

Charles signaled for the check and then led Trevor out of the restaurant. A light spring breeze greeted the men as they strolled up Madison Avenue past New York's finest galleries. Along the way, Charles asked his companion to comment on the paintings in gallery windows. Trevor discussed the individual merits of the American and European paintings they saw, sometimes presenting whole treatises on individual works of art. Charles was amazed at the breadth of Trevor's knowledge.

But he needed to know more about Trevor, so at Baedeker Fine Art he steered him into the gallery, and up to a William Merritt Chase landscape of the beach at Shinnecock.

Trevor didn't say anything for a moment. Then he asked Charles if he would mind if they talked back outside.

Once out of the gallery Trevor said nervously, "I hope the owner isn't a friend of yours, and I hope you don't think I'm crazy, but I think that Chase painting is a fake."

"Why?" Charles asked.

"It's too composed, for one thing. There's no sense of the ease and pleasure that Chase painted with at his summer home. The paint is applied too thickly — it doesn't have that slapdash quality. I even think the colors are slightly off, too pastel pale. It's hard to put a finger on it — it just doesn't seem right."

To Trevor's surprise, Charles slapped him on the back. "Well done! The first time I saw that painting Sid and I thought it couldn't be right. But just to be sure, we had the Chase expert come in and take a look

18

at it. He agreed with us — the painting was a fake. We returned the painting to the owners, and since not all dealers have good eyes — or good ethics — the painting keeps coming back on the market every few years."

"So this was a test?" Trevor asked good-naturedly.

"Yes. I had to know. No one succeeds in the art world without a good eye. You can't be wasting money on fakes. Or lawsuits. You only get a couple of mistakes in this business before people start distrusting everything you do. And once that happens, you might stay afloat, but you'll never be a big player."

"So that's it? You're in?"

"Yes, young man, I'm in."

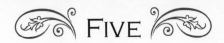

FIVE

"*...So Charles agreed to work with Trevor,*" Bernard said. "*But he didn't tell him that he had to convince Mary too. Of course, she gave in. I always wondered if she regretted it....*"

"*We can't worry about that, Bernie,*" Lewis said. "*I'm sure she saw how happy it made Charles. Anyway, no one can predict the future.*"

Mary came home the evening after Charles' meeting with Trevor to find her husband at his desk in the study, reviewing old files. She came around the back of his chair, kissed him and teased, "Are you suffering from nostalgia?"

Charles winced, and said, "Well, in a way. I met someone today who wants me to go back into the business, as his partner."

"Oh, no." Mary's face was all concern. "You said no, didn't you?"

"No." Charles put up a hand to stop the protest on the edge of Mary's lips. "Hear me out, honey. Let me tell you why.

"You know that retirement has been peaceful. But, truth is, it's also been a little bit boring. I miss the business.

"And with you still working, it's not like we have all this time to spend together. Mostly it's me and Whistler during the day. Whistler's a great companion, but...."

Mary laughed a little, and Charles gained confidence. He stood up and continued.

"Mary, this young man — Trevor Whitney is his name — is offering me something no one else in the world ever would. A full partnership, in exchange for my expertise. Do you know how good that makes me feel? All my life I've craved recognition in this field, and along comes a twenty-six year-old who wants to give it to me in spades. He doesn't care about anything except my knowledge."

"But does he know anything? He's so young — you'll have to do all the work."

Charles laughed at that. "Once you meet him you won't think so. The boy has more enthusiasm than a puppy with a new toy. He's also charming, extremely wealthy, and has a great eye. And he may not know much about the business yet, but he sure knows his way around American paintings."

"But Charles, is this what you really want? You're not just caught up in the flattery of it all?"

"No, Mary. This is what I really want."

Mary still didn't look convinced, so Charles asked her, "Why do *you* still work, Mary? You know we've got the money for you to quit."

"But you know the patients need me. And I'm just a few years short of retirement."

"And?" Charles prompted.

Mary sighed. "And I love nursing."

Charles smiled. "That's what I'm trying to say, Mary. I love the art world. I never wanted you to know how much I've missed it. But I do."

Mary gave him a rueful smile. "Then I guess you're as doomed as I am to keep at it."

Charles hugged her. "I don't think it's such a tragedy to be doomed to do something you love."

"I guess not. But Charles, promise me that if it's not all you expect it to be — if you're not truly happy — you'll quit again. And let's make a vow not to keep this up until we're too old to enjoy a real retirement. We deserve that. I want to have some golden years with you."

"You will, Mary. We're both healthy as horses! We've got many good years left together, I'm sure."

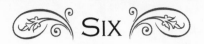

Six

"When Charles joined with Trevor, there were only two obstacles to opening the gallery," Bernard said. "They didn't have a building, or any paintings. Luckily, they had us, because Charles and Trevor had to acquire a gallery full of artworks in time for the opening. And that required a long road trip..."

When Charles asked, Lewis and Bernard were delighted to accept the challenge of finding and furnishing the perfect gallery space – especially with Trevor's generous budget.

"We'll have to find space on the Upper East Side, preferably in the sixties or seventies," Bernard told Trevor, "where the other major historical American art galleries are. Clients like to be able to see everything in town in one afternoon, especially if they've come in for the big sales at auction.

"But the chances of finding an empty gallery space are remote. We'll undoubtedly have to remodel whatever space we can find."

"Will that take long?" Trevor asked. "I'm hoping to open in September."

"Trevor, with your budget we can overcome mountains of red tape. Besides, Lewis and I know workmen who can be trusted to complete the job on schedule. That's one of the few advantages of having lived in this city our whole lives!"

Lewis and Bernard's involvement in the gallery had an unexpected benefit: people started talking. The art world was soon abuzz with the news that Lewis and Bernard were involved in a new gallery, and were helping their "dear friend" Trevor Whitney get started in the business. The New York art scene was soon dying to meet this Trevor Whitney. Much to Lewis and Bernard's glee, however, they could state in all honesty that meeting Trevor was out of the question because he was off acquiring paintings.

Many an art gallery owner spent sleepless nights wondering just where Trevor Whitney was getting his acquisitions. Meanwhile, other devotees of the art world began claiming to have "Trevor spottings" in which the new dealer was purportedly seen at any number of trendy New York events.

But all this growing excitement took place without Trevor's knowledge, because Charles had taken Trevor on a foray around the East Coast to introduce him to various collectors and contacts. Their task was formidable: they had to bring back enough good quality paintings to put the gallery on the map the day it opened.

Great paintings were not sitting around waiting to be plucked up by galleries. They were hidden in family attics, sitting in storage at country auction houses, or even hanging in full view on living room walls — in the possession of owners who had no intention of parting with them.

Their first big break came in Delaware, just two days into the quest.

They stopped at the home of Victor Whitehead, a gentleman who in the 1950s had amassed from Steinman Gallery an excellent collection of Hudson River School paintings. Although he had been unwilling to part with any of them in the ensuing years, Sid had always kept in touch with him, occasionally making offers to buy something back when he had a client looking for just the kind of Frederic Church or Albert Bierstadt landscape that Whitehead owned. Charles hoped that Victor Whitehead, now in his late eighties, might have finally reached a point in life when divesting of possessions was as satisfying as acquiring them had once been.

They parked the Volvo station wagon they had rented on a tree-lined street near the University of Delaware, and walked up a brick path to the front door of a large, colonial mansion. They rang the doorbell and waited. After a few moments a middle-aged woman came to the door. She was wearing blue jeans and a rolled-up denim shirt and was obviously frazzled. Her graying hair was flying out around her face from the ponytail meant to hold it neatly, and there were smudges of dirt on her arms and clothes. She took one look at the two men at her door and began smoothing down her hair and brushing dust off her pants.

Trevor exuded charm from every pore of his body. He was wearing his favorite outfit: a soft brown Italian suit, dark loafers and a silk shirt. He stood casually, rocking on his heels with his hands in his pockets. A section of brown hair that refused to stay back on his head fell impishly over his forehead. His eyes, sparkling blue, were smiling.

At his side, Charles looked serene and professional in a gray suit that complemented his complexion and his salt-and-pepper hair. A blue shirt, a dark blue bow tie. His soft gray mustache and a pair of glasses completed his air of scholarliness.

"Can I help you?" the woman at the door asked, blushing.

Trevor spoke first. "I'm Trevor Whitney, and this is Charles Brightman. We were wondering if Victor Whitehead was at home?"

"Oh. Oh dear, no. No, I'm afraid he isn't." She paused, as if uncertain how to continue. "Are you friends of his?" she asked, with every indication that she hoped they weren't.

"Well, no," Trevor admitted. "In fact, I've never met Mr. Whitehead. He knew Mr. Brightman, however. Charles worked for many years at the Steinman Gallery."

"Mr. Whitehead was always one of our favorite clients," Charles said.

"Oh! Well... what a coincidence! I was trying to get in touch with the Steinman Gallery, and then I found out that they'd closed! Please, come in."

They followed the woman into a large drawing room, and it

25

immediately became evident that packing and moving were taking place in the old Whitehead home. Some of the furniture was covered with white sheets. In the living room, boxes were filled with books from the now-empty bookshelves that flanked a large marble fireplace. Over that fireplace was a faded spot where a painting must have hung. Charles and Trevor exchanged a glance of alarm.

"Please sit down," the woman said, pulling a sheet off the couch and settling herself in the armchair across from it. "I'm Angela Whitehead Burns, Victor's daughter. I'm afraid that my father had a stroke a few months ago, and I'm in the midst of moving him to assisted living."

Trevor offered condolences, and Charles recalled what a vibrant man Victor Whitehead had been and expressed hopes for his speedy recovery. Angela Burns brightened at his words.

"Yes, my father has always been very strong. He's already made miraculous strides in his rehabilitation. But I'm afraid this big house is just too much for him, and he really can't come back here." She looked with sadness around the room. "I grew up in this house. It's hard to sell it, but it has to be done."

"Mrs. Burns," Trevor said, "you mentioned that you'd been trying to get in touch with the Steinman Gallery. May I ask why?"

"Yes! It's such an amazing coincidence. My father asked me the other day to pick out the paintings I wanted for my own home, and to sell or consign the rest to Steinman. I guess he was unaware that the gallery had gone out of business. When I discovered they were closed, I didn't know what to do." She looked at her guests apologetically. "Dad didn't trust many dealers. I knew I had to ask him to recommend another gallery, but I was putting it off. I didn't want to distress him, you see; it's hard enough for him to part with the paintings."

Trevor leaned forward and spoke earnestly to his hostess. "Mrs. Burns, I don't believe in coincidence. I believe in fate."

He let that sink in, then continued.

"I'm starting a new gallery in New York, and Charles is helping me meet collectors. That's why we stopped here today. But if you need someone to handle the paintings, I think I'm your man." He glanced toward Charles before continuing with a smile. "I can promise you that Charles will make sure I treat old Steinman Gallery paintings with all the love and tenderness they deserve. He understands how much the paintings meant to your father, and he'll help me make sure they go to equally appreciative homes."

"Absolutely, Mrs. Burns," Charles chimed in. "I wouldn't be here today with Mr. Whitney if I didn't have total faith in his integrity."

"Oh, this is wonderful!" exclaimed Victor Whitehead's daughter. "It's such a weight off my mind. Let me take you around and show you what's available."

The tour through the house demonstrated that Angela Whitehead Burns had inherited her father's good taste, for a number of the best paintings that Charles remembered were safely hanging on her own walls. Nevertheless, there were four beauties that Angela had decided just wouldn't work in her home: a romantic Thomas Cole landscape of the White Mountains from the 1830s; a large Sanford Gifford of a summer field with cows; a vertical Asher B. Durand woodscape with a hint of a rainbow visible through the trees; and a grand-sized view of the Wyoming River by Albert Bierstadt. "That one was Dad's favorite," Angela Burns noted of the Bierstadt, "but it won't fit anywhere in my house." Trevor could hardly contain his joy.

When the final numbers were hammered out, both parties felt they'd struck a very advantageous deal. Trevor arranged for a New York art handler to come pick up the paintings, and then they parted with great good will.

Once seated back in the Volvo, Trevor threw his arms around

Charles and kissed him on the cheek. "You're incredible!" he cried. "I can't believe you brought me here at just the right time. You're a genius!"

Charles laughed. "I'd love to take all the credit for our good fortune, but I think it was a combination of timing and your good looks. That woman was obviously smitten."

"Well, whatever..." Trevor said, dismissing the idea of his personal appeal. "All I know is that I wouldn't have been here if it weren't for you, and I am forever in your debt."

Charles chuckled, then decided Trevor needed a dose of reality. "Young man, I hope you're aware that we are unlikely to encounter another such bit of good fortune."

Yet, incredibly, their luck was far from exhausted.

SEVEN

"...*They went everywhere!*" *Lewis exclaimed. They went to New Hope and met the descendants of Daniel Garber and Edward Redfield. Do you know who they are? Pennsylvania Impressionists, beautiful landscapes. They didn't give Trevor any paintings, but a relative of Robert Spencer consigned that big painting of mill workers. Remember, Bernard?*"

"*I do. And they went to DC and met with Ted Cooper at Adams Davidson Gallery – that was an old Georgetown institution – and Hollis Taggart and Carl Jorgensen when their gallery was brand new. Hollis turned out to be a good friend later. And they had the most amazing luck in a Georgetown antique dealer's shop. They walked in just as the owner was unwrapping an Abbott Fuller Graves painting of a midsummer flower garden. Trevor bought it on the spot.*"

"*It was so lovely!*"

"*And he got that Childe Hassam Parisian street scene from the collector in Kalorama – what was his name? Charles told Trevor to offer him a price that ended all discussion of 'getting a few other dealers in to take a look.'*"

"*And then where did they go? Ah, yes. Shepherdstown, West Virginia to see William Glackens' son, Ira. Not an easy man to get along with, but he took a shine to Trevor and sold them a café scene. Then they swung up through Pittsburgh, where Trevor and Charles attended a fundraiser for the Carnegie Institute and hobnobbed with the city's collectors.*"

"*And that's where they met Waldo Picker!*" *Lewis said.*

"*Who's that?*" *I asked.*

Bernard answered. "*One of Charles' secret weapons. He's a runner – one of those people you hear stories about that dig around in people's attics. The art world depends on them. But Waldo has the touch – he's the one who finds all the great treasures.*"

The days were passing by, and Trevor and Charles had to be back in New York in a few weeks to oversee the final details of the gallery. They were gambling that their swing through New England, a part of the country well plumbed by the other dealers, would produce some miraculous results.

In Massachusetts, Charles took Trevor to meet the Vose brothers of Boston — owners of the oldest American art gallery in the country. Terry and Bill invited them to come along to a reception at the Museum of Fine Arts, where Trevor met Ted Stebbins, head of the American art department and an expert on the works of Martin Johnson Heade. Again Trevor's charm was in effect, for in Dr. Stebbins' entourage was a female collector who suddenly decided her Heade marsh scene was for sale. Soon that painting, too, was on its way to the Trevor Whitney Gallery.

While in Boston, Trevor acquired a small Maxfield Parrish painting illustrating a scene from the fairytale *Rapunzel*, a poetic Arthur Dow beach scene, and a pretty, Impressionist landscape of a Connecticut farm by Willard Metcalf.

During the trip back down through Connecticut, Trevor and Charles stopped at a small auction in Mystic. There Trevor bid on an early John Twachtman snow scene. But in the excitement of his first auction, he paid more money than he'd intended. Charles realized Trevor needed a lesson in the fine art of bidding at auction:

"You got off on the wrong foot and that forced you to go over your limit to get it. Next time make sure you jump into the bidding so that your bid will be the one to hit at your high mark."

Trevor nodded.

"And don't jump in so early — you got away with it this time because there weren't many dealers there in person. But at the New York auctions you won't want to tip your hand so early. Better to wait until others have dropped out of the fray before you see if you want to get in it. Remember, the less others know of your business, the better off you'll be."

Since this was not the first warning Trevor had received about the New York galleries, he asked, "Are they really that bad or are you just trying to scare me?"

"You'll find out soon enough," was all Charles would say.

There were only a few days left of their trip, and they still didn't have enough paintings. Charles was unconcerned; he assured Trevor he had saved one of the best stops for last.

Yet when they arrived at a small farm in upstate New York, Trevor couldn't imagine that the owners of such a modest place could actually have any paintings worth seeing. He was stunned when the manager of the farm brought them out to a large barn and invited them to look around while he went to find the owner. Inside the barn were stacks and stacks of paintings, all carefully wrapped and labeled.

"When you meet the owner, Josias Brimley," Charles instructed Trevor, "tread carefully. Don't accept any liquor he'll offer you — ask for water or lemonade instead. Don't accept a cigar; and when his wife Clara brings out her homemade ham biscuits, eat many and praise them to high heaven. Don't mention parties or women, no matter how encouraging Josias seems. If you can admire the religious artifacts he has, do that too."

Charles saw that Trevor was gaping at him, uncomprehending.

"You see, the Brimleys are Mormon, and most of the dealers have insulted them over the years by refusing to keep that in mind. Josias loves to trick unsuspecting dealers into confessing how ungodly they are. But for Josias, following the Lord's will is a sign of character, and Josias has yet to meet the dealer whose character is good enough to justify his selling any paintings."

"But where did they get all these?" Trevor asked, pointing in amazement toward the stacks of paintings.

"The Brimleys live modestly, but they've spent all their spare money on paintings — at auction. They love the Luminists and the American Impressionists. They see art as the evidence of God's grace flowing through the hands of the artist."

"You know so much about them. Did Sid ever work with them?"

Charles shook his head, and smiled wryly. "Sid had an ironical streak. Josias could always tell he was just humoring him. Josias has to believe in you if you're going to pull this off."

"Jeez, Charles, I'm not the right candidate for this. You seem a lot more godly than I do. *You* talk to him."

Charles considered this. "Will you go along with whatever I say?"

"Absolutely. Talk away; I won't contradict you."

Charles smiled. "Okay. But remember, just play along."

The door to the barn opened and Josias Brimley entered. He was a tall, lean man with a white beard and a brimmed hat. It was impossible to tell his age — he could have been an old-looking forty or a youngish eighty. His voice, however, was firm and strong, and so was the handshake he offered his two visitors. Charles introduced himself.

"I'm Charles Brightman, Mr. Brimley. I'm a dealer in New York City, and this young man is a friend of mine who just finished his degree in art history. We were over in the next county looking at some paintings, when I remembered hearing that you had a great collection of Luminists. Trevor, here, did his senior thesis on Francis Silva."

"Did you now?" Josias' face, which had been frowning since Charles mentioned he was a dealer, lit up at the name Francis Silva. "Do you know that I have the largest private collection of Silvas in the country?"

"No, Sir, I didn't. I mean, I knew that some good ones were in private collections, but I didn't know they were yours. I'd be honored if you'd show them to me." Trevor hoped he sounded like a person well acquainted with Silva's art, since in reality his senior thesis had been on the Connecticut Impressionists.

"Help me move these," Josias said in way of an answer. A large stack of paintings was lifted aside so they could reach some long horizontal works in the rear. "You go ahead and unwrap those four over there, and I'll get these two big ones."

When the paintings were unwrapped, Trevor and Charles found themselves looking at the six most poetic Luminist seascapes they had ever seen. In some the sun was rising or setting, casting a red or yellow stream of light across the sparkling water and quiet dunes. Boats either sailed in silent glory across the waters of the Hudson River, or lay half-broken and long deserted upon the sands of the New Jersey shore. The last and best of the paintings was a moonlight scene of Boston harbor that actually shimmered.

"These are stunning, Sir. Absolutely stunning," Trevor said.

"Thank you, Son. I've been buying and selling Silvas since Clara and I first got the art bug. I kept refining my collection until I was sure I had the best. I don't think there are any others out there better than these."

"He's so rare, Mr. Brimley," Charles noted. "You've had amazing luck getting all of these at auction."

Josias shot Charles a suspicious glance. "So you know that I don't work with dealers?"

"Yes, Sir."

"But you stopped here anyway."

"Well, I didn't want Trevor to miss the opportunity of seeing your collection, just because you've managed to torture all the other dealers before me."

Trevor actually gasped, but to his surprise Josias burst out laughing.

"Torture! That's a good one. My friend, it took nothing to 'torture' those other dealers — they jumped on the rack themselves before they'd been three minutes in my company." He chuckled again and shook his head. "Come on up to the house, boys — I like you. I'll get Clara to whip up some biscuits for us."

They walked up toward the white clapboard house. On the way, Charles paid attention to the fields and the livestock, complimenting his host on the condition of both. He stopped by the house garden to comment on the fat tomatoes and huge cucumbers, and he and Josias began a long discussion about the advantages of chicken manure as a fertilizer. Charles acted as if he had all the time in the world and didn't care if they never mentioned the paintings again.

Inside the house, Trevor sat politely on the sofa, afraid to move or speak, but Charles walked around the parlor, nodding at the few small paintings on the walls, but pausing to examine closely some religious statues and some religious tracts on the bookshelves. The items he was looking at seemed to satisfy him, for he mumbled "Fine, fine" under his breath, then deftly refused the drink Josias offered him, asking instead if "he and the young man could have some water." Clara brought out a tray full of biscuits and three glasses of apple cider, and Charles was quick to ask if she had made the cider herself. She had, and she was delighted to meet someone who understood the effort of pressing all those apples for just a few gallons of sweet, pure juice.

After their third helping of biscuits, Trevor declined a cigar from his host who, laughing, said he knew it was worthless to offer one to Charles. Josias then asked Trevor all sorts of questions about his life and his school, all of which Trevor — in a state of panic that he would say the wrong thing — answered very carefully and politely. He even remembered *not* to say that his family had been in the tobacco business for generations, instead substituting lumber when the subject came up.

Throughout Trevor's grilling, Charles sat quietly in the armchair next to his friend, his hands lightly tapping together in his lap while he quietly hummed just under his breath. When the grill ended the room was silent, except for Charles' humming. Suddenly Josias began singing along to Charles' tune: "And when the Lord shall reach me, I shall rise to meet the Lord. Then let the angels carry me up where I belong.' Goodness, I love that old hymn. Haven't heard it since I was a child."

"We still sing it every Sunday," Charles said.

"What church?" Josias asked.

"Methodist."

Josias nodded. "Methodists have always known a good hymn when they hear one."

There was a companionable silence between the two older men for a few moments more. Then Josias suddenly said, "Let's go look at the rest of my paintings. There might be a few I'd consider parting with for the right price."

When Charles and Trevor left the farm a few hours later, they had eight new paintings stacked in their Volvo: a small but jewel-like John Frederick Kensett of Newport beach, a powerful Winslow Homer watercolor of a Cullercoats woman waiting for her husband to return from the sea, two Martin Johnson Heade hummingbird paintings from the 1863 series, a charming William Merritt Chase portrait of a little girl in a white dress, a large Frank Weston Benson watercolor hunting scene, a small John LaFarge still life of flowers, and the pièce de résistance — a monumental scene of Gloucester harbor by the master Luminist, Fitz Hugh Lane.

EIGHT

During the drive back to New York City, Charles suddenly said, "You know, Trevor, now that we're nearing the end of our trip, I want to compliment you."

"On what?"

"On fairness. I like the fact that you didn't try to cheat anyone."

"Cheat anyone? Why would I do that? I mean, wouldn't it be bad for my reputation?"

"You'd think so. But it rarely turns out that way — even when dealers get caught. That's why so many of them do it."

Trevor was quiet for a moment, digesting this. "Give me an example — what would you consider cheating?"

"It's not definitive, but I'd say that if you know you're going to make more than double or triple your money off a private client, you've probably crossed the line. I know a dealer who rooked an old lady out of a John Singer Sargent portrait for $50,000; then turned around and sold it for $750,000. Of course when you're buying from auction or other dealers, that's different. You make as much as you can there."

"What happened to the dealer who ripped off that little old lady?"

"Nothing. *Caveat emptor* — it's a 'buyer beware' system. I don't even know if the original owner found out."

"Well, I'd never do that."

Charles smiled at Trevor's certainty. "I hope not. But greed can change people. I've seen it happen over and over again."

"Did Sid ever cheat anyone?"

"No, never. On the contrary, I once saw his father, Harry, send a family a check for $5,000 because he'd sold their painting for much more than he'd expected when he'd originally bought it from them. Harry believed strongly in karma — 'what goes around comes around' — so he always treated his clients with as much honesty and respect as he could. He passed that idea down to Sid and me."

"That's the kind of dealer I'm going to be," Trevor said without hesitation. "I'm in it for the long haul; I'm going to build relationships that will last."

Charles didn't bother telling Trevor that in the art world, ethics were challenged almost every day. Trevor would find that out soon enough, and Charles would see just what sort of moral fiber the young man was really made of.

When they got back to New York, Trevor dropped his luggage off with the doorman at his Fifth Avenue apartment building and rushed over to see the gallery. When he first arrived on the street and looked up at the building exterior it was just the way he'd pictured it, but he had not anticipated the powerful effect of seeing his name etched in large gold letters on the front window.

The building that Lewis and Bernard had rented for The Trevor Whitney Gallery was located on 70th Street between Madison and Park Avenue. A more prestigious location would have been hard to find. It was just down the street from two renowned American art galleries — Berry-Hill Galleries and Hirschl & Adler — and across the street from two more: Leo Maxwell Gallery and Kaufmann-Kramer.

The gallery occupied the first two floors of a four-and-a-half story gray stone townhouse. The half-story was a basement floor of the building that was half-above street level, and had a separate entrance. This floor was a psychiatrist's office. To enter the main building one walked up stone steps, elegantly flanked by curving stone banisters, and entered through a beveled glass door into a small entryway. From there one could take an elevator to the top two floors of the building, or enter straight ahead through another glass door into the "exhibition hall" of the gallery.

Charles and Trevor were given the grand tour by an excited Lewis.

"We went with mahogany on the first floor. I know it's a bit dark but it's very expensive — we wanted your gallery to ooze prosperity. Of course, it's also very nineteenth-century, and we did want to create an authentic salon feeling. The lights counteract all the darkness anyway. Just look at that ceiling! Original patterned tin. We had to paint it to keep the reflection down, but it's still gorgeous."

"I like the window seat in the front bay window," Trevor said.

"It's deep enough for a large painting stand," Lewis told him, "and it doubles as a place for clients to rest. Oh, and what do you think of this fabric?" Lewis pointed to the luxurious beige textured material that covered the walls. "Watch this." He pulled out a nail, tapped it into the wall and pulled it out again. "No marks!" he declared, "The fabric hides them."

"Won't we be using the brackets to hang?" Trevor asked, looking toward the ceiling.

"I hope so; they cost a fortune," Lewis answered, laughing. "But sometimes a painting won't sit right unless you pound it into the wall. And besides, this fabric protects from scuff marks too. You'd be amazed how often galleries with painted walls have to touch up the paint."

"The rug is beautiful," Charles said. The center of the floor was covered with an exotic Persian carpet in rich hues of beige, burgundy, and gold.

"Shh! We stole that at a Topper's sale. Bernie has a friend in the rug department there, and he spread a rumor for us that it wasn't authentic. The pedestal and matching benches came from Topper's too," Lewis said, gesturing toward a mahogany stand in the center of the room. It was large enough to hold catalogues, a guest book, and an enormous vase; nearby were accompanying benches upholstered in beige to match the walls.

"Where did you get the mahogany desk?" Charles asked, pointing toward the reception area at the back of the room. "I've never seen anything so massive."

"Oh, the desk and wing chairs came from Sotheby's. They were pricey, but they matched so beautifully we had to have them. We had the chairs re-upholstered to match the carpet. Now, are you ready to see your offices?"

Lewis led Trevor and Charles through an arched portal at the center of the back wall, into a hallway. On either side of the hallway were two large offices behind glass-and-mahogany doors. One said "Trevor," etched in gold, and the other "Charles."

"Oh, Lewis, thank you!" Trevor said, explaining to Charles, "I made him put your name on the door. I thought we could get away with it, and I wanted to do it for you."

Charles was visibly moved. "Thank you, Trevor. That was very thoughtful."

"Now look inside!" Lewis said impatiently. In each office was a delicately carved desk, beautifully appointed, surrounded by walls of elegant bookshelves. Each also contained an old-fashioned wooden painting stand, "so you can contemplate your acquisitions in private," Lewis explained.

At the back of the hallway was a huge service elevator for carting paintings of all sizes up and down between floors. Next to the elevator was a stairway leading upstairs.

The second floor contained a hallway leading past three doors (a kitchenette, a bathroom and another office) to the front of the building. There, another large gallery space had been arranged as a private viewing room.

This space was decorated to resemble a contemporary living room, with soft gray wallpaper and recessed lighting. There was an over-stuffed sofa in a floral pattern and two matching striped armchairs — the material being variations on the colors gray, green and pink. "Good neutral colors for complementing Impressionist paintings," Lewis explained.

A chrome-and-glass coffee table offered a place to rest catalogues and papers. There was room for only medium-sized paintings and works on paper on the walls, but the furniture ensemble faced three large painting stands for displaying larger works of art. Behind the stands was a thick gray curtain that hid the "stacks," or storage area, for undisplayed paintings. Trevor pulled back the curtain and was amazed at the amount of space.

"I wonder if we'll ever fill it," Trevor mused, and Charles assured him that they would.

"And here's my favorite acquisition," Lewis announced, pointing to the side wall. "I found this portable bar at a rummage sale in the Hamptons. Look, you can serve everything from brewed coffee to martinis! Perfect for entertaining those discriminating clients."

"Who occupies the upper stories of this building?" Charles asked.

Lewis shuddered. "Actuaries and accountants," he said. "But at least it's always deathly quiet up there."

Soon, Trevor and Charles were thrust into a frenzy of last minute preparations for the grand opening. Lewis and Bernard had hired one of the best caterers in the city, but final menu decisions had been left until the last minute. A florist had been engaged, but precise color arrangements had been put off until the paintings were in place so that the flowers would complement the art. A photographer was hired to take transparencies of the paintings. Trevor and Charles spent the days hanging works of art, setting lights, and typing labels and information sheets while the caterer, florist and photographer careened in and out

41

of the building, frantically trying to finish everything on time.

Finally the details fell into place, and The Trevor Whitney Gallery was ready for business. At six o'clock on the third Thursday evening of September 1983, the gallery was officially opened.

The exhibition hall looked fabulous. The paintings sparkled. Generous vases of flowers were placed around the gallery, and caterers in tuxedos stood ready with trays of peeled shrimp, Gruyere tarts and baby lamb chops. Trevor paced the floor nervously, but Charles, Lewis and Bernard composedly poured themselves glasses of champagne, and sneaked hors d'oeuvres off the caterers' trays when no one was looking.

The three had good reason to be complacent: everybody who was anybody was coming to the opening, and the paintings were spectacular. When hung together, the bounty from the road trip formed a collection of quality that even the most discerning eye would have to acknowledge. The gallery was a force to be reckoned with.

The crowds started flocking in at twenty minutes past six, and then never ceased. No one, it seemed, wanted to miss this chance to get a look at Trevor Whitney and his gallery.

Charles stood at Trevor's elbow and introduced him to the collectors, dealers and auction house representatives as they entered, which left no doubt in anyone's mind that Charles was a significant force behind Trevor Whitney's entry into the art world. Lewis and Bernard stood by, spreading their munificent presence on the company, occasionally whispering some tip about a collector into Trevor's ear. They were waiting for members of the press, so they could commandeer their attention and give them their "unbiased" opinion on the opening.

But despite the crowds, few guests had a kind word to say about Trevor's gallery.

"He's an upstart," said the dealer Sonny Kaufmann, one of Trevor's new neighbors. He sniffed at his glass of wine with disdain as he downed it. "He's nobody. I give him a year."

"Of course he won't last," said Leo Maxwell, another dealer from across the street. "If none of our clients deal with him…."

"You wouldn't happen to be jealous?" asked Ellen Finlay, from Sotheby's. "This is the most beautiful collection of paintings I've seen in one space in a long time."

"Oh yes, it's beautiful," said Mrs. Doris Ogilvy, a collector. "But the prices!"

"Do you think they're too high?"

"Well, of course they are," came the reply. "They must be! How else can the young man pay for these expensive renovations to the building?"

"Well, I'm only annoyed that none of these paintings came from our auction houses," said Arthur Woodman, who worked in Christie's American Paintings department. "Trevor Whitney should have made more of an effort to meet with us. With his money we could have found a way to put him together with some important collectors."

"He seems to have done fine by himself," Ellen noted. "He even got Josias Brimley to sell some things."

"You see, Sonny," Leo Maxwell whined, "Josias Brimley has already broken ranks and sold to him. He's never sold to a dealer before!"

"Calm down, Leo," Sonny said. "I have a tight rein on my clients. You just worry about your own clients and trust to time. Trevor Whitney is a flash in the pan. This is probably his proudest moment, right now. It's all downhill from here. Trust me."

"I certainly hope you are right, Sonny." Lavinia Worthington, another dealer, had walked over, and she spoke with venom. "I've never liked Trevor Whitney."

"Oh, did you know him before?" asked Ellen.

But Lavinia ignored the question and stalked off.

All in all, the guests walked around with strained smiles on their faces, speaking cattily under their breath but publicly making a great show of being nice to Trevor. As the evening wore on more and more people came, and though all those bodies jammed in the gallery made it unbearably hot, no one seemed inclined to leave. All the food and most of the liquor were consumed. The guests seemed to expect that if they just waited long enough, something exciting would happen.

At ten minutes to ten, Bernard took Trevor aside and whispered something in his ear. Trevor walked across the room and stood before the large Bierstadt landscape of the Wyoming River. Then, with a boyish flourish, he placed a red dot on the wall label.

"My first sale," he whispered to a pretty young blond standing next to the painting.

Turning to the crowd, he announced: "I want to thank you all for coming. I'm looking forward to working with you, and I hope this will be the beginning of many great friendships between us."

Trevor Whitney was handsome, young, very rich, charming; he had a good eye, great paintings, and he had even sold a work of art at his very first opening. Most dealers decided right on the spot to hate him.

It was time to leave. A few of the most sour dealers congregated on the street outside the gallery to angrily wonder among themselves who had spoiled the evening by buying a painting. Most of the other guests hailed cabs and took off for their respective homes — the men wondering how long Trevor would last, and the women wondering if Trevor had a girlfriend.

But back inside the gallery, Lewis clapped his hands with glee. "That was magnificent!" he cried.

"But they hate me," Trevor said. "I could see it in their eyes."

"That's why it's so wonderful!" Lewis said. "The more they hate you, the more they think you're a real player. If they had liked you more, it would have meant they felt sorry for you. The fact that they hate you means you've won their respect!"

Trevor turned to Charles. "How do you think it went?"

Charles laughed. "We couldn't get rid of them. That's a very good sign."

"What happens when they find out that the Bierstadt didn't really sell?" Trevor asked his friends.

Bernard beamed at Trevor. "They won't. Lewis and I are buying it and donating it to the Cleveland Museum. Lewis grew up in Cleveland."

"Oh, thank God!" Trevor exclaimed. Then he recovered himself. "I mean, thank you! You've already done so much for me. But I was wondering what I would do to hide a painting that big! I thought you were crazy when you suggested pretending it had sold."

"You needed a sale, Trevor," Charles said. "The first sale is the most important. It breaks a wall. You'll see — tomorrow you'll begin seeing collectors and dealers casually wandering in here, feeling you out for your best prices."

"Oh, yes. That Bierstadt move was a stroke of genius. Bernie was absolutely right to insist on it," Lewis said. "Besides, even if we hadn't bought the painting, it would have been an easy thing to get around. No one would ever have known."

Trevor wondered how in the world they would have prevented it, but he didn't ask.

Charles suddenly started laughing. "Now do you see, Trevor, that these folks are piranhas? They practically asked to be hoodwinked."

Trevor couldn't help laughing too, remembering a few comments he was surely not meant to overhear. "Is there *anyone* we can trust in New York?" he asked Charles.

"I'll make you a list tomorrow. Who you can trust, who is your friend as long as you're scratching their back, and who you should never, ever let up your guard with."

"Come now, Trevor, don't worry," Lewis said. "Give me a hug." Lewis gathered everyone to him and spread his arms around the group. "We were magnificent. We must take a moment to bask in the glory."

"We can't quite bask until we've read the papers," Bernard said in a muffled voice from under Lewis' arm.

"Don't ruin the mood, Bernie," Lewis said, waving his arms as if pulling good feelings toward the group. "Bask, bask."

NINE

The New York press reported that the opening had been an astounding success:

"The gallery space and paintings are of the highest quality," announced the *New York Post* in its gossip column, "and everyone who is anyone in the art world attended the opening."

The *New York Times* reported that "the night was crowned by the announcement of the sale of a magnificent Albert Bierstadt landscape, rumored to have been purchased for the Cleveland Museum."

New York magazine even wrote that "the other dealers will have to work hard to keep up with Mr. Whitney." Whether or not they believed this, the magazine printed it to antagonize the dealers who were resisting *New York's* advertising rates.

The highest praise came from *The New Yorker*, that bastion of taste, or snobbery, depending on your point of view. They covered the entire opening in their "Talk of the Town" section, writing with unabashed glee at the discomfort of the other dealers. "Most of the dealers were frowning," they reported, "although with smiles plastered on their faces. Trevor Whitney had done the unthinkable — he had impressed the old guard. We can only say, ain't art grand?"

The favorable press notices brought throngs of people to the gallery. Many of them were art lovers who couldn't afford the paintings, but as predicted by Charles, the big collectors began coming in right away too. Trevor and Charles refined their system of managing the clientele - Trevor dealt directly with most of the clients, but always under the express direction of Charles.

Serious collectors were ushered up to the second-floor gallery where they were treated to drinks and a private viewing of the paintings. Many of them had been openly disparaging at the opening, but suddenly didn't have the slightest compunction about doing business with Trevor. Occasionally, however, a collector would casually mention that he or she had a "relationship" with such-and-such gallery, and would appreciate it if Trevor would keep their purchase a secret.

By the end of the first week it was obvious that Trevor and Charles needed more help to run the business. Trevor was up until midnight every evening sending information to potential clients and compiling a mailing list; and every day it was a struggle to decide in what order each visitor should be handled. There were times when so many potentially important contacts were in the gallery at the same time that Trevor and Charles couldn't greet them all. Luckily, Lewis and Bernard hung around during those first days of business, and soothed a lot of egos.

Finally Charles called a temp agency. "Send us anyone," he said, "anyone with a pretty face, a sweet personality and some brains. We'll teach her the business."

The sexist nature of this request went unremarked by the temp agency. Galleries were notorious for hiring only attractive women as assistants.

Thus began a steady stream of young women who tried to be The Trevor Whitney Gallery receptionist. Their only job requirement was to be pleasant to the visitors, answer all questions they could and refer the other questions to one of the two owners.

It proved to be amazingly difficult to find a person who could handle this without making some faux pas.

One young woman seemed to recognize every rich individual who entered the gallery and gushed about how thrilling it was to meet them. Another, through a misplaced sense of loyalty, took great umbrage if anyone said anything the slightest bit unflattering about the gallery. Still another young lady developed such an intense crush on Trevor that she spent her days doodling hearts with their initials twined together, to the neglect of her other duties.

Trevor and Charles began to despair of ever getting any capable help. Maybe we've approached it wrong," Trevor said. "Temp agencies just don't have the right type of person. We need someone with art gallery experience."

"I guess we'll have to advertise," Charles said. "I'll put an ad in the paper."

But putting an ad in the paper turned out to be complicated. One could say to a temp agency that one required good looks and a female body to sit at the reception desk, but since that was blatantly illegal one couldn't put that in a newspaper ad. Charles knew a bit too much about discrimination to turn employees away for that reason, so he procrastinated, and for a few months young women came, worked for a while, committed some unforgivable act of indiscretion, and were sent away again.

Meanwhile, the gallery prospered. Sales were steady enough that the main problem was how to keep restocking paintings.

Charles made a suggestion. "Let's contact a few of the galleries we like and offer to buy some paintings in shares. They should be eager to work with us while we have so much business coming through the door."

"How does that work?" Trevor asked.

"It's common practice. We buy a painting with one or two other dealers. We spread our wealth and our risk further that way."

So Trevor talked with the few dealers that Charles liked, and soon the gallery had acquired eight new paintings for the cost of four.

A steady stream of runners visited the gallery as well. Not all dealers had the financial pockets of Trevor Whitney, so he became the first dealer approached by this underclass. But by far the most prosperous relationship was forged with Waldo Picker, the runner they had met in Pittsburgh.

Waldo traveled up and down the East Coast in a battered old Chevy station wagon, carting paintings he'd "found" in attics or purchased from small antique shops and estate sales. Like all runners, a lot of what he peddled was basically junk, but unlike many runners Waldo had a good eye, and he always knew just what he was hauling. His eye and his knowledge of painting condition enabled him to disregard coats of old varnish or dirt, and he sometimes turned up valuable paintings that other runners had passed over. Once he began doing business with Trevor, he was encouraged to take even more chances. He knew that if a painting was good, Trevor would definitely buy it.

One day in late November, Waldo surprised Charles and Trevor with an unplanned visit. "You won't believe what I've got in the car," he whispered to Trevor, although the only other visitors in the gallery at the time were three young people who appeared to be art students. "Where's Charles?"

"He's on the phone with the photographer. We keep running out of transparencies to give to people; the poor photographer has to come back every week. Why are you whispering?"

"Shh!" Waldo answered with alarm. "Get Charles as soon as he's off the phone and meet me at the car. I'm parked illegally."

Waldo always had to park illegally — that was status quo in New York City — so Trevor wondered why Waldo didn't just bring in whatever it was he had. But he dutifully got Charles and brought him outside to Waldo's station wagon.

Waldo began explaining. "I was afraid to take this out of the car. I don't want your neighbors to catch wind of it." He tossed his head with derision toward the Leo Maxwell and Kaufmann-Kramer galleries.

"Why? Do you think they're watching us?"

Waldo snorted. "My presence is usually duly noted, I'm sure."

"So what do you have?" Charles asked. He was cold and eager to return to the gallery.

"Just this, my boys." Waldo opened the back hatch of his station wagon and pulled a blanket off the top painting. Beneath it was a magnificent portrait — unmistakably by John Singer Sargent. It showed a beautiful young woman in a pink dress, charmingly playing with a string of pearls around her neck.

"Holy Toledo! Where did you get this?" Trevor gasped.

"I was at this estate sale in Springfield, Massachusetts. I didn't think they had much — just the usual junk — when all of a sudden they pull this painting out of a closet. Seems the grandmother of the house's owner was once some sort of Boston *grande dame* - had her portrait done by Sargent in the 1890s. I bought it before anyone had time to blink."

"How much?" Charles asked, rubbing his hands together for warmth but now not quite as eager to leave.

"To you, one hundred and twenty thou. I won't do better than that. Every gallery in the city would kill for this."

Trevor looked at Charles. He was still feeling his way around pricing. Charles nodded. "It's not worth negotiating. Waldo's right."

"Okay." Trevor said, turning back toward the gallery. "Bring it in and I'll write you a check."

Charles put his hand on Trevor's sleeve to stop him, and Waldo blurted out, "What are you, crazy?"

"What's wrong?" Trevor asked in bewilderment.

"You can't just walk into your gallery with this — you don't want anyone to even get a whiff of this one. This one's a real jewel!"

"I don't get it. Why not?"

"Why not? Jeez — this kid's such a novice! Tell him, Charles."

"The reason," Charles said carefully, not wanting to hurt Trevor's feelings, "is that if anyone knows about it, they can start disparaging it. Dealers hate to be outdone. So if someone else has a better painting, their best defense is say it's junk."

"But they could do that to any of our paintings," Trevor noted, still a bit confused.

"Yes, but if they don't know about *this* one, they can't. And this one is worth a fortune."

Trevor began to see how secrecy could be the wisest course. Charles had told him that Doris Ogilvy had been wanting a great Sargent portrait for years. He could imagine her response to one that had been off the market for almost a century ...unless she'd already been "warned off" the painting by one of their competitors.

"Okay. Good point. But how do we get it in the gallery?"

"We'll have to be clever," Waldo said. "What time do our friends across the street close up for the night?"

"Six o'clock," Trevor told him. "We're all on the same schedule."

"Okay. I'll come back around about 7:00. Leave a light on for me."

"Hold on," Charles said. "You're not going anywhere with our painting. Who knows who you'll run into?"

"Hey, I'll go visit my sister in Hackensack. Honest! I won't stop at any other galleries until this beauty is safely in your hands, I promise."

"I've got a better idea. What else do you have in your car?"

"Just some early American portraits, and a ship painting. Stuff you don't usually like."

"Let's see."

Waldo gingerly lifted the Sargent to show Trevor and Charles what was underneath. Charles did some quick measuring in his head.

"Looks like your two other portraits are just about the right size. I think we need to make a Sargent sandwich."

Waldo's face lit up. It was a simple solution: carry the Sargent into the gallery in between the two other paintings, and no spy would be the wiser. Then, when Waldo carried the extra paintings out again, it would just be assumed that he and Trevor couldn't agree on a price for them.

"Brilliant!" Waldo slapped Charles affectionately on the back. He added to Trevor with a flick of his thumb, "Told you you were lucky to fall in with this guy."

Things were going very well indeed for Trevor Whitney. And in early December, when Trevor made his first big decision about the gallery on his own, Charles discovered that Trevor had a good eye for more than just art.

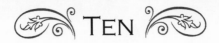

TEN

"...and then Claire came!" Lewis said.

"Don't get Lewis started on Claire," Bernard said. "We'll never get to the end of the story. Lewis can wax rhapsodic about her for hours."

"But she's important! If it wasn't for her... I mean, that's when things really took off for the gallery."

"Twenty thousand. Twenty thousand. I have twenty thousand. Do I see any more? Twenty thousand going once, twice... sold to the gentleman in the back. Your paddle, Sir? Number one forty-four."

"Claire? Aren't you supposed to be manning the catalogue desk?"

Claire MacKenzie was diverted from her concentration on the auction by a tap on the shoulder from her boss, Ellen Finlay. This was the third time in two months that Ellen had discovered Claire was missing from her post and had found the young woman in the sales room. Claire was not surprised to see the frown on the older woman's face.

"Sorry, Ellen. There was no one at the counter, and the sale was so intriguing, I just thought I'd slip away for a minute."

Ellen sighed. "What am I going to do with you, Claire? Have you talked to the people in American art recently? Do they expect to have any openings?"

"No. Oh, Ellen, I have to get into that department! I've been here two and a half years already! How long can they make me wait?"

"You know as well as I do that you can't transfer unless there's an opening. Even then you'd have to apply for the job; there's no guarantee they'd give you a chance."

Claire wrinkled her brow in annoyance. She knew more about American paintings than most of the people working upstairs. American art was her passion, her life! She'd been studying constantly ever since she'd graduated from Bryn Mawr.

It was Claire MacKenzie's great misfortune to have discovered her passion for American art at the end of her college career. Her business degree was almost complete before she took an art history course for diversion. How could she have known art history would change her life, and lead her to take a grossly underpaid job as a Sotheby's receptionist in the hope that she might somehow manage to get promoted to the American painting department?

Claire's boss was sympathetic but not very encouraging. She had seen too many young women come to Sotheby's with the same dream, and most of them left disappointed. An important American Paintings department like Sotheby's demanded credentials, and all the knowledge in the world paled beside a Master's degree in art history.

"You'd better get back to work," she told Claire. "And think about what I said before. You really should go back to school and get your degree if you want a promotion."

As Claire walked back to the catalogue desk she once again told herself there had to be a way to get what she wanted without a degree. Not that she wouldn't kill for the opportunity to get one, but graduate school cost money. And if there was one thing Claire and her family didn't have, it was money.

Claire was the fourth of eight children, the second eldest girl. She had grown up just outside Pittsburgh in a small town where her parents ran the local theater. Her mother was playwright, director, seamstress and actress; her father was set designer, box office manager and sometimes the musical accompanist. The kids had, throughout their youth, taken turns ushering, sewing costumes, manning the box office, and selling homemade refreshments during intermission. Only Stacey, the eldest, and Charles, the second son, had any real interest in acting, although all of them had found themselves upon the Silver Theater stage at one time or another. Every season the theater barely made ends meet, which meant the MacKenzie family was poor. Their father supplemented the family income with piano lessons and tunings, but every child reaching the age of sixteen had to work after school to bring in extra money.

Claire's theatrical upbringing was considered by many of her friends to have been the height of fun and adventure, and she knew that an outsider looking at her family might well consider them fodder for a musical play along the lines of "The Seven Little Foys." Claire loved her family, but she couldn't wait to move out. She had dreams of being rich and glamorous, and she knew those dreams were not going to come true in her little town outside of Pittsburgh.

Claire was the sophisticate in the family: the one who knew the difference between merlot and cabernet sauvignon, the one who made her own prom dress from a design she copied out of Paris *Vogue*, the only gourmet cook in the family, and the one who learned to speak French fluently because it improved her general diction. Claire pictured herself living in a Park Avenue penthouse one day, collecting art, attending opening night at the opera, and taking her terrier named "Tosca" out for walks in Central Park.

Claire's dream wasn't selfish. She planned to make enough money to put the rest of her family on sound financial footing as well.

Falling in love with art history had put a serious damper on her plans. Her business degree could have been funneled into a corporate job with plenty of upward mobility, but following her heart had landed her in a position where simply being one of the Sotheby's "chosen" was expected to make up for lack of pay.

"Sotheby's girls" were a group of beautiful young women — all poised, polished and elegant — who worked the jobs that had the most client interaction but required minimal brains: coat check, reception, the catalogue desk. No one was expected to actually make a living at these jobs — they were "centerpiece" positions that enabled eligible young women to meet eligible wealthy men. When Claire had first moved to New York she had been unaware of the job's limitations, but she vividly remembered that when she had questioned the amount of the salary at her interview, the personnel manager had replied with sincere surprise, "Don't you have a trust fund?" Claire had taken the job anyway, but she had to wait tables at night to make ends meet.

With these thoughts in mind, Claire returned to the catalogue desk. She didn't pay particular attention to the young man who accosted her for a catalogue until he began to fret.

"Did I miss much? What lot number are they on? I can't believe the cab driver didn't know where Sotheby's was; we drove around in circles for twenty minutes."

Sotheby's had moved to a new building at York Avenue and 72nd Street the year before, and a number of clients had complained that the taxi drivers in the city were oblivious to this fact.

"Don't worry, you've only missed about ten lots. I have the sales prices marked down in my own catalogue. Here, take it to mark the numbers in yours," Claire offered.

"Thanks. Where do I register to bid?"

"At that table right over there. The woman in the black suit will help you."

"Okay. Thanks. I'll return the catalogue as soon as I can."

"Sure; I'll come find you at the break." The big sales went from 10:15 a.m. until noon, then broke for lunch and recommenced at about 2:00.

As he walked away, Claire suddenly thought she'd seen him before. Then it hit her: he was Trevor Whitney! She'd been at his opening – standing near the Bierstadt when he placed the red dot.

Claire spent the next hour-and-a-half straining to hear what was going on in the sales room. As the first collectors began leaving for lunch, she went to find Trevor.

She found him sitting alone in the auction room, still looking intently at the catalogue despite the emptiness around him. She slipped into the seat next to him.

"You'd better go get some lunch if you intend to make it back for the afternoon sale," she said. "Every restaurant for blocks around will be a mob scene."

Trevor looked up from his catalogue and blinked at Claire, as if seeing her for the first time. "Do you work here? Oh, of course you work here; you're the one who gave me the catalogue. Can I ask you something?"

Claire smiled and shrugged. "Sure," she said. She couldn't help finding him a little amusing. Claire wasn't used to people not remembering her. Most men took one look at her and had trouble peeling their eyes away.

"I was wondering if you'd had a chance to examine this painting, lot number 190." He pointed to an open page in the catalogue. "It says 'artist unknown' but I think it might be the work of Jerome Thompson."

Claire didn't respond for a moment. Then she said, "You're Trevor Whitney, aren't you?"

"Do you know me?"

"You whispered in my ear when you sold the Bierstadt at your opening. My name is Claire MacKenzie."

Trevor shook her hand. "I do remember you! So what do you think about this painting?"

Claire paused, unsure whether to say anything. Catalogue girls were never supposed to offer their subjective opinions. But the impulse to show off and a general feeling of frustration with her job impelled her to lean over and say confidentially, "Oliver Clark also thinks it's by

59

Jerome Thompson, but he isn't saying anything because he wants Gerald Townsend to get it at a good price."

"You mean Professor Oliver Clark, from Cincinnati, the one who wrote that book, *Allegory in American Art*?

"Right. He was here the other day, and I overheard him telling someone at Townsend Galleries that the painting was a missing Thompson. Since he didn't bother mentioning it to anyone here, it was obvious he wanted to keep his discovery a secret."

Trevor chuckled and shook his head. "So Oliver Clark is in cahoots with Gerald Townsend. Charles told me a lot of the scholars were employed on the side by dealers." He looked down at the catalogue picture again. "Do you think the painting is by Thompson?"

Claire was flattered that he wanted her opinion. "I thought it might be when they first brought it in. But I don't work in the American Paintings department, so I didn't say anything."

"Hmm. I wonder how much Gerald Townsend will pay to get it?"

Claire lifted her eyebrows. "If you're planning to go head-to-head with Townsend Galleries, be prepared to go pretty high. They've been selling everything to Oscar Manning — you know, that big collector in California. He's building a huge collection and price is no object."

Trevor said, "I know. Charles told me."

"Who's Charles?"

"My partner. Charles Brightman. He used to work at Steinman Galleries."

Claire was impressed. "That was a great old gallery. Probably the greatest. I don't know if we'll ever see the likes of the Steinmans again. They were such gentlemen."

Trevor apparently noted Claire's appearance for the first time, for he said, "Weren't you just a baby when the Steinmans were in business?"

Claire tossed her head indignantly. "I'm twenty-four. And I can read, you know. I've tried to learn everything I can about American art history."

"Really? Does eavesdropping on scholars' conversations come under the heading of 'everything I can'?"

Claire laughed. "It was a public phone. And I can't help it if I was following Professor Clark around like a puppy dog, trying to get him to notice me so he'd give me a scholarship to his Master's program."

"So you want to go back to school, huh?"

Claire sighed. "Not really. I just want a job where I can use my knowledge. And it seems all those jobs require an advanced degree."

"Well, you seem pretty knowledgeable to me." Trevor looked thoughtfully at his new friend. "Listen, I know this is out-of-the-blue, and you don't know anything about me, but I don't suppose you'd be interested in a job at my gallery? We could really use someone, well, intelligent. We've been having an awful time finding employees who know what they're doing."

Claire's heart took a leap, but she told herself to tread carefully until she knew what Trevor Whitney was offering. "I don't know. What would I do there?"

"Everything. Charles and I are desperate for help. You can probably do whatever you want and we'll be grateful. You'll have to answer the phones and greet people at the door and all that, though. If that isn't too demeaning."

Claire smiled wryly. "You're talking to a girl who sells catalogues all day and waitresses at night. I don't think 'demeaning' is in my vocabulary. What can you pay me?"

"Probably not as much as you're making here," Trevor said, frowning.

Claire felt her heart sink, but then it occurred to her that Trevor Whitney might have no idea how much she was currently being paid. "Try me," she said.

Trevor quoted a number, and Claire broke out in an ear-to-ear grin.

61

"When do you want me to start?" she asked.

"Really? You don't mind leaving Sotheby's?"

"You really are new, aren't you? Let's get some lunch and discuss this in private. I know a take-out place around the corner that should have emptied out by now." She looked at her watch. "But we'd better hurry, we only have about forty minutes left."

Ellen Finlay was not happy when Claire returned from lunch and announced she was quitting her job, but when Claire explained that she intended to sit with Trevor during the rest of the auction, Ellen had no choice but to consider her an ex-employee.

Claire was a very valuable auction buddy. She knew most of the dealers and collectors by sight, so she was able to watch the room and keep track of who was bidding on which lots. She had inside information on many of the paintings — including their condition — that helped Trevor decide whether to bid. And she taught Trevor the nuances of the auction room, such as the fact that the biggest dealers liked to sit in the front row, so the rest of the room behind them could only guess when they were bidding or making deals among themselves. Claire also taught Trevor to watch out for syndicates — groups of dealers who bid up certain lots for their personal benefit — even though the practice was illegal.

Trevor did not bid on the Jerome Thompson. But by the time he returned to the gallery he was filled with admiration for Claire MacKenzie, and thrilled that he had managed to hire her. "She's going to be a great addition to the business, Charles. A great addition!" he boasted.

Charles had never seen Trevor express more than the most casual interest in any female, so he was curious to meet the woman who had actually inspired Trevor to such heights of praise. But he noted that Trevor talked entirely about her brains, and not once mentioned her appearance. So much so, that when Claire walked into the gallery for the first time Charles was truly astonished.

ELEVEN

"She's like Botticelli's Venus — all she needs is the half-shell!"

That was Lewis' reaction to Claire MacKenzie, and Charles could only agree. Trevor's description had given him no preparation for Claire's heart-shaped face, her soft blond hair that fell in cascading waves, her bright green eyes, and her infectious dimpled smile. At first glance she made many men think of the Goddess of Love.

"But she's so unpretentious," Bernard noted. "She's really very 'girl-next-door'."

That was the paradox of Claire: she was gorgeous, but quite unimpressed with her own looks; she wanted to be sophisticated, but was actually quite down-to-earth and approachable. Men regularly fell in love with her; Claire didn't notice. She was too busy wallowing in her beloved art history to be distracted by a romance. In that, of course, she was just like Trevor.

Claire instantly loved the gallery, and Trevor and Charles soon realized she was worth her weight in goldleaf. She was enthusiastic about the paintings and could talk intelligently about them. She was warm and gracious with the customers, and knew how to get even the stuffiest to relax and smile. Best of all, her years studying business had trained her to work efficiently and professionally. She took on all sorts of administrative tasks that had previously plagued Trevor, and freed his time for the more important work of finding and selling paintings. Trevor and Charles felt a bit like Henry Higgins and Colonel Pickering in "My Fair Lady" when they suddenly realized it was delightful to have Eliza Dolittle around.

But though Trevor appreciated Claire's talents, he seemed completely unaware of her beauty. Claire reacted to Trevor's good looks with the same apparent indifference. Charles found himself in the amusing position of working with two young people who were extraordinarily attractive, but seemed absolutely immune to each other's physical charms.

Nevertheless, people began to speculate on the nature of Claire and Trevor's relationship. Lewis fueled most of the rumors, for he quickly became convinced that the two were secretly in love.

"Isn't it delightful?" he said to Bernard after meeting Claire. "True love is blooming in our garden of art."

"What in the world are you talking about, Lewis?"

"Trevor and Claire! You know it's only a matter of time. He swept her away from the drudgery of Sotheby's and installed her as his princess in the gallery! She doesn't know it yet, but he's in love with her."

"Lewis, never let it be said that you don't have an active imagination."

"You'll see, Bernie. Just wait."

Claire quickly developed a special bond with Charles. She eagerly sought his advice on all aspects of the business, and Charles was the first to discover that despite Claire's polished appearance she struggled hard to make ends meet.

"That's a beautiful suit," he remarked to her one day. Claire was wearing a new lilac two-piece by Perry Ellis.

"Thank you. I'll tell you a secret," she said, smiling like a mischievous child. "I get all my clothes at a little consignment shop in the garment district. You can't believe how many rich people wear things once and then discard them."

Charles laughed. "Well, you have excellent taste. But I happen to know that we pay you enough to shop at Barneys or Saks. Are you one of those people who just loves a bargain?"

Claire explained that she sent some of her salary home. "My family needs the money, and I really have more than I need now. I'm used to being frugal. You see, there are eight of us kids. I want to make sure the younger ones get to college. Not all of them will qualify for a scholarship, like I did."

"Eight kids! I was an only child."

"How did you get started in the business, Charles? I've been meaning to ask you that."

"My mother was a singer at the Cotton Club in Harlem. She met Harry Steinman at the club, and talked him into taking me on. I was only fourteen at the time. I think she was afraid I would follow my father into show business. He was a musician, you see, and always on the road. She wanted to keep me in New York City."

"Hey, my parents are both in show business! They own a theater outside of Pittsburgh — the Silver Theater. I've spent my whole life around theater folks. There isn't any money in it, but my parents certainly are happy. I never wanted to follow them into it, though, myself." She grinned. "I'd be making a lot more money if I'd stuck with business. My plan was to be a millionaire by now."

Charles laughed. "Even on Trevor's salary you've got a long way to go before you're a millionaire."

"I know. It doesn't seem fair, does it? You follow your dreams and you end up starving. But at least I'm happy!"

"...*Remember the first time Claire handled a client on her own? We have to tell that story.*"

"*What happened?*" *I asked.*

"*Well, Charles and Trevor were nervous about leaving her alone in the gallery.*"

"*Charles was, really,*" *Bernard said, "but Charles was always protective of her.*"

Lewis continued. "Anyway, that's how they met Barney Digglewelder!

That was probably when they first fell in love – chasing Barney's painting. I mean, how could you not fall in love after an adventure like that?"

After Claire had been working a few months, Trevor and Charles went to Christie's to view some paintings in an upcoming mid-season sale, and Claire was left in charge.

"Don't let anyone into the building unless you know him," Charles said. "I'm going to call in exactly one hour to check on you."

So when the phone rang at that exact time, Claire expected it to be Charles, and decided to have some fun.

"Thank you for calling The Trevor Whitney Gallery," she said in her best answering machine voice. "No one can come to the phone right now. The employees are fighting off rapists and murderers."

"Oh dear. Oh dear me. I must have a wrong number." The man's voice on the other end of the line definitely wasn't Charles.

"Oh no! Don't hang up! You do have the right number. I'm dreadfully sorry! I thought you were someone else."

"Is this The Trevor Whitney Gallery?"

"Yes! Please forgive me. I was just playing a silly prank."

"My! You gave me quite a scare. I believed you. You know what they say about New York City."

Claire was truly ashamed of herself, but she couldn't help suppressing a giggle at the idea that anyone could have actually believed her!

"My name is Claire MacKenzie," she offered.

"My name is Digglewelder. Barney Digglewelder. I'm calling from the Eastern Shore."

"The eastern shore... of Long Island?" Claire asked.

"No, no. Maryland."

"Oh. What can I do for you, Mr. Digglewelder?" As soon as she said

66

the name out loud she realized it was hard to say without smiling.

"I have a painting. It's been in my great-aunt's house since I can remember, and she's just passed away. She left it to me."

"Oh, I'm sorry. About your great-aunt, I mean. I'm sure the painting's lovely."

"I wanted to find out if it was worth anything."

"We'd be happy to do an appraisal for you. But maybe I can spare you that expense." Claire knew from experience that most paintings that turned up in this way were worthless, except sentimentally. "Why don't you describe it?"

"It's a landscape. There's a field, and some trees. Some sheep, too. And a shepherd."

It was a description of any number of 19th century paintings.

"Is it signed?" Claire asked.

"I think so. It's hard to read. It looks like an 8, and then J-N-N-E-S-S. And then a date, 1875."

Claire wrote down what Mr. Digglewelder had said. "Is it an oil painting?" she asked.

"Yes."

"How large is it?"

"Oh, about two feet by one foot."

"On canvas or wood?"

She could hear her caller turning the painting over. "I think it's on wood," he said.

"Okay." Claire was carefully gathering facts. The more Mr. Digglewelder talked, the more it became possible that what he actually had was....

"Mr. Digglewelder, do you think that the 8 could be a G? And the J maybe be an I?"

"Maybe...." Mr. Digglewelder said with uncertainty.

"Because if it is," Claire continued, "then you may have inherited a George Inness!"

"A who?"

"A George Inness! He's an important 19-century American painter!"

"Is that good?"

"Yes, very. The painting may be worth quite a bit of money."

"Oh, dear. I was afraid of that." There was a sigh on the other end of the line. "What would I have to do with it, then?"

"Do? What do you mean?"

"Don't I have to give it to a museum or something?"

Claire was as confused as her caller. "I don't know. Why would you? Is it in the will?"

"What will?"

Claire was becoming exasperated. "The will that your great-aunt left that caused you to inherit the painting."

"I don't know. I don't think it said that in the will."

"Then why would you have to give the painting to a museum?"

"I thought I had to. I thought everyone had to if they had important art. To avoid taxes or something."

It seemed Mr. Digglewelder, whoever he was, was a man of many preconceptions. Claire told herself it would be a kindness to offer to help him.

"Mr. Digglewelder, would you like to send the painting to me? Then we can look at it and let you know if it's really an Inness. If it is, we can tell you what it's worth. There's no charge unless you need a written appraisal, then it's a flat fee of seventy-five dollars. That way you'll know for sure what you have. And then you can decide whether to keep it, or sell it, or donate it."

"Oh, no. I couldn't do that."

"Which part couldn't you do?"

"Send it to you! I wouldn't know how to send it."

"There must be someone in your area who could crate the painting for you."

"No. I have a better idea. I'll take it on the train! Oh, but I've never been in New York City. Is it safe?"

"Perfectly. I could even meet you at the train."

"Could you meet me at the train stop in Wilmington? I have cousins in Delaware. They'd probably put me up for the night."

Claire was taken aback. "I don't know..." she began.

"Oh please!" Mr. Digglewelder said. "Don't make me go to New York!"

Claire thought it was crazy to go to so much trouble for this man, but if it really was an Inness....

"Well, all right. Let me have your phone number. I'll call you back in a little while and let you know what day I can do it."

"Oh, how lovely of you! Next Wednesday would be good for me."

"All right. I'll see about next Wednesday."

"Good. Thank you. Now I won't have to call all these other galleries on my list. Good-bye!"

Claire hung up the phone. Other galleries on his list! What did that mean? Had he been planning to peddle the painting to every gallery in New York?

The phone rang again and Claire grabbed it.

"Claire, I'm sorry. I couldn't get to a phone. Everything all right?" It was Charles.

"You won't believe the conversation I just had!" Claire filled Charles in on the details. "What do you think? Should we pursue it?"

Charles was laughing. "He sounds like a nutcase," he said.

"I know, but maybe it really is an Inness. And if we don't go, maybe he'll call the other galleries!"

"And maybe he's a great con artist. The whole thing sounds fishy."

"Oh, please Charles. Talk it over with Trevor. I really want to go!"

"Here, tell him yourself." Charles handed the phone to Trevor.

"What's this about an Inness?" Trevor asked as soon as he had the receiver.

Claire told the story again. "Don't you think it's worth at least seeing the painting?" Claire asked.

"Why not? Worst that can happen is you'll drive to Delaware for no reason." There was a voice in the background, and Claire knew that Charles was protesting.

"Wait, Claire, Charles doesn't think you should go by yourself. It might not be safe."

"He sounded completely harmless. I'm sure I can handle him!"

"No, I think Charles is right. One of us should go with you. I'll tell you what. I'll drive you down to make sure your Mister Digglewinder..."

"Digglewelder," Claire corrected.

"Right... is all right, and then I'll make myself scarce seeing some museum collections, and you can handle the whole thing. I'll pick you up when you're through, or you can take the train back if you'd like."

"Okay. Thanks, Trevor!"

Over the next few days Claire spent hours poring over LeRoy Ireland's catalogue raisonné of Inness' work, especially concentrating on the photographs of paintings from 1875. The more she read, the more excited she became. The subject matter, and size, were right for the date. So was the fact that the painting was on panel instead of canvas. And there were some wonderful paintings from the year that were listed as "location unknown." Claire began to feel certain that the trip to Delaware was worthwhile.

Neither Trevor nor Claire owned a car, so they rented one. Trevor splurged and picked out a Lincoln Continental on the basis that a three-hour drive required comfort. They arrived at the Wilmington train station about fifteen minutes before the train was due, and decided to walk down and meet Barney Digglewelder on the platform.

If there had been any doubt that they would be able to pick him out in the crowd, it was quickly dispelled when a small, round, late middle-aged man in a crumpled, ill-fitting suit exited the train and looked around with both alarm and discomfort. He was carrying a suitcase and a briefcase and struggling with both as if they were very heavy. Claire quickly walked up to relieve him of his burdens.

"Mr. Digglewelder? I'm Claire MacKenzie, and this is the owner of the gallery, Trevor Whitney. Here, let me carry that for you." She reached for the briefcase and Trevor took the suitcase while greetings were exchanged all around.

"Oh, thank you!" Mr. Digglewelder said with relief. "There was so much to carry on the train, and I was afraid the whole time that someone would steal the painting."

The three began to walk out of the station toward the car. "I'm sure no one would suspect that you had a painting in your suitcase," Claire remarked as they strolled along. "Thieves don't usually take paintings anyway. They rarely know if they're valuable."

Barney Digglewelder stopped dead and looked around him in confusion.

"What's wrong?" Trevor asked.

"Who has the painting?" Mr. Digglewelder said.

"What do you mean?" Claire asked. "Isn't it in your suitcase?"

"No. I wrapped it up. I put it on the rack over my seat. Oh, dear, I must have left it on the train!"

Claire and Trevor stared at him. "You what?!"

"Oh, my god!" Claire exclaimed. "What do we do?"

"Don't panic," Trevor said. "We've got the car. We'll race the train

71

to Philadelphia."

"Race the train! Trevor, are you crazy? We'll never make it."

"We will too. Stop talking and get in the car. Hurry!"

They pulled Mr. Digglewelder into the back seat of the Lincoln, and within seconds Trevor had peeled out of the parking space and was gunning down the highway like a professional race car driver.

Claire gripped the armrest and prayed that Trevor wouldn't kill them, while Mr. Digglewelder rolled about in the back seat and tried to utter protestations. "Don't you... I don't think... Really, is this necess..." and finally, "Help!" escaped from his lips, but Claire and Trevor ignored him. If there was an Inness on that train, they had to retrieve it before someone else decided to pick it up as unclaimed freight.

Claire thought the odds of catching the train were against them, but she began hurling questions at their guest just in case. "Where, exactly, were you sitting on the train, Mr. Digglewelder?"

"I don't know. I don't remember. Wait, I got up to go to the snack car. I walked back through two cars to get there."

"Good. Now, which side of the train were you sitting on?"

"Going which way?"

"Going the way the train was going of course!"

"Oh. On the right. I had a window seat. We passed through some lovely towns...."

"And you said the painting was wrapped. What did you wrap it in?"

"Newspaper. Yesterday's. You can check the date." He said this as if he quite expected other newspaper-wrapped packages to be prevalent on the train. Claire threw an exasperated glance toward Trevor.

"Don't worry," Trevor stated with utmost assurance. "We'll find the painting."

After only fifteen minutes and the miracle of not getting pulled over for speeding, Trevor left the highway and pushed his way through the city streets. He finally came to a screeching halt in an illegal parking spot in front of the 30th Street Station in Philadelphia. Trevor and Claire jumped out of the car. "Wait here!" they shouted in unison to Mr. Digglewelder, and they took off at a run toward the station door.

There were a dozen trains listed on the huge schedule board, all arriving at different times from different locations. Claire was the first to get a grip on the information. "I think it's platform 3B!" She grabbed Trevor's arm and pulled him toward an escalator, where a line of people were casually making their way downstairs, displaying tickets to an agent before they descended.

"Excuse us. Sorry," Trevor kept repeating as they pushed past passengers. They reached the front of the line and the agent blocked their way.

"These people are in just as much of a hurry as you are...." she began to scold.

"I'm so sorry," Trevor said. He paused to assess the agent — a slightly plump, 30-ish female who looked worn and tired — and then flashed his most endearing smile. "You must think we're so rude, but it's only because our client has left a valuable package on the train, and if we don't get there before everyone else, it may disappear."

"Oh," the agent replied, staring into Trevor's blue eyes.

"Trevor," Claire whispered, poking him in the back to get him to keep moving.

"I'm afraid we really must hurry," Trevor said, and the agent moved aside demurely and let them through.

They got to the platform just as the train was arriving. Claire counted forward from the snack car and leaped onto the steps of the second car as it slowed to a stop. A conductor was moving out to assist the passengers. "Emergency!" she cried in response to his astonished expression, and she dashed into the railway car. A number of passengers looked up in surprise as she ran down the aisle toward the middle seats. There, completely undisturbed, was a newspaper-wrapped package in the rack on the right side. "Got it!" she yelled to Trevor, who was just entering the train.

"Great, let's go!"

The two of them climbed down from the train — and smack into a uniformed guard.

"Whoa! Hold on there. Just what do you two think you're doing?"

Claire, taking her cue from Trevor's earlier conduct, batted her eyelids. "Oh, sir, we were *so* panicked. Our client left this package on the train and he was distraught. We simply had to retrieve it for him!" She lowered her voice to a conspiratorial whisper. "He's Barney Digglewelder," she said, as if the name were famous. "You know how important clients can be sometimes difficult. I was afraid he'd fire our firm!"

The guard, who really had no idea what she was talking about, said "Barney Digglewelder, eh? Okay. But next time try not to disrupt the station. I've got complaints coming out of my ears about you two cutting in line and pushing people out of the way."

"We're so sorry, sir, really we are," Claire said.

"Yes, we are," Trevor joined in. "It will never happen again." This he could certainly say with complete confidence.

"Well, okay then. Have a nice day and try to stay out of trouble!" The guard smiled at Claire.

"Let's see what we've got." Trevor took the package out of Claire's hands and began taking off the newspaper.

"Do you think we should?" Claire asked. "I mean, should we wait for Mr. Digglewelder?"

"I didn't drive like a maniac and practically get us arrested just to hear Mr. Digglewelder babble for a half hour before he lets us unwrap the painting. Come on, over here." They had emerged into the upper waiting room, and Trevor found a corner bench that was unoccupied. He suddenly handed the painting back to Claire. "You do the honors," he told her. "I said you could handle it, remember?"

Claire smiled and removed the final piece of newspaper from the painting. Both Trevor and Claire gasped.

"God, it's beautiful!" Claire exclaimed.

"To think it was just sitting on the train, where anyone could have picked it up."

It was indeed a George Inness, and a spectacular one at that. The image was of a shepherd herding his flock through an Italian meadow toward a farmhouse half-hidden in a copse of trees. But there was a dreamy stillness over the landscape and a quality of light that elevated the work with a spiritual feeling.

"It's so Swedenborgian!" Claire proclaimed. Inness had become a devout follower of the mystic Swedenborg during the 1860s, and the best of his subsequent work reflected Swedenborg's special veneration for nature.

"Do you remember this one from Ireland's catalogue?" Trevor asked.

"I think so. Oh, darn, I should have brought the book."

"That's okay, I'm sure it's right. There's no question this is an Inness. Now, how should we handle our Mr. Digglewelder?"

"Well, obviously we'll have to tell him what he's got," Claire said. "And hope for the best, I guess."

"I don't like those odds. The man's so strange."

"But if we offer to buy it, I think we'll scare him off."

"I agree. Let's buy some time," Trevor suggested. "We'll say we think we should get a second opinion. Then after a few days we can announce that it's definitely an Inness. By then the painting will have been out of

75

his hands for a while, and he might be more comfortable letting it go."

They re-wrapped the painting and tucked it under Trevor's arm, then exited the station and found Mr. Digglewelder pacing nervously in front of the Lincoln. "My painting!" he cried when he saw them, then added, "What took you so long? I've been frantic!"

"It took a little longer than we expected to get through the crowd," Claire said. "But here it is. Safe and sound." She handed the painting to him.

"Thank you. Thank you so much." He paused and looked at his package critically. "A bit untidy, isn't' it? I thought I'd wrapped it more neatly than that."

Claire flushed. "I probably mussed it up when I grabbed it," she said.

"Well, no harm done." He turned to Trevor. "Oh, you have to move the car, Mr. Whitney, I had ever so much trouble convincing the policeman not to ticket you!"

"No problem. Hop in." The three climbed into the Lincoln and Trevor leisurely turned the sedan back toward Wilmington. "I assume you still want to go visit your cousins," Trevor said.

"Oh yes. Dear me, how worried they must be by now."

"So," Claire began, after they'd been driving for a few minutes, "would you like to show us the painting?"

"Now? While he's driving?"

"I promise I won't crash, Mr. Digglewelder," Trevor said.

"Well, I suppose it's all right. After all, you've been so kind." He unwrapped the Inness and turned it shyly toward Claire. "What do you think?" he asked.

"Can I hold it?" she inquired.

He passed it up to the front seat.

"It's nice...," she said with deliberate hesitation. "I can't tell more than that. What do you think, Trevor?"

Trevor glanced at the painting and stated, "It certainly looks like an Inness. But we'd need to get a second opinion. Ireland's catalogue dates back to 1965. It's always prudent to get another opinion with Inness."

"What catalogue?" Mr. Digglewelder asked.

"Well, there was this man, LeRoy Ireland, and in the 1960s he catalogued all the known paintings by Inness," Claire explained. "But naturally some have come to light since then, or some have been discredited. There are always discrepancies with important artists."

"Oh. Who could give you a second opinion?" Mr. Digglewelder asked.

"I could ask one of the curators at the Metropolitan Museum to take a look at it," Trevor told him, hoping that sounded impressive. "That is, if we had the painting in New York," he added.

Barney Digglewelder thought about it for a moment, then said, "By all means. Take the painting to New York. I thought it was lost for good, so a few days in New York won't do it any harm."

Claire and Trevor exchanged a smile.

The three co-adventurers were on the best of terms by the time they returned to Wilmington. Mr. Digglewelder spent most of the trip telling them stories about his great-aunt, whom he obviously missed. He was reluctant to talk about himself, but did reveal that he lived on a large farm he'd inherited from his father, and raised chickens. As he stepped out of the car at his cousins' home, Mr. Digglewelder said good-bye with the plea that from now on they would call him "Barney."

Claire and Trevor laughed all the way back to New York, and couldn't wait to tell Charles the story. When they finally reached the gallery they took turns telling about their escapade in spurts, each eager to imitate Barney Digglewelder and all his buffoonery. Charles listened appreciatively and then told them his own bit of news.

"Barney Digglewelder is ignorant like a fox," he announced. "I made a few phone calls today, and the man is one of the largest chicken producers in Maryland. He's a multi-millionaire!"

"He can't be!" Claire protested. "He's so innocent and absentminded!"

"I don't know," Charles suggested. "Perhaps he left that painting on the train just to see how badly you wanted it?"

After weeks of negotiation, Mr. Digglewelder finally agreed to sell the Inness for a sum that proved he was smarter than he seemed, but Trevor and Claire were just happy to have it.

TWELVE

Trevor stood in the middle of the gallery, noisily opening a large wooden crate with a crowbar and the claw end of a hammer. The crate had been nailed shut, so the gallery's brand new battery-powered reversible screwdriver was of no use. Trevor couldn't help ribbing Claire as he struggled to open the crate — it had been her idea to buy the electric screwdriver, just as it had been her idea to update their accounting system, and replace the typewriter with a word-processing writer. Lately she'd begun talking about getting a facsimile machine, but Trevor was convinced that would never catch on. It was 1984, and he still thought it was unnecessary to get things Federal Expressed overnight.

Claire was hovering around the crate in anticipation. Inside were four Winslow Homer watercolors — the centerpieces for a pristine little exhibition on Gloucester artists that was going to coincide with the spring auctions. Charles had magically pulled most of the paintings for the exhibition out of thin air. He had remembered great paintings that had been sold by Steinman over the years, and had painstakingly written to each owner asking if for old times' sake the paintings would be lent. Astonishingly, many of the owners had expressed a desire to have the paintings appraised for sale, so an exhibition that had been conceived mainly as a loan show to attract auction-goers was now looking as if it might generate a healthy profit.

Finally the crate was opened. Trevor and Claire pushed aside the straw packing material and gingerly lifted out the four Homers. One was of two little boys sitting on Ten Pound Island looking out to sea, two were of fishermen in boats along the Gloucester shore, and the fourth was a charmer of a little girl in a blue dress carrying berries in her pinafore along a seacoast hill.

"Oh, I just love this!" Claire exclaimed as she lifted up the final watercolor. "I could kill for it!"

Trevor laughed at her. Claire wouldn't even squish a fly.

Charles came out of his back office to survey the paintings. "Even better than I remembered," he declared. "What are we still waiting for?"

"The Theodore Wendel hasn't arrived yet, and I think Vose Galleries is sending down a Charles Woodbury on consignment," Trevor said.

"I'd like to start hanging," Charles said. "I'll leave a space for the Wendel, and if the Woodbury comes we'll fit it in."

There is an art to hanging paintings, and Charles was an expert. It is no easy task to take a number of works by different artists working in different styles and make them look cohesive. Years of experience had honed Charles' instincts and he rarely had to change his mind once he'd lined the paintings up on the floor. When he was done, it was Trevor and Claire's task to do the physical hanging. Trevor had wondered, at first, why they couldn't hire someone to help with the job. But Charles, with his Depression-era belief in the value of self-sufficiency, had told him, "Do it yourself for at least a year, Trevor. It's an important skill to learn."

"The florist called," Claire said as Charles left them. "They'll be here tomorrow by four. And the caterer called to say they'd tracked down enough of that wine from upstate that you like. The winery is delivering a case here by noon tomorrow."

Trevor wasn't worried about the flowers or the wine, but he appreciated the fact that Claire was on top of things.

"Oh, and one other thing," she added. "A gentleman named Oratius Monk is coming in later today. He claims he has a Prendergast watercolor."

"Oratius Monk?" Charles came flying back out from the rear hallway. "Did you say Oratius Monk?"

"Yes. Do you know him?"

Charles grimaced. "Last I heard he was in jail."

"Wow," Claire said. "There was something about him that seemed... funny. That's why I kept forgetting to tell you guys he had this Prendergast. I had a hunch it might not be right."

"Oh, it'll probably be right," Charles said. "But I wouldn't do business with him anyway."

"Why not?" Claire asked.

Charles continued. "See, Oratius was a legitimate dealer, but he liked to live the good life, and sales couldn't always keep up with his expenses. So he came up with a couple of schemes.

"One was to take a painting to sell on consignment, sell it, and then never tell the consignor. He lived off the money until the consignor threatened to sue if he didn't return the painting. So then he took a painting from another client to sell, sold it, paid the first consignor, and didn't tell the second client. You can see how this could go on for a long time."

"What finally tripped him up?" Trevor asked. "Did someone catch on?"

"I'll tell you. After a while one creditor at a time wasn't generating enough money for Oratius. So he added a layer to the scam. Every time he got a painting on consignment, he sold a share of it to another party."

"But he didn't own the painting in the first place. How could he make enough on the sale to satisfy everyone?" Claire asked.

"He couldn't, but for a time it worked. Let's say he took a painting on consignment at $60,000, planning to sell it for around $120,000. He immediately sells a half-share in the painting at, say, $25,000 — just to have some instant cash to spend. Then he sells the painting for $120,000 and tells the partner he sold it for $80,000. He gives the guy

$40,000 — not a bad return on $25,000 — and then tells the original owners he's got an offer on the painting, and asks them to take $50,000. He makes $55,000, *and* has the consignor's $50,000 to play with for as long as he can stretch out the deal.

"He apparently had ten or twelve of these deals going on at the same time, for years."

Claire said, "You'd need an iron-clad memory to keep all of that straight in your head! What finally happened?"

"He annoyed the wrong person. One of the consignors sued him before waiting the usual amount of time for Oratius to string him along. Once word of the suit got out, everyone else demanded their money or paintings immediately, and before he knew what hit him he was arrested, convicted and behind bars."

"You know," Claire noted, "that's awful, but maybe he's turned over a new leaf?"

Trevor added, "If he used to be legitimate, he might still have a few contacts around who will work with him. The Prendergast could be okay. How in the world will we know?"

"It won't be easy. The wisest course is just not to deal with him."

"You're right," Trevor said, then added, "But it couldn't hurt to look at it. I don't want to seem like I'm holding the past against the guy."

"Well, just be careful," Charles warned. "He's no sap who got in over his head. Oratius Monk is a professional con man."

If there was an expectation in Claire's mind about what a professional con man looked like, it was not the image of Oratius Monk. Oratius was a short man in his early forties with curly blond hair, bright blue eyes and a bloom in his cheeks as if he'd never had a care in the world. He bounced into the gallery — jauntily balancing the watercolor under his arm — dressed in khaki pants, loafers and an argyle L.L. Bean sweater. He looked as if he'd be more at home on the deck of a yacht than in jail. And he laughed easily — at himself, at his circumstances, and at the "ironies of life that had enabled him to re-enter the business he so loved." Claire, despite herself, was rather charmed.

So was Trevor. He examined the Prendergast – a 1901 beach scene with a hot air balloon – and quickly decided it was not fake. So that left Trevor in a dilemma. Should he trust the man, or not?

"We could take the painting on consignment," Trevor offered. That was the safest course. That way if it turned out to have uncertain ownership, the gallery could return it without losing money.

"I'd love to oblige you, Trevor my-boy, but you know how it is. Starting up again, and all. I need cash. Can't wait for my ship to come in this time. Gotta hit the floor running."

"I'll have to discuss this with Charles," Trevor said. Charles had discreetly stayed out of sight in the back office. He didn't particularly care to see Oratius Monk, and he had wanted Trevor to handle the situation himself.

But Trevor was so enamored of the painting that he really didn't have the heart to toss the man out of the gallery.

He brought the watercolor back to Charles, and they began an exchange in whispers.

"I don't know what to do, Charles," Trevor started. "Look at it! It's a beauty! I hate to let it go."

"I like to think I'm as forgiving as the next guy, Trevor, but I've seen these things over and over in this business. A leopard doesn't change his spots. You can't trust Oratius as far as you can throw him."

"But what if it's okay? We'd be crazy not to buy it! Look — it's even got an estate mark on the reverse. He says it comes right from the Prendergast family."

"He can say whatever he wants. We can't prove it. I just don't trust him."

"What if he got a letter from the family? Would that do it for you?"

Charles was getting exasperated. "Look, Trevor, I can't tell you what to do. You can make your own decision. But if it were my money, I'd do the safe thing. We don't *need* this painting, any more than we need a lawsuit down the road."

It was the word "lawsuit" that finally got to Trevor. It wasn't worth finding out the hard way that he was wrong.

Oratius took the news cheerfully. "No problem. Got to prove myself again. Have to build your trust. We'll do some business later." He was so gracious about the whole thing that Trevor and Claire felt a little ashamed.

But only for a short while. A few days later, a visitor to the "Gloucester Artists" show pulled Trevor aside to ask him a question.

"I'm with IFAR. I wonder if you happen to have seen any Prendergast watercolors lately?" The man handed Trevor his card.

"The International Foundation for Art Research?"

"Right. I'm investigating a piece of stolen art."

Trevor swallowed hard before admitting the truth. "Do you know Oratius Monk? He was in a few days ago. He had a Prendergast watercolor he was trying to sell. But we didn't buy it," he quickly added.

The visitor smiled. "Oratius Monk! Is he out of jail?" He shook his head, smirking. "Well, I guess you should know that Williamstown College in Massachusetts, which is compiling the catalogue raisonné of Prendergast's work, just reported that one of the watercolors from the estate seems to be missing. Can you describe the painting?"

A few days later the news was out that Oratius Monk had been arrested again, caught red-handed with the missing Prendergast. Trevor and Claire were chagrined, but Charles only smiled ruefully.

"So you two have met your first art crook," he said. "Don't worry — you'll be wiser next time. A few Oratius Monks pulled the wool over

84

my eyes when I first started in this business."

"...The Gloucester exhibition was a success, but Trevor was disappointed that the show wasn't reviewed in the papers," Lewis said.

"That's really not unusual – once you've had the kind of glowing reviews like we had at the opening, the press always seems unwilling to do anything else for you," Bernard said.

"But then Claire came up with the idea for Anna..."

"Wait a minute, Lewis, you can't skip over the American Pastoral exhibition. That's what led to the whole NYHADA thing..."

"Oh, yes, the whole NYHADA thing...," Lewis slapped himself on the forehead. "That's important later...."

THIRTEEN

The Trevor Whitney Gallery's first scholarly exhibition was held to coincide with the big American painting sales in December of 1984. Charles and Trevor agreed that in order to be recognized as a serious gallery they would have to mount museum quality exhibitions at least once a year. This meant not only having a well thought-out theme and excellent paintings, but also producing a scholarly catalogue. This turned out to be no problem for Trevor. His major talent, besides his great eye, was his ability to write beautifully and to develop new insights in the study of American art.

For this first exhibition they chose the theme "American Pastoral — 19th Century Artists and the New World." Trevor's theory, which he expounded on at length in an introductory essay, was that 19th century America was largely viewed by its inhabitants as the New Eden — a paradise on earth — and that the paintings of the era reflected that viewpoint.

Trevor drew together sources ranging from the writings on nature of Ralph Waldo Emerson and Henry Thoreau, to the religious sermons of Lyman Beecher, to the poetry of Walt Whitman and the psychological theories of William James. He challenged the tradition of viewing 19th century American art as a reflection of art movements that came before and concurrently out of Europe, and instead claimed that American art reflected ideas all its own.

Trevor's thesis was important, and he chose paintings that perfectly illustrated his point of view. The artists included Hudson River School masters such as Albert Bierstadt, Frederic Edwin Church, Thomas Cole, and George Inness. Most of the paintings were from the gallery's own collection — some carefully acquired during the months leading up to the exhibition with an eye to filling in deficiencies. A few were on loan from museums and collectors, and a few had been coaxed out of their owner's hands for sale at the last minute by Charles, whose memory of the whereabouts of almost fifty years of Steinman paintings once again proved crucial.

Recognition for the exhibition was slow at first. In the midst of sale-season frenzy every major gallery was mounting exhibitions to attract the buyers who flew in only twice a year for the auctions, and the competition to get noticed was fierce. But soon, those in the academic and museum worlds began to take notice; art lovers flew back to New York for another look at the exhibition. Word got out to the press and soon even the media couldn't ignore the buzz. The Trevor Whitney Gallery was treated to another round of great art reviews, generating even more crowds.

But Trevor's most important accomplishment was that with one essay he had proven he was not just a gallery owner, but a bona fide scholar.

It was then that the New York Historical Art Dealers Association decided to blackball him.

The NYHADA was an old organization that had always had a remarkably welcoming philosophy. This was perhaps because they actually *did* nothing. Oh, they occasionally released an opinion on a legal decision regarding art, or agreed to sponsor a school contest, but mainly they simply existed to provide a benign moniker for New York galleries to splash on their letterhead. For an annual fee of $100 any gallery that had been in business for one year could join, and as long as the dues continued to be paid membership was automatically renewed. In the rare event that a gallery needed to be thrown out — say because of fraud — a quorum of members could vote to do so. In the eighty-five years of its existence, the NYHADA had never once actually thrown out a gallery — possibly because a quorum of members had never managed to attend a meeting. And in its entire history the NYHADA had never refused membership to any new gallery.

Unfortunately for Trevor, in 1982 a change had occurred in the leadership of the NYHADA. Some of the more prominent galleries in the city had staged a take-over. They wanted the organization to become more exclusive, and to act as an arbiter of quality. In short, they wanted the phrase "member of the NYHADA" to mean something.

They also wanted the association to do something splashy and important. They had decided that in 1988, on the 75th anniversary of the famous New York Armory Show, the NYHADA would sponsor a members-only exhibition at the 67th Street Armory. Thus, the leadership's unannounced goal was to weed out before then any gallery whose contribution to this exhibition might be less than stellar.

A covert elimination had been taking place. Membership renewal bills had mysteriously been "lost in the mail" and not re-sent. Persistent, but unworthy, galleries had been quietly advised that new membership requirements had been passed by the organization, and that they would not continue to qualify unless they could meet these requirements. The "new requirements" were then custom-made to be out of that gallery's reach. With systematic cruelty, galleries that had been members of the NYHADA for years or even generations were deemed unacceptable and silently ousted. Since no gallery wanted to admit they'd been dropped, the victims did not publicly complain.

Leading the change was the NYHADA's new president, Lavinia Worthington. Lavinia was a dealer in American paintings who had scratched her way to acceptance in this traditionally male-dominated field with persistence, ruthlessness, and the help of a behind-the-scenes sugar daddy — the collector Alfred Cummings with whom she'd been adulterously sleeping for ten years. In gratitude for her favors Alfred Cummings made Worthington Gallery his exclusive supplier, which meant that any other dealer who wanted to sell art to him had to go

89

through Lavinia. This arrangement provided an exceptional living for Miss Worthington.

In the normal course of things, Trevor's gallery would have been just the kind of shop the NYHADA wanted in its membership. However, most of the new leadership hated Trevor. And none more so than Lavinia Worthington.

Lavinia's hatred had festered for three years, and dated back to a time before Trevor was even an art dealer. It stemmed from one of those occurrences that men often forget and women often remember — especially narcissistic women who feel they have been insulted.

It had happened at a private party on a yacht harbored off the Costa del Sol of Spain, during the time that Trevor had been training his eye at the great museums of Europe. The yacht's captain — an old Lawrenceville friend of Trevor — also happened to know Lavinia Worthington from his college days. He had invited both American travelers to the yacht, and knowing of Trevor's insatiable interest in art history he had introduced the two with the hope that they might hit it off.

Trevor, in his usual way, enjoyed talking art with Lavinia but never comprehended that he was supposed to find her irresistibly attractive. As soon as she tried to steer the conversation to more personal subjects, he became bored and wandered off to meet other people — leaving Lavinia feeling mortified.

Little did he know that this small example of gracelessness would come back to haunt him.

At the January 1985 meeting of the NYHADA, a dealer of European art named Charles Goulet made the suggestion that the group consider The Trevor Whitney Gallery for admission. As a few members began murmuring agreement, Sonny Kaufmann, of Kaufmann-Kramer Gallery, jumped up on a chair and demanded the floor.

"Are you all insane? I have enough of that man just being across the street from him. The last thing I need is his competition in the Armory show as well."

"The exhibition is getting very crowded," concurred Gerald Townsend. "Although unlike Sonny, I'm not afraid of a little competition." He paused to sneer at his colleague. "But I don't want the Armory to look like a garage sale. I don't think we should let any new galleries join at all this year."

"Are you saying that you want to blackball all new members between now and the Armory show?" asked Charles Goulet. "That's three more years!"

Lavinia spoke from the front of the room. "Not everyone. But definitely Trevor Whitney."

The room became silent as the members looked expectantly at Lavinia, waiting for her to explain.

"Let's be honest," she said. "Ever since he came to town Trevor Whitney has been the bane of our existence, and I for one am sick of him. Somehow he gets great paintings, great reviews, steals away our best clients — and now with the attention his essay is getting the man thinks he's God's gift to art scholarship. And has he earned this luck with years of hard work? No. He simply came to town and — boom! — everyone fell all over him." She paused for effect. "I think he needs to be put in his place."

"Hey, I thought we *wanted* successful galleries to join," protested Charles Goulet, but to no avail.

Sonny Kaufmann addressed the room again. "Lavinia's right. Just look around this room; we've all been had by Trevor Whitney."

"Stuart," (he pointed to Stuart Feld of Hirschl & Adler Gallery) "remember that John Kensett you were chasing in Connecticut? Who ended up with it?

"And you, Jim," (he nodded toward Jim Hill of Berry-Hill Gallery) "didn't Mrs. Ogilvy used to be your exclusive territory? None of us ever tried to sell her a painting without going through you, but Trevor Whitney ran right over you with that Sargent.

"And Leo, my dear friend," (he walked over and put his hand on Leo Maxwell's shoulder) "do you remember how much work you did to try to track down the old Steinman clients? Trevor hired Charles Brightman and took away any chance you had.

"My friends," Sonny addressed the crowd, "it may seem unfair, perhaps even unseemly, for us to blackball anyone. But sometimes a man has to be taught a lesson. There are rules to how we do business here; dues that all of us have had to pay that Trevor Whitney has not paid. If we let Trevor Whitney into the NYHADA, we will be saying in essence: 'Let all newcomers in. We have no standards. We have no principles.'" He surveyed the room and let this sink in. "Is this what we've worked so hard for these past years? I think not. I think the NYHADA is better than that, and I for one think it is our duty — yes, our duty — to blackball the likes of Trevor Whitney."

Sonny Kaufmann sat down.

Lavinia, who had been grinning like a Cheshire cat during Sonny's speech, began to clap. Around the room other claps joined hers. It was not a unanimous approval of the blackball, but it was sufficient. The big players were on board; the little ones had no power to contradict.

"I see we're in agreement," Lavinia stated. "From now on I forbid nomination of Trevor Whitney to this organization unless I myself suggest it. Any discussion? Good. Then this meeting is adjourned until March."

It was Lewis and Bernard who first got wind of the NYHADA blackball. Charles Goulet felt obligated to call the couple so they could warn their friend. They discussed what to do with the information

92

over lunch at La Côte Basque:

"Should we tell him, Bernie? It will only distress him." Lewis deftly stuck his fork into a baked oyster and savored its aroma before devouring it. "Delightful!" he exclaimed.

Bernard was carefully slicing a pâté appetizer. "Has Trevor ever mentioned wanting to join the organization?" he asked. "If not, I think we should let it go. That silly emblem on the letterhead doesn't make any difference to the average collector."

"What about the Armory exhibition, Bernie? Trevor will want to participate in that!"

"That's not until 1988. Minds can change between now and then."

"That Lavinia Worthington is a bitch!" Lewis proclaimed with passion.

"Now, Lewis," Bernard said, pointing his fork toward his companion, "none of that! After all, the poor woman had to sleep with Alfred Cummings to get where she is today."

Lewis giggled. "You're right — a fate worse than death!" he said.

And the two raised their glasses of wine in a toast to the horror of it.

FOURTEEN

On a lovely June day in 1985, Sonny Kaufmann pounded his fist onto his magnificent English Regency desk, then stood and began pacing around the office, growling. He had just taken a call from the art dealer Alex Acevedo, who had mentioned in passing that Trevor Whitney had sold a very nice Childe Hassam to a woman who used to be a client of Sonny's former partner, Al Kramer.

Sonny felt like committing murder. Ever since Trevor Whitney had opened across the street, the new kid on the block had had the most astounding success. If it wasn't a great painting dug up from only God knows where, it was another client who'd left his or her old gallery and done business with Trevor. At first Sonny thought it would be a passing phase, and that in the course of things Trevor's luck couldn't hold. But it had been well over a year, and Trevor was only getting more popular and more successful. Blackballing Trevor from the NYHADA wasn't enough. Sonny wanted to destroy him.

Sonny Kaufmann was neither boyish, nor "sunny." He was in his fifties, six foot three, and about one hundred pounds overweight. He had dyed black hair, bushy black eyebrows over beady eyes, and a greasy black handlebar mustache. He also had a horrible temper. But none of this kept him from being extremely successful.

Sonny Kaufmann was the sole owner of Kaufmann-Kramer Gallery, one of the two galleries across the street from Trevor Whitney. He had joined forces with Al Kramer back in the 1960s, when Kramer had the respected, old gallery and Sonny had the money Kramer needed.

Sonny had inherited a fortune from his father, a garment man who rose to immense wealth on the backs of starving immigrant seamstresses. Like many a child of the nouveau riche Sonny had disdained his father's occupation and wanted to pursue something more genteel. He took a shine to the art business, which had the veneer of old money, respectability and refined taste.

Yet Sonny was not eager to work his way up from obscurity. It was so much easier to merge with a gallery that already had a pedigree. When he heard a rumor that Al Kramer was having financial problems, Sonny adopted his most charming demeanor and offered to spill money into the gallery in exchange for half of the business. Al Kramer, in his late fifties and worried about entering retirement with something more to show for his efforts than his good name, jumped at the opportunity. Sonny quickly became the dominant force in the gallery, and Al Kramer lived only long enough to regret the merger.

Sonny succeeded on his own because of the power of the old Kramer name, and because he was a bully. It is a strange fact of the art world that some clients respond well to being told — really ordered — what to do, instead of trusting their own eye or sense. And Sonny was an expert at intimidating almost anyone into buying almost anything.

He played on his clients' insecurities. The right name-drop, as in, "so-and-so wants this, but I decided to give you first shot," or a simple lift of the eyebrow which implied "surely you can't be so stupid as to hold that opinion which is contrary to mine" — even a small smile which clearly meant "you know you are going to buy it so why even bother to argue" — all these were trademark Sonnyisms. Clients were strangely complacent about his methods. In fact a number were heard to say they had "a good working relationship with Sonny" — a phrase meant to imply that Sonny appreciated them, which was only wishful thinking.

His employees were mainly terrified of him. He thought nothing of berating them in public for the most minor infractions, especially when these infractions were actually his own fault. However, Sonny did have one employee who had learned to make himself so indispensable that he was not only tolerated, but also confided in. That employee was the gallery manager, James Hardwick.

Sonny buzzed the receptionist, and demanded James' presence in his office. He needed a new plan for putting The Trevor Whitney Gallery out of business.

James found his boss sitting behind his massive desk, his chair turned around to face the window and his back to the door. His hands were in a prayer-like gesture, resting on his huge stomach, and he appeared to be contemplating the view out his back window — a view that consisted of one straggly tree in a concrete and dirt "backyard."

"Why do you think I've been so successful?" he asked without turning around.

James was used to this type of puzzle and knew the answer. Plus, he had a pretty good idea why his boss was on a rampage. The receptionist had hinted that the words "that damn upstart" had been heard emanating from Sonny's office.

"Because you never let anyone or anything get in the way of your success," he replied.

"Precisely," Sonny said. "And do you know who has been getting in my way of late?" he asked.

"Trevor Whitney."

"Yes." Sonny turned his chair around and faced his employee. "What we are going to do about him?"

James pulled up a chair and sat down. Seeing that Sonny was in a conspiratorial mood instead of a "blame it on James" mood, he looked forward to the rest of the conversation.

"I did have a thought on that," he suggested. "It seems to me we are at a disadvantage because neither Trevor nor Charles is one to talk. They keep their business remarkably close. What they don't say, we can't use against them."

"True. True," Sonny remarked. "So we need some way to get at their secrets. We need a spy."

"Yes!" James was thrilled. He had a plan, and it was perfect. "I was thinking," he said, "that if we had someone on the inside, someone who would unknowingly give us the information.... They've got that assistant — Claire MacKenzie. I was thinking that if I...."

James never got a chance to finish the sentence.

"Forget the inside. They're too smart for that. I was thinking of the outside. Now there's where some spying could take place. The alley — behind their building — I believe that's where they dispose of the trash every night."

James flushed. He'd had visions of a romantic interlude with Claire MacKenzie. Now it looked as if he'd be pawing through garbage instead.

"But, Sonny," he tried to protest. "This woman, Claire, is single. She's from Pittsburgh — probably doesn't know too many people. She's probably lonely. I thought if I could take her out, show her a good time, get her to trust me...."

Sonny snorted. "I suppose that would be a real hardship for you. Glad to know you're willing to date a beautiful woman just to do your duty for the gallery." He laughed out loud. "Kid, you've got a snowball's chance in hell of getting a date with Claire MacKenzie. Besides, word is she and Trevor are an item. But if you want to try — by all means, go ahead." He narrowed his eyes and looked hard at James. "But in the meantime I expect a garbage report. Weekly."

James was furious, but he opted for a response that would better serve him. "I'll have to work late at night," he began. "Extra hours, dangerous work."

He didn't even have to continue; Sonny caught his drift. "You'll be compensated. As usual."

James stood up. Money always made him feel better. "I'll start tonight."

"Good."

James turned to leave, then paused. "By the way, I have it from a reliable source that Trevor and Claire are *not* an item. And I *will* get a date with her. If it's the last thing I do."

Sonny didn't even look at him. "Whatever you say, kid. Always good to have a goal in life."

James stalked out of the office.

FIFTEEN

Claire was in her element. While the gallery was closed for two weeks for summer vacation, she was overseeing the change in gallery lighting — replacing the regular bulbs with halogen lamps. As she weaved around the electrician's ladder and surveyed each painting's appearance under the new lights, she was pleased. She had read in *Art News* that halogen lights were whiter, so paintings with old varnish looked less yellow. She had convinced Trevor and Charles to let her make the change. It was already obvious it was a good decision.

Claire loved new technology. She had recently placed an order for the gallery's first computer; and had convinced Trevor to try some new packing boxes with triple layers of foam. Claire felt that keeping everything in the gallery up-to-date gave their business an aura of progress and prosperity. Since she didn't have the most knowledge of art history, a long client list, or any money to invest in the business, it was the one contribution she could make.

Trevor walked in the door and smiled at her. "I guess they do look pretty good," he admitted, admiring the new lights. He walked over to a box full of the old lighting fixtures and picked one up. "Are you sure we won't have any trouble installing these in the booth?" he asked.

Claire repressed the desire to tease him. Trevor was not a mechanical genius. "Don't worry, they'll pop right into the lighting tracks," she told him.

Trevor and Claire were taking the old lights to Dallas in the first week of September. They had reserved a booth in a big art and antiques extravaganza being held in the convention center to raise money for charity.

It would be the first time the gallery exhibited outside of New York, and the first time they set up a booth by themselves. The details — choosing a color for the walls, arranging for the shipping of paintings, renting fine furniture and rugs, installing a phone line, and making sure they packed every tool and picture hanger they could possibly need — were making Claire's head spin, but she didn't mind the extra work. This was a chance to show off the gallery to an entirely new audience.

Charles was going to be running the gallery in New York for the five days they were gone, with the help of Lewis and Bernard. Lewis was quite enthusiastic about aiding in Trevor and Claire's departure.

"A few days alone together..." he said, "and they'll be announcing the wedding!"

Trevor and Claire arrived in Dallas early on a Thursday morning, and went directly to the convention center to begin setting up the booth. They soon found themselves disagreeing about everything, from where to place the desk and phone jack to which arrangement of paintings looked best.

By four o'clock in the afternoon the booth was only half hung, Trevor and Claire weren't speaking to each other, and they were faint with hunger.

"Truce," Claire suddenly said. "How about taking me out for one of those famous Texas steak dinners? I have a feeling everything will seem much easier after we've eaten."

"Well, we're not getting anywhere here. I'm starving too. Let's go check into the hotel, and then we'll ask the concierge for a dinner recommendation."

They started gathering up their luggage, but as they left the booth Trevor suddenly stopped and looked back at their work. He contemplated it for a moment, and then he said, "You know, it doesn't look half bad. We do make a good team, don't we, Claire?"

"Of course we do," she said quickly. "We're just tired and irritated."

Just then one of the show's organizers, Mrs. James Halverson III, came running up.

"Ooh!" she cooed. "Your booth looks fabulous."

Claire raised an eyebrow at her, since the booth was only half-fin-ished, but Trevor said, "It's mostly Claire's work. She really knows what she's doing; I'm only along to make her life difficult."

He risked a smile at his assistant, and Claire returned her first smile of the day.

"Well," Mrs. Halverson said, "my ears have been ringing all day about you, Claire. Every man in the building wants to know who you are."

"Oh, I doubt that..." Claire replied, glancing down at her dirt-streaked jeans. "Look at me; I'm a mess."

Mrs. Halverson ignored her protests. "I want to introduce you to my nephew tomorrow night," she went on. "You'll adore him! And Trevor, you must join us for dinner after the opening. Say yes now so the other ladies can be jealous of me!"

"Of course. It will be my pleasure," Trevor replied. "Speaking of dinner, Claire and I are running off to get some. We'll see you back here tomorrow."

As they walked away, Claire remarked, "Mrs. Halverson certainly likes you."

"What do you mean?"

"She was fawning. 'Ooh, your booth is fabulous! You simply must have dinner with me.'"

Trevor laughed. "I'm not the one apparently making everyone's head spin in the building. I wouldn't talk if I were you. People in glass houses...."

"Oh, yes. I'm irresistible," Claire replied. "Especially in this stunning workshirt."

Trevor made a show of letting his eyes run analytically over Claire's appearance. "You'd be surprised how good you look," he finally announced.

Claire couldn't suppress a blush.

Later, over a hearty dinner, Trevor made a suggestion. "Let's hire some local guy to hang the rest of the paintings. That way we won't wear ourselves out before the opening."

"Good idea. It's easier to argue when you don't have a heavy painting in your arms," Claire rejoined.

"Very funny. You know, I meant what I said to Mrs. Halverson. You do know what you're doing."

"Thanks, Trevor. But if you think so, why do you insist on disagreeing with me so much?"

Trevor smiled. "Don't you know it's very bad to go through life always getting your way? I'm doing you a favor."

A good night's sleep and a mutual desire not to experience a repeat of the day before had a profound effect on Trevor and Claire's ability to finish the booth quickly the next day. So they were in a very good mood by the time they returned to the convention center that evening for the opening.

To Trevor and Claire's astonishment, during the hours they'd been resting up before the opening the vast exhibition hall had been decorated as a Venetian moonlight scene. The walls were painted with all the sights of Venice, and with gondolas floating down glistening canals. Costumed gondoliers had been hired to stroll through the exhibition singing Italian arias, and a huge spread of Italian treats was laid out on tables among the aisles of exhibitors. The lighting and many fragrant flowers created the illusion of sweet evening air and moonlight.

"Can you believe they've transformed this place so completely?" Claire asked, taking Trevor's arm as they entered the building. "Just a few hours ago it was a mess. It's so beautiful now!"

It was customary for charity art shows to allow their biggest supporters an hour of undisturbed browsing and hors d'oeuvres before the other attendees were allowed into the event. Within minutes of the early opening, the exhibition hall was thronged with Dallas' most prominent citizens.

Mrs. James Halverson III — called "Missy" by her friends — ran over to the Trevor Whitney booth as soon as the show opened, dragging along her husband and her husband's great-nephew. Although Missy was a very attractive brunette in her forties, her extremely wealthy husband was about eighty-five.

"Oh, Trevor," she gushed. "I want to introduce you to my husband, James." She dropped her voice. "He's a little hard of hearing, so you'll want to speak up."

"Hello, Sir," Trevor said loudly. "Delighted to meet you. You must be very proud of your wife. She's done a wonderful job organizing this show."

The elder Halverson nodded. "Missy takes great pride in her charity work."

"And this is our... nephew, Edgar Halverson." Missy carefully skipped over the word "great," not being fond of pointing out the age discrepancy.

"Nice to meet you," Edgar said. "Call me 'The Colonel.'"

Despite Trevor's social polish he was momentarily knocked off balance. The man in front of him was only in his late twenties. He was not dressed in military uniform, although he was impressively tall and did have an incredibly straight back. Trevor had a moment to collect his wits because Edgar Halverson kept talking.

"Love your paintings. Real beauties. Quite impressive." He seemed only able to speak in phrases. Trevor mischievously remembered this was the person Missy had wanted Claire to meet.

"Let me introduce you to my assistant, if I can get her attention." Claire was over on the other side of the booth with her back to

105

Trevor and his guests, showing off a William Trost Richards watercolor to another visitor. "Claire," he called over, "When you have a minute...?"

Claire turned around. The Colonel let out an audible gasp.

Missy smiled, Trevor felt a twinge of annoyance, and James Halverson III didn't react because he hadn't heard anything. But Claire, who had dressed in a stunning, bare-shouldered red Givenchy dress, was in the mood to be appreciated. So she excused herself from her company and walked over. She immediately offered her hand to Edgar.

"I'm Claire MacKenzie," she said to him. To her surprise, Edgar pounced on her hand and held it fervently in a firm grip. Claire was in pain, but managed to smile. Then she turned to Missy, lifted her eyebrows and said, "So this is the nephew you told me about?"

"Yes, this is Edgar. But we all just call him 'The Colonel.' Let go of her hand, Colonel. And this is my husband, James."

If Claire found Edgar's title surprising it was lost in her gratitude for having her hand released. "My, you're strong," she murmured, causing the young man to smile proudly. Then Claire turned composedly to Missy's husband. "Pleasure to meet you," she said. "Are you enjoying the exhibition?"

James Halverson III grunted. "I'd be enjoying it more with a drink in my hand. Why don't I go get us all a round?"

"Let me, Uncle," The Colonel immediately piped up. "Miss MacKenzie?"

"Oh, thank you. White wine, please."

"Good choice," The Colonel responded. "Mr. Whitney?"

"Wine would be fine."

Edgar Halverson disappeared, and returned minutes later with a waiter carrying a tray of drinks. As soon as Claire had picked up hers, he asked, "May I get you a plate of hors d'oeuvres?"

"Oh. No thank you. I don't like to eat during openings."

"Then perhaps you would allow me to escort you to dinner at the end of the event?"

Claire wondered what she was getting herself into. She knew she looked good, and didn't mind flirting a little with someone in front of Trevor. But this young man seemed rather... overeager. She looked toward Trevor, hoping he'd make some excuse for her, but Trevor only smiled. "Go ahead," he told her. "This will give you a chance to see some of the city."

Claire gave him a look of displeasure, but The Colonel went on pressing her for an answer.

"It would be an honor to give you a tour. By *real* moonlight," he said.

Claire felt she had no polite choice but to accept.

The rest of the opening was busy with collectors and fresh contacts, yet whenever Claire had a moment to look around she would find The Colonel within eyesight, often staring quite unabashedly at her from across the room.

"He's smitten," Trevor pronounced, and Claire felt slightly alarmed.

"Why do you think he calls himself 'The Colonel'?" she whispered to Trevor.

His eyes laughed at Claire as he answered, "I guess he's a military man."

"There hasn't been a war in years. I mean, you can't just call yourself 'The Colonel' without earning it somehow, can you?"

Trevor shrugged. "Maybe it's some sort-of Texan conceit. Everyone here is a bit bigger-than-life."

"It sounds so strange on a young person. I don't think I can bring myself to call him 'The Colonel' all night."

"Sure you can. Just look at those puppy-dog eyes! How could you deny a man like that his military moniker?"

Claire rolled her eyes, but wished Trevor would come up with some excuse to get her out of her date. In the end, he tried to be helpful.

"We have an early day tomorrow," he told The Colonel pointedly when he came to collect Claire at the end of the evening. "I'll need her home by midnight." It was nine o'clock. Trevor had at least limited her discomfort to three hours.

"I'll call you when I get in," Claire said, as Trevor went off to fulfill his dinner obligation with Missy and her husband.

Edgar Halverson offered his arm to Claire, and when she took it she realized the arm was as solid as a rock. Claire prayed he wouldn't try anything. But as it turned out, The Colonel was honor personified.

He'd ordered a limousine to give them a private tour of the city. He held the door for her, but politely sat across from her in the car instead of next to her. After showing her the highlights of the city he had the driver bring them out to The Mansion on Turtle Creek, one of Dallas' finest restaurants. There he ordered the chef's specialties without even looking at the menu. The waiters — obviously familiar with The Colonel — fawned over them, and Claire was impressed despite herself. He was a perfect gentleman, even when he dropped her off at the hotel. He did not attempt a goodnight kiss, but only took her hand warmly — and gently — in his, and swore he'd never had a more wonderful evening.

The next morning a dozen yellow roses arrived at the booth for Claire, with a note from The Colonel restating his admiration. It included a plea that she would allow him to see her again when he traveled to New York. Trevor teased her relentlessly for the remaining three days of the art show.

The exhibition was a success for the gallery. They sold four paintings, met numerous new collectors, and became friendly with the curators of the Amon Carter — a museum in Fort Worth specializing in American art.

But the first thing Trevor made a point of reporting to Charles, Lewis and Bernard when they were all reunited at the gallery was that Claire had an ardent admirer in The Colonel. This came as no surprise to any of them, however, because a dozen yellow roses were already waiting on Claire's desk for her return.

Claire was visibly embarrassed by this discovery and made a point of refusing to comment on Edgar Halverson, prompting Lewis to pull Bernard aside and complain woefully, "Doesn't this Colonel person know when he's not wanted? Obviously Claire doesn't know how to get rid of him, but meanwhile poor Trevor's heart is breaking."

"Lewis," Bernard remonstrated, shaking his head, "you're out of your mind."

Charles, however, had some news of his own that he was anxious to focus on. "I got a disturbing call from our friend Barney Digglewelder yesterday. He said that another dealer in New York called him out of the blue wanting to know if he had any paintings for sale. Since he claims we're the only gallery he's been in touch with, we need to figure out how someone else got his name."

"Did Barney say who it was?" Claire asked.

"Our friends across the street, Kaufmann-Kramer."

Claire shuddered. "Ugh. They're the last people I'd want knowing our business."

"My thoughts exactly. Trevor, any idea how they could have figured it out?"

"None. I didn't tell a soul. I'm sure none of us did. But I wouldn't put it past Barney to just be having a little joke at our expense — you know, shaking us up a bit."

"That's true," Charles admitted. "Still, we'd better be extra careful from now on. That's the kind of leak we can't afford. So all of us need to be especially alert now. If you notice anything unusual, Claire, anything at all, make sure you tell Trevor or me."

Bernard offered to help too. "We'll keep our ears to the ground," he said. "People have a tendency to brag when they've put one over on someone."

For the next few weeks everyone connected with The Trevor Whitney Gallery was particularly careful. But although it soon became clear that the one leak was not an isolated incident, none of them could figure out where they were failing in security.

SIXTEEN

In October of 1985, The Trevor Whitney Gallery mounted its second major exhibition. It was timed to coincide with the annual meeting of the American Museum Association, which was holding its convention in New York City that year.

Ever since Trevor had written his senior thesis on the Connecticut Impressionists, it had been a dream of Trevor's to present an exhibition of the works of Gerald O'Connor. Gerald O'Connor had once been considered the "third musketeer" of his more famous Connecticut colleagues: John Twachtman and Willard Metcalf. All three of them had a similar brilliant approach to painting landscape — a shimmering style of Impressionism that delighted the eye. Just about 1905, when the three names were being linked in commentary about the strength of landscape art emerging from Connecticut, Gerald O'Connor suddenly abandoned the art scene. Twachtman and Metcalf were eventually considered two of the most important practitioners of American Impressionist landscape. Gerald O'Connor was soon forgotten.

Trevor had always wondered what happened to the artist. Had he died young? Become incapacitated? It was a mystery no one had yet solved. Trevor determined to resurrect O'Connor's reputation, and discover the reason for his sudden disappearance from the art world.

Even Charles, with all his years of experience, had only seen two or three O'Connors. A few others were known from book reproductions. But most of the artist's oeuvre remained unknown and unlocated.

Rather than discouraging Trevor, the situation presented an exciting opportunity. For it was just possible that there was a stash of O'Connors somewhere, in some family member's attic, waiting for the right person to come along and ask about it.

Trevor and Claire began spending hours at the New York Public Library, pouring over old Connecticut newspaper articles, hoping to find some personal information about O'Connor that would aid their search. Finally Trevor found something he could use: Gerald O'Connor had married a Miss Frances Hodgson in June of 1903. The Hodgson family was from Newport, Rhode Island.

Trevor photocopied the page of "Hodgsons" from the Rhode Island phone directory and returned with it to the gallery. For the entire afternoon, Charles, Trevor and Claire took turns phoning through the list of names, hoping to find a Hodgson who knew something about Gerald O'Connor. Finally it happened. A young woman in Providence told Claire that her husband's great-grandfather's sister had been the Frances Hodgson who'd married O'Connor, and that her husband's mother had recently inherited a number of the paintings.

Trevor held his breath for three days, waiting for this young woman's husband to phone his mother and get permission for Trevor to contact her. When permission came, Trevor lost no time in making arrangements to fly to Rhode Island to see the paintings.

The woman he went to see, Janice Somers Hodgson, knew very little about O'Connor or the fifteen paintings she'd inherited, as she had married into the family and never been told much about the artist. So she was very impressed with the information Trevor brought to her, especially when he was able to identify the location of the scenes in many of the O'Connor paintings. Mrs. Hodgson was perfectly willing to sell most of the works, as she had nowhere to keep them all, and was glad to loan the rest for the exhibition. However, she had no information that explained why O'Connor had apparently stopped painting so suddenly, nor did she know of anyone else who owned any paintings.

It seemed a dead-end in terms of the O'Connor mystery. But that night in his hotel room Trevor suddenly bolted awake at 3:00 am. He had remembered something Mrs. Hodgson had mentioned in passing — something about a painting that had been donated to charity.

The next morning Trevor drove to the headquarters of the Rhode Island Society for the Blind. Trevor looked around the reception room and noticed plenty of sculptures, but no paintings. The receptionist didn't know if there was a painting by Gerald O'Connor on the premises, but she told Trevor that if he didn't mind waiting a few moments, she'd ask the Director to speak with him. After a while the Director appeared — a tall, burly redheaded man with an air of intellectualism. He introduced himself as Dr. Clarence McCoy, and ushered Trevor into his private chambers.

As soon as Trevor entered Dr. McCoy's office he recognized the painting behind the desk as an O'Connor. It was a glorious garden scene painted at Twachtman's house in Greenwich, Connecticut. Trevor couldn't help exclaiming out loud, "Ah, there it is!"

"Yes," Dr. McCoy replied, "and we have two others in storage. Tell me again what your interest is in Gerald O'Connor? You're the first person who's ever come by to look at the painting."

Trevor explained about the exhibition he was planning.

Dr. McCoy nodded approvingly. "I've always thought O'Connor deserved some sort of retrospective. I'm no art connoisseur, but I can recognize genius when I see it. Are you going to include the sculptures as well?"

"Sculptures?" Trevor was taken aback. He had never heard of any O'Connor sculptures.

"Yes. You do know about the sculptures, don't you? That's what O'Connor did after he went blind."

Trevor's jaw dropped. "When I heard that a painting had been donated here I wondered if it was something like that! I knew he'd stopped painting abruptly around 1905, but I couldn't discover why."

"Yes, he went blind from an infection when he was forty-five. He was quite desolate for a while. I'm told he even destroyed some of his paintings one day in a fit of anger. But apparently his wife convinced him to try working in clay, and he became quite adept at the medium."

"He must never have exhibited the sculptures," Trevor said. "I searched every reference on O'Connor I could find and nothing about sculpture ever came up."

"O'Connor became a very private man after his blindness. I only know so much about him because our archivist researched the artworks in our collection."

Dr. McCoy reached into a desk drawer and pulled out a pamphlet for Trevor. "We must have about twenty O'Connor sculptures here in the building," he told him. "He donated them to us in gratitude for the aid the Society gave him. You can take this booklet and make a little walking tour of the halls to see them. In the meantime, if you'd like, I'll call someone to pull those two other O'Connor paintings out of storage so you can have a look at them."

Once Trevor realized that the sculptures he'd passed earlier in the hallway and the reception area were by O'Connor, he saw that he himself had been blind not to notice them. They were extraordinary works — all figurative — in a style that seemed to foreshadow the fragmented surfaces of Giacometti but in rounder bodies, with a vibrant sense of human interaction. Men, women and children were depicted in everyday situations: a farmer pushing a cart down a road; a city man in top hat and evening coat swinging a cane as he sauntered down the street; two children pulling on their nursemaid's arms in opposite directions; two lovers holding hands and gazing into each other's eyes. In many ways, Trevor immediately realized, the sculptures were far more inventive than O'Connor's paintings.

The receptionist came to retrieve Trevor back to Dr. McCoy's office, and there leaning against the wall were the two other paintings. One was an early landscape, probably painted in Brittany during

O'Connor's student years in France. It had more broad and flat areas of color than his later works. The other was a vertical work of an elm tree by a stream — in the later style but not terribly interesting in composition. Dr. McCoy made an abrupt offer: if Trevor would donate part of the proceeds of the sale of those two paintings back to the Society, then he would authorize the sculptures to go on loan to the exhibition. It was an offer Trevor couldn't refuse.

Trevor's exhibition and catalogue made another splash in the art world. Although the press ignored it, independent scholars and museum professionals were thoroughly impressed with Trevor's accomplishment, and he was highly praised in private circles. A number of the friendlier dealers made a point of congratulating Trevor on solving the O'Connor mystery, and art collectors soon began coveting the sculptures as much as the paintings. Although the exhibition offered no sculptures for sale, a few subsequently came out of the woodwork and Trevor sold them for hefty numbers.

It should have been a glorious time for Trevor, but unfortunately it was at that time that Trevor realized he was being blackballed by the NYHADA. A second rejection, with no explanation, arrived in the mail.

The first rejection had been accepted as a matter of course, for the NYHADA had been requiring a longer time in business than one year. But the second, with its curt denial, greatly annoyed Trevor. As Lewis had predicted, he was particularly angry that he would be unable to participate in the planned re-creation of the 1913 Armory show.

All lovers of American art history held the 1913 Armory show in special veneration. It was a watershed event, marking the date when modern art was introduced to the American public. That its fame stemmed from the European artists who exhibited there, not the Americans, made no difference. It was the Americans who had the genius to mount the show and bring the works of their European counterparts to a new audience.

Most of the public at the time thought the art in the exhibition was appalling. They had no appreciation for cubism, abstraction, synchronism or futurism. Newspaper articles reported that the art world was degenerating to depths never before dreamed. Immense crowds came to see and to mock, people were rude and unruly, the police had to be called in. All in all it was considered a huge success.

To re-create the exhibition on the same spot seventy-five years later — with new sponsors but many of the same artists' works — was a grand idea and one the NYHADA could justifiably be proud of. It nagged at Trevor not to be able to take part in it.

But the NYHADA rejection also bothered Trevor for another reason. At this point, Trevor had been in business for two very successful years and felt he had worked hard to deserve the clients and rewards that had come his way. At the beginning when the other dealers had insulted him, he had not minded much. The fun and adventure, and success, had mitigated any serious need for his colleagues' approval. But now he felt he'd earned some respect; it bothered him that clients, scholars, and museum directors were willing to give him the credit he deserved, but he still could not get a complimentary word out of the other big galleries.

One day, in contemplating the rejection, Trevor made an offhand comment to Claire about the possible reason. He wondered out loud, "Do you think the NYHADA is rejecting me because of Charles?"

Claire was horrified at the idea. "That's ridiculous, Trevor!" she exclaimed. "How could you even suggest such a thing?"

"It was just a thought. Charles was so sensitive about his race when we first went into business together, but we haven't seen anything like that. I wondered if this was the first example."

116

"Well, I'm glad Charles isn't around to hear you say it. Anyway, Charles always warns you how vindictive the art dealers in New York are. This is probably just their way of getting revenge."

Trevor actually agreed with Claire that it was highly unlikely the gallery would be rejected because of Charles' race, but didn't say so.

He later had cause to wish he had.

SEVENTEEN

"...*Just when the whole NYHADA thing came to Trevor's attention, The Colonel came to town.*"

"*We never will know what his relationship to Claire was,*" Bernard mused.

"*Oh pooh, Bernie, he was never more than a distraction! But it was terrible timing. Poor Trevor was devastated.*"

"*I really think he was much more upset, at the time, about the NYHADA,*" Bernard said. "*And the leaks. That was a serious problem.*"

"*Well, The Colonel didn't help things. This is when it all started to go wrong....*"

"I can't believe it!" Claire exclaimed to Trevor in frustration a week after the O'Connor exhibition opened. "Gerald Townsend is going to bid against us for the J.G. Brown!"

She was on the phone with Waldo Picker, who was calling from Kentucky. He'd just run into one of Townsend's employees at a little estate sale he'd discovered outside of Frankfort. The Trevor Whitney Gallery had been hoping to buy the Brown painting — a charmer of a little girl picking cherries — for a song. Somehow they'd acquired competition.

"How the devil did they find out about it?" Waldo demanded on the other end of the line. "I've been scoping out this part of the country for weeks, and I've seen no one. No one! Then here, out of the blue, shows up one of Townsend's lackeys."

"I don't know. It's weird. Everything we do lately seems to be known before we do it. I'm beginning to think our phones must be tapped!"

"Well, give me Trevor or Charles. I need to know how high to go on this thing — now that we have competition!"

Claire handed the phone to Trevor, then went into the back office to tell Charles.

"Waldo's on the phone. Someone from the Gerald Townsend Gallery just showed up at that sale in Kentucky," Claire announced as way of greeting.

Charles winced. "This is getting really strange," he said. "Ever since that thing with Barney Diggleweder, it's like we have a spy in the building."

"Do you think it would be paranoid to call the phone company and ask them to check for wire taps?"

Charles pushed his telephone toward Claire. "Do it," he said. "We have to get to the bottom of this."

But New York Bell could come up with no sign of wire-tapping. They suggested the gallery do a thorough search for bugs, so Claire spent part of the afternoon unscrewing the phone receivers and running her fingers under desk edges and behind paintings. She felt like Mata Hari, but nothing turned up.

The phone company's other suggestion was to call the police, but Charles and Trevor didn't want to take it that far. The last thing they needed was to publicize the leak.

The Trevor Whitney Gallery bought the J. G. Brown in Kentucky, but only after paying twice what they'd wanted to. It became a point of honor to Trevor to acquire it no matter how high they had to go, so naturally they paid well over what was sensible. In the end it was little satisfaction to have thwarted Gerald Townsend, because the painting couldn't be sold at a profit.

"This has got to stop," Charles told his colleagues. "Rack your brains until we figure out how our competitors are getting information about us!" But try as they might, they couldn't find the leak.

Across the street, Sonny Kaufmann was laughing into his hands. At first James had been only getting tidbits during his night prowls, but then one day he'd hit the jackpot. He'd come back with a used

120

phone message pad, the kind where an impression of the message is left behind in the book. Kaufmann-Kramer had knowledge of every phone message The Trevor Whitney Gallery had taken in the past four months — revelations about who they were working with, and what they were working on.

At first Sonny had used the information James supplied him himself, but he'd soon realized it would be wiser if no suspicion fell particularly on his own gallery. So he'd begun to be cannier. His latest coup — offering to go half-shares on a J.G. Brown in Kentucky with Gerald Townsend if Gerry sent one of his employees to bid — had worked even better than he'd planned. It was actually more fun not to get the painting and to see Trevor Whitney spend too much in frustration.

The phone pad was a gold mine, but Sonny had to admit James was not the best choice for the job of trash spy. He didn't like to get his hands dirty, and only grabbed the obvious items — like the message pad — instead of carefully reviewing every tossed bit of paper. Sonny had no intention of letting James stop this extracurricular activity, but in the meantime he looked for other ways to cripple The Trevor Whitney Gallery.

Sonny decided it couldn't hurt if James attempted to romance Claire MacKenzie. After all, Sonny had nothing to lose by the attempt — only James. If James was willing to make a fool of himself so be it, and if by some miracle he was successful — well, that would be icing on the trash cake.

When Sonny mentioned to James that, after all, he could see no harm in his trying to date Claire, James' mind went into overdrive. He needed a convincing, and brilliant, plan. It would do no good to simply pad across the street and ask Claire out directly. If she didn't refuse him outright, Trevor or Charles would no doubt throw him out of the building anyway. He would have to approach her outside of work, perhaps in an environment where she might drink too much. After weeks of contemplation he finally hit upon the perfect place.

It was December of 1985, and the big American painting sales were coming up at Sotheby's and Christie's. James knew that Claire would not only be at the Sotheby's cocktail reception, but would probably be there alone. That same night there was a special reception at the Metropolitan Museum, and Trevor would have to make an appearance. As for Claire's other protector, Charles rarely ventured out to evening events. He preferred to catch the train home to City Island and spend his evenings with his wife.

Back across the street, the morning of the Sotheby's reception, Charles and Claire were downstairs in the gallery when Claire received a telephone call. She appeared so nervous afterward that Charles couldn't help asking if everything was all right.

"Oh, it's nothing," Claire assured him, "It's just that The Colonel is in town, and wants to see me."

Charles raised his eyebrows and tried once again to fathom Claire's feelings about her Texan admirer. Claire always refused to speak of him, yet every first Monday of the month, like clockwork, a dozen yellow roses arrived at the gallery door. Claire's reaction was always the same. She dutifully stopped whatever she was doing to place a phone call to Dallas and thank him. They would speak for a few minutes — sometimes a bit longer — but Charles and Trevor were left clueless as to any additional conversations they might be having outside of business hours, or, in fact, what exactly Claire thought of it all.

So Charles wasn't quite sure what to say about The Colonel's sudden arrival, and simply asked, "So, are you going to see him?"

Claire looked at Charles as if she was surprised at the question, and said, "Oh, I told him it would be all right if he wanted to meet me at Sotheby's tonight."

This was still cryptic to Charles. It wasn't a refusal, but it didn't sound like a date either. Charles could see he'd get nothing further out of Claire, so he amused himself by telling her, "Too bad Lewis will be at the Met tonight. He's quite dying to meet The Colonel, you know." To which Claire turned beet red, but offered no comment.

James arrived early at the Sotheby's reception. He wanted to make sure he cornered Claire the moment she arrived. When she finally entered the room he almost lost his nerve. She was wearing a little black Halston dress and sexy black slingback shoes, and had artfully arranged her hair to swoop up from her face and then cascade down her back. Every male head in the room turned to look at her, but Claire made straight for the paintings being displayed for the auction and seemed intent on memorizing every one.

James sidled up next to her. She seemed unaware of his presence. He cleared his throat.

"You look very beautiful tonight, Claire," he said.

Claire turned a blank expression toward him. "Oh. Thank you, James," she said.

"Can I get you a drink?"

Claire seemed to consider this for far longer than was normally necessary. "Yes. I will. White wine, please."

By the times James returned with their drinks, Claire was half-way farther down the first wall of paintings. She looked at him as if surprised to see him again, but then took the drink. "Thank you," she offered. She seemed disinclined to say anything more.

James knew enough about Claire to know that the way to her heart was through American paintings. So he began trying to engage her in conversation about the works in front of them. "I think that Cropsey's quite good, don't you? The estimate may be a bit high, but I think a collector could pay it. How about that Bricher on the far wall? I'm not much of a Bricher fan, but I have to admit, that's probably his best beach scene. Did you get around the corner yet to see those Glackens? Gloucester pictures, real beauties. And wait till you see the Frieseke they've got of a woman with a parasol in a garden. I think the Terra Museum might go after it."

To all these comments Claire smiled politely, or shook her head, but said virtually nothing. It finally dawned on James that she seemed incredibly nervous.

Before he had a chance to ask himself if he might be the cause of this, they were interrupted.

"Claire?" A tall young man — with remarkably good posture — tapped Claire on the shoulder from behind. Claire jumped; the wine in her glass jumped too and sploshed all over James' jacket.

"Oh! Oh, James, I'm so sorry. Edgar! How nice to see you... Oh James, do let me clean that up for you. Let me introduce you. James Hardwick, this is Edgar Halverson... umm, The Colonel. Edgar, please run and get us some napkins. I'm so sorry, James!"

The Colonel raced off to find napkins, and Claire was left smiling apologetically at James.

"Old friend?" he asked.

"No. I mean, yes. He lives in Texas; I haven't seen him in some time."

"Old boyfriend?" James asked more pointedly, but just then The Colonel returned and handed Claire a pile of napkins far outweighing the needs of the situation.

Claire gave James a helpless look, and James valiantly offered, "Here, hand them to me. I'll do it myself."

"If you need to have that dry-cleaned...." Claire began, but by now James had recognized the absurdity of the situation, and wished only to extricate himself.

"Oh, it will be fine. You two run along. I'm sure you have plenty to talk about." And with that, James turned and crossed to the other side of the room, where he could observe Claire's next move and curse his bad luck.

Claire and The Colonel took their time viewing the rest of the paintings up for auction. James saw that Claire seemed suddenly animated, and spoke nonstop and with expansive gestures about the paintings. It occurred to him that it might be an additional sign of her nervousness, but James didn't know her well enough to be sure it wasn't also enthusiasm. After about forty-five minutes The Colonel strolled up to the bar and returned to Claire with another drink. She downed it in one gulp, and then the two of them left and got into a cab together and took off into the night.

"Damn," James said to himself. But since this Colonel fellow was from Texas, perhaps there was hope yet.

In a perverse mood, James decided to pay attention to Jean Downing, Gerald Townsend's mousy new registrar. With thick-framed glasses, skinny legs and limp brown hair, she was decidedly not his type, but James had heard a rumor that she thought he was "cute." With forced charm he descended upon her, plying her with compliments and then with drinks. Eventually he wangled an invitation back to her apartment, and when he finally got her into bed, he made a point of pretending to himself that it was Claire he was making love to.

⌇⌇ EIGHTEEN ⌇⌇

The morning after the Sotheby's reception, Trevor asked Claire if she wanted to accompany him to the auction. As they rode over in the taxi, Trevor remarked, "I hear The Colonel was in town last night."

"Yes. He's staying a week."

"What exactly does he *do*, anyway?" There was a slight tone of annoyance in the question. Claire chose to ignore it.

"Investment banking. He's looking into investing in a technology company here."

"So that's what you have in common," Trevor said, with sarcastic amusement. "You both love gadgets."

"You shouldn't make fun of him." Claire said sharply. "He's very, very sweet to me."

"I didn't mean anything by it, Claire."

Trevor suddenly wished he'd never mentioned The Colonel. He felt as if he'd skated onto thin ice, and that at any moment Claire might turn to him and say something he didn't particularly want to hear.

They were both visibly relieved when the cab pulled up in front of the auction house.

During the sale, Trevor noticed that Claire kept getting up from their seats and going over to other dealers to visit. He felt as if she were punishing him for something, and he wished again he'd never mentioned The Colonel's name. By the time the lunch break came though, he had stopped feeling guilty and was simply annoyed at her.

"I don't suppose you'd care to have lunch with me," he said as he pulled her away from a conversation with M.P. Naud of Hirschl & Adler Galleries.

"Of course I want to. Hey, Glenn Peck wants to know if you want to go in with him on the Louis Ritman coming up this afternoon." Claire was all smiles, and Trevor was confused. "He said to meet him back here ten minutes before the sale to discuss it."

"Oh, okay."

"So where do you want to eat?"

Trevor's favorite restaurant near Sotheby's was Zucchini, a few blocks away. As they munched on pasta salad and large glasses of peach iced tea, Claire kept up a running commentary on the sale so far, and Trevor found his good mood returning. The only reference he made to their disturbing morning was as they walked out of the restaurant.

"You know, Claire... did anyone ever tell you you're a bit incomprehensible sometimes?"

"Am I?" Claire responded, smiling to herself.

Trevor went in with Glenn Peck on the Ritman, and managed to bid successfully despite robust competition from two phone bidders. Paintings were routinely setting new auction records, and the December sales of 1985 were no exception. The art world was full of confidence that demand for American art was still skyrocketing. The only drawback to this healthy market was a rapidly dwindling supply.

Charles expressed concern about this. "We're seeing too many second and third-tier paintings coming up at auction," he remarked at the end of the sales week. "The good stuff is getting harder and harder to find."

It was perhaps no surprise that a small number of unscrupulous people should see this market condition as an ideal one for forgery.

In February of 1986, Claire received a phone call from a woman named Alice Boswell. She was coming to New York from Tulsa to visit cousins, she said, and would it be all right if she brought along the Mary Cassatt drawing she had recently inherited to get it appraised for possible sale?

"Of course," Claire eagerly told the caller. "What day will you be here? I want to make sure both owners of the gallery are available to meet you."

A date was set. On a cold, wet February afternoon, Alice Boswell walked into The Trevor Whitney Gallery.

She was the spitting image of a Norman Rockwell grandmother: gray hair in a bun, sensible shoes, plump figure. She came in wearily, dragging in a gust of icy wind, and carrying in her arms a brown paper-wrapped package, a heavy shopping bag from Saks and an oversized black umbrella. She wore a thick wool coat with a fur collar, and rubber boots, and her nose and cheeks and ungloved hands were red from the bitter weather. Claire quickly offered to take the packages out of her arms, find a stand for the umbrella, hang up her coat and brew a cup of hot tea. Alice accepted all the attention gratefully and sank into an armchair next to the reception desk.

Claire disappeared into the back hallway and returned with the cup of tea, and Charles. He shook Alice's hand, and explained that Trevor Whitney would be back any moment. Trevor had just stepped out to check on a painting at the restorer's, he said, but in the meantime, would Alice care to show them the drawing?

Alice sighed as she unwrapped the brown paper. "I hate to part with it, but I'm just a little old lady on a widow's pension. I sure could put the money to good use."

The drawing was exquisite. In soft pencil on fine Arches paper, it depicted a fully dressed mother sitting on a boudoir chair, hugging her naked infant to her body with fierce love. The lines were fine and delicate, and the expression on the mother and infant's faces clear and readable. It was signed on the lower right and framed simply, with a little gold label indicating the artist, Mary Cassatt, and the title, "A Mother's Caress."

"Is that a preparatory drawing for the color print, *Maternal Caress*?" Claire asked.

Alice Boswell's face lit up. "Yes! How did you know?"

129

"I used to work at Sotheby's," Claire explained, "and one of the prints came up at auction a few years ago."

Charles beamed at Claire. "We have a very sharp employee," he told Mrs. Boswell with pride.

Just then another gust of wind brought Trevor through the door. He quickly joined the group at the desk and apologized for his tardiness.

"We were just looking at Mrs. Boswell's Cassatt," Charles told him. "Claire recognized it as a preparatory drawing for one of Cassatt's colored prints."

Trevor took the framed image in his hands. It was about fourteen by ten inches. He turned it over and examined the back. For a few moments he thoughtfully considered it. Then, "It's quite beautiful," he said. "Did you have a figure in mind for it?"

Alice looked pensive. "A friend of mine said he thought it must be worth around ten or twelve thousand," she said hesitantly.

"It would be," Trevor said without hesitation, "on the retail market. But if we were to buy it, Mrs. Boswell, we'd have to be able to sell it for that. We'd have to pay you a little less."

Alice looked visibly relieved. "I don't mind taking less," she said. "If you can pay me in cash." She looked at her three hosts, who were looking back at her in obvious surprise. "If I take cash," she explained, "I don't have to declare it. I don't think a little old lady like me, on a pension, should have to pay too much in taxes, don't you agree?"

Claire furrowed her eyebrows, and Charles opened his mouth to protest, but Trevor held up a hand and stopped him. "Sure, Mrs. Boswell, I understand," Trevor said. "If you come back here tomorrow, at the same time, we can have cash for you. Will six thousand be all right?"

As soon as Alice Boswell expressed gratitude for the gallery's generosity, she was bundled back up, received her Saks bag and umbrella, and left the building.

Trevor immediately began taking the frame of the drawing apart.

"What are you doing?" Claire asked in surprise.

"It's a fake," Trevor stated.

Charles smiled and was about to say something when Claire exclaimed, "I knew it! Guess what was in her shopping bag? Peter Kaiser shoes and two cashmere sweaters!"

"How do you know what was in her shopping bag?" Charles scolded, "And anyway, what are Peter Kaiser shoes?"

Claire flushed. "I looked. Sorry! I couldn't help myself, I was just curious. Anyway, Peter Kaiser is a German brand. Very exclusive and very expensive. As soon as she told us she needed cash because she was on a pension, I knew she was lying."

"What tipped *you* off, Trevor? I only noticed that the drawing seemed too elaborate for a preliminary sketch," Charles said.

"What does that mean?" Claire wanted to know.

"I've seen hundreds of Cassatt drawings over the years, and when Mary Cassatt did sketches that she wanted to work into prints, she only drew in the essentials. She put the details in later, directly on the plate. Look, this one has the pattern of the dress and wallpaper already included, and even the design details of the sleigh bed in the background.

"Anyway," he added, "I never trust anyone who wants to be paid in cash. Which brings me to another question. Why in the world did you invite her back, Trevor? We're not going to pay her in cash tomorrow, even if the drawing turns out to be right."

"Don't worry – I have no intention of paying her. I just needed an excuse to get her back here. I'm going to call our friend at IFAR and ask him what to do."

"Wait a minute," Claire said. "What to do about what?"

"About Mrs. Boswell. She drew this herself."

"I don't get it? How can you be sure? I mean, the elaborate drawing, the cash, and the expensive shoes — it all looks suspicious, but how do you know she actually faked this drawing?"

"It's the watermark." Trevor held the drawing, which was now completely out of its frame, up to the light. "Look carefully, there. See the initials P.M. at the Arches watermark? That stands for Perrigot-Masure. They produced hand-made paper for Arches, but not until the early 20th century. It was specifically designed to look 'old,' which makes it a perfect choice for a forger. But if this were a preliminary drawing for the Cassatt print, it would have to be circa 1891.

"Besides, this is expensive paper. Mary Cassatt would never have used such fine paper for a preliminary drawing."

Claire looked over Trevor's shoulder. "It sure is well done, though, you have to admit. I mean, the paper does look old. And the drawing is very, well... very Cassatt-like! I mean, in a vacuum I would certainly believe it.

"But maybe her mother was the forger, or the person her mother bought the drawing from?"

"I don't think so. Look at the frame. It's been aged with stain and scuff marks very carefully. But here, inside the corner, is a spot someone missed. Perfectly fresh wood, probably just off the sawmill."

"And there's the timing," Charles chimed in. "It's just too propitious. We all know that Adelyn Breeskin is so ill that she hasn't been able to do any work on the Cassatt catalogue raisonné. That's pretty convenient for Mrs. Boswell, isn't it? Without the expert, buyers are on their own."

"Yes," Trevor agreed. "And if Adelyn dies, it will be a few years before anyone takes over the Mary Cassatt project. That gives Alice Boswell a nice span of time to get away with this."

"Clever! I wonder how many of these she's done?" Claire mused. "And I wonder if Alice Boswell is her real name?"

Claire didn't have to wait long to find out. The next day, when Alice Boswell arrived at The Trevor Whitney Gallery, a tall man in a severe brown suit approached her. As he whipped a badge out of his breast pocket, he declared, "I'm Agent Simpson, with the FBI, Ma'am, and I'd like to ask you a few questions."

An apparently stunned Alice Boswell did not attempt to flee, or deny anything. Instead she sat down weakly in the same chair she'd graced the day before, and began pouring out her story. She hadn't meant to become a forger, she said, it had just sort-of happened one day, when a dealer in Tulsa mistook her drawings for Cassatts. One thing led to another, and the next thing she knew....

"How many drawings have you sold as Cassatts, Mrs. Boswell?" Agent Simpson asked.

"Let's see. About twelve." Alice Boswell looked over at Charles, Trevor and Claire, who were trying to maintain a respectful distance during the interrogation — but not so distant that they couldn't hear what was being said. "They're the first people to ever suspect anything!" Alice announced with surprise, and a touch of admiration.

After Alice Boswell was taken away, Charles turned to Trevor and suddenly held out his hand. As Trevor shook it, Charles said, "Well done. I don't know any other dealer in this city who would have known that much about watermarks. If I'd been on my own I might have bought that drawing. If, of course, she'd have taken a check," he added with a twinkle in his eye.

"And you, young lady," Charles turned to Claire, "I should scold you for snooping in a client's personal belongings, but in this case I think you added a very nice touch of detective work."

"Trevor really was the brilliant one. Don't you think he deserves some public recognition for this?"

"I'm sure the story will hit the papers as soon as Alice Boswell is arraigned," Trevor said.

"But they may not credit you for being the only dealer smart enough to see she was a forger! Just like no one bothered to write about how you solved the O'Connor mystery. I have an idea... Remember, Charles, how you said a long time ago that it would be great if we had our own press agent? A friend of one of my sisters — Anna Lipski is her name — just graduated from NYU and is looking for PR or marketing work. I bet she could write a wonderful press release about Alice Boswell, and Trevor's role in unmasking her."

"What would she charge for something like that?" Charles asked.

"Not much, I'm sure. But Anna is special. She's smart, and adorable, and she loves art — even though she doesn't know much about American art history. And, you know, we really are getting too big to run the gallery with just the three of us. We desperately need some additional help, even just to answer the phones and help with the filing...."

"You want us to *hire* her?" Trevor asked.

"Why not? You'd get another staff person, and your own personal press agent!"

"Charles, does any other gallery in the country have a press agent on staff?" Trevor wanted to know.

"Well, you don't have to *call* her that," Claire protested.

Charles was amused. "It couldn't hurt to meet her, Trevor. We could use the help."

And so Anna Lipski, twenty-two years old, came to work at the gallery. She was tall, with shoulder-length brown hair, a long, swan-like neck and large brown eyes. She was chronically shy, and was over-whelmed by her surroundings at first. But she could write as if she were the ringmaster at a circus — singing the praises of her new employers

134

with flair and confidence that was completely at odds with her retiring personality. The simple energy of her words, as well as the huge list of publications she regularly corresponded with, resulted in her press releases being picked up quite often. At the end of six months she had increased the gallery's press coverage from about six notices a year, to two notices a month.

But only a few weeks after she was hired, Anna was plunged into the biggest coup of The Trevor Whitney Gallery's history.

NINETEEN

"....The day they discovered the Tarbell, that was probably the biggest coup of Trevor's career. It's still funny to think about Anna and how she was thrown into it – I bet she'll be telling her grandchildren that story."

Lewis nodded, but then sighed. "I think that was the apogee in the gallery's life. It slowly started to unravel after that."

In April of 1986, Waldo Picker paid an unexpected visit to the gallery. He rushed into the building in a frenzy, thoroughly startling Anna, who was sitting at the reception desk and hadn't yet made his acquaintance. His obvious disappointment in not immediately seeing anyone he knew didn't encourage her to be outspoken, and when he flew past her into the back hallway — shouting for Charles or Trevor, or even Claire, to make an appearance — it took all her courage to follow him. Finally she found the voice to tell him they had all stepped out to pick up some lunch, but would be back any moment.

A thoroughly agitated Waldo tried to settle himself into a chair to await their return, but could not sit still. He kept jumping up — as if he planned to run out after his gallery friends — and then sitting back down again. When Trevor finally appeared in the doorway Waldo practically bowled him over trying to pull him into the building faster.

"Waldo, hey, what's all this? What's the matter?" Trevor asked in concern.

"It's the find of a lifetime. The find of a lifetime, Trevor! At least I think it is. That's why I need your help. I don't know if I'm right, and I've got to be sure."

"Slow down! What are you talking about?"

To his surprise, Waldo suddenly ran a finger across his lips. "I won't say yet. My lips are sealed. I want Charles to hear this at the same time as you."

With that, he folded his arms across his chest and sat down, his eyes twinkling mischievously and a smile playing at the corners of his mouth.

Trevor looked at him with exasperation, then shrugged. "Any messages?" he asked, turning to Anna.

Waldo was instantly on his feet again. "You're not even going to try to drag it out of me?"

Trevor started laughing, and then Anna, shyly, did too. Waldo looked at the two of them and broke out with his own guffaws. Then he walked over to Anna, held out a hand, and introduced himself.

"I realize I've not made your formal acquaintance. I'm Waldo Picker. I do business with the boys here. And you are?"

"Anna Lipski. I'm new."

Trevor, who had already learned how shy Anna could be, stepped to her side as she answered to check Waldo from teasing her. "Anna's our press agent and general Girl Friday," he said. "We already don't know how we got along without her."

Anna smiled gratefully, but Waldo began looking around in anticipation again. "Where *is* Charles, anyway?" he demanded, just as Claire and Charles walked up to the door. "Ah, the gang's all here! Quick, you two, get inside. I have momentous news."

Claire and Charles were hustled into the building in much the same way Trevor had been, and as soon as they had caught their breath Waldo made an announcement:

"I think I've found a missing Tarbell."

There was a moment of silence while everyone absorbed the news. Edmund Tarbell was one of the founding members of The Ten — one of the fathers of American Impressionism — and one of Boston's greatest artists. His paintings were renowned for capturing the elegant lifestyle of the turn-of-the-century New England elite.

Claire, Trevor and Charles all began talking at once:

"Where? Can we see it?"

"Which one? Is it a figurative piece?"

"How much do they want for it?"

Waldo started laughing again. "I love you guys!" he declared. "Okay, I'll start at the beginning. I was in Topper's this morning. You know Toppers, the fifth-rate auction house? Up past Harlem? Well, I was checking out some carnival glass for my sister when all of a sudden I notice there's this large painting behind a bedroom dresser. Now, the place is packed with things — you can barely move anything an inch — but I manage to get a peek around the furniture, and — I swear to God — that painting is a Tarbell if there ever was one."

"What's the subject?"

"It's a living room scene from maybe the nineteen-teens, with this lady sitting on a couch — beautiful dress, all pensive like, looking off to the side and looking bored — and next to her sits this guy in a suit, reading the evening paper and ignoring her. It's classic Tarbell!"

"Could you see if it was signed?" asked Trevor.

"The thing's filthy dirty. It might be, might not be. Anyway, I couldn't pay too much attention to it, you know, 'cause that would make the place take notice. Everyone there knows me; they know what I do for a living. The thing's got an estimate of only three to five thousand!" Waldo added. "We don't want anyone there thinking about that estimate."

"When's the sale?" Charles asked.

"Tomorrow night. We don't have much time."

"Let's go then. I'll get a cab...." Trevor started toward the door, but Waldo stopped him.

"No, no. I can't go back today, and you certainly can't. Someone might recognize you! If word gets out that Trevor Whitney is looking at a painting at Topper's we're doomed. There will be dealers crawling all over there!"

"But we have to see it before we bid on it."

The group tried to think how they could handle it, but Waldo kept insisting it was too risky for any of them to go in person to see it.

"I know," Claire suggested. "Trevor and Charles can wear disguises."

"Disguises?" Trevor made a face.

"I'm serious! It's not that difficult — just a wig and some makeup — maybe a fake mustache."

Charles laughed appreciatively. "Claire knows what she's doing — she grew up in the theater."

Trevor wanted to protest, but before he could, Claire had Anna calling the nearest wig store, and she was running out to the theatrical supply shop to get pancake makeup and props. She sent Charles out to buy a pair of blue jeans, a sweatshirt, and a baseball cap — an outfit he normally would not be caught dead in.

In no time at all, Claire transformed the two owners. Makeup, a wig and one of Charles' bow ties made Trevor look like a gentleman about twice his age. Black shoe polish in Charles' hair took ten years off his face, and his new clothes made him look like any average guy who frequents junk sales.

Waldo was thrilled with the results. He instructed the two men to leave in separate cabs, and not to talk to each other while they were there.

At Topper's, Trevor and Charles played their parts with gusto. Trevor walked stiffly, as if his joints ached, and although he spent some time examining the painting, he spent far more time scrutinizing some sofas and chairs at the other end of the room. Charles appeared to look at everything but the painting, and seemed to only glance at it because he was trying to see the back of a dresser.

When they each returned to the gallery, they were bursting with excitement.

"It's incredible!" Trevor exclaimed. "It's probably one of the best Tarbells ever painted."

"I'm dying to know where it's been all these years," Charles said.

"I doubt it's ever been reproduced."

"There's no question it's a Tarbell, though. Waldo, you're a genius. I think your hometown should erect a statue in your honor."

"Aw, shucks, Trev, you're making me blush," Waldo said sarcastically, but with good humor. "Anyway, how are we going to handle this? I want in on it."

"Of course! Do you want a half share?"

"That depends on what it costs you," Waldo replied.

"You don't think we'll get it for the estimate?" Claire wanted to know.

"I'd love to think so, sweetheart, but I've lived too long. It would be a miracle if we had no competition, and I don't think it's smart to count on miracles. You guys will have to decide just how high you'll go if you have to."

"Five hundred thousand," Charles said without hesitation. "It's worth a million."

"A million dollars! Do you really think so?" Claire was impressed. In 1986 it was still a special event if an American painting brought a million dollars, even in private sales.

"I'd stake my reputation on the fact that once it's cleaned and reframed we can sell that painting for over a million dollars," Charles assured Claire. "Just think how rare great Tarbells are! All of the others are in museums."

"How are we going to bid?" Trevor asked. "By phone?"

Waldo shook his head. "That's gonna be a problem. They don't do phone bids. You have to be there in person."

"Can *you* do it, Waldo?" Claire asked.

"Too risky! You guys still don't get it — if you want to pull this off with even a prayer of success, then none of us can do it. We're all too well known!"

"Even with disguises?" Trevor asked. He had found it rather fun to be incognito.

"Too risky. What if someone got a really good look at you? Besides, what name you gonna give when you go to collect your painting?" Waldo pointed out.

"How about Anna!" Everyone turned to look at Anna as Claire continued. "She's perfect! No one knows her yet...."

"Brilliant idea!" Waldo exclaimed.

Anna's eyes grew wide with alarm.

"Oh, I don't think I could..." she began.

"Sure you can!" Claire assured her. "It's easy. I'll coach you."

"But it's so much money — so much responsibility! I don't know if I should."

"We know we're asking a lot of you," Trevor told her, "but we have complete faith in you. Don't we, Charles?"

"We'll coach you, Anna," said Charles. "Don't worry, you'll do fine!"

But Anna's natural reticence made it extremely difficult for her to find the courage to face the task with confidence. Although Claire and Charles worked with her for a few hours, her hands still shook whenever she pictured herself at the actual auction. She was terrified she'd make a mistake and lose the painting for them.

"It's not the auction itself that scares me," she said, "It's just the bidding. What if I get off on the wrong foot, or get scared and stop too soon, or forget myself and go too high? I don't want you guys to be mad at me!"

"You won't. And we won't be mad at you, I promise," Claire said.

But Trevor, who had overheard Anna's worries, couldn't help

wishing out loud that they had a way to be in contact with her during the sale. "It's too bad we can't set up some sort of walkie-talkie or something, so we could talk to her."

"Oh!" Claire suddenly exclaimed. "I have the best idea! Portable telephone!"

"You mean one of those car phones?"

"Yes! You don't have to use them in a car, you know."

Anna was ecstatic. "Oh, I'd feel so much better if I could talk to you while I bid!"

Trevor agreed to buy the car phone, which came in a not-so-subtle bulky carrying case. Nevertheless, Anna was relieved.

The following night Anna set off for the auction in a cab — her head full of instructions, her hands nervously clutching the portable phone bag. Her colleagues dimmed the lights in the gallery so it appeared they'd gone home, then gathered around the telephone to await Anna's call when the bidding started.

Across the street, James Hardwick set off on his weekly raid of The Trevor Whitney Gallery trash. He whistled softly to himself as he entered the alley, quite in a good mood. He was no longer afraid of getting caught — months of not being detected had allayed that fear — and he'd begun to look forward to these night prowls. It allowed him to spy on Claire, which was far more interesting than spying on the gallery. For example, he knew that The Colonel was history, or soon would be. He'd found a letter Claire had drafted to Edgar Halverson and then torn up — a letter in which she'd tried to explain why he had to stop thinking of her as "his girl." James thought it was only a matter of time before he'd have a clear shot at Claire himself.

The alley was unusually dark. Charles usually turned on the light over the back door before he went home, but apparently had forgotten this time. Well, no matter. James knew his way around well enough. He felt his way to the first trash can and quietly lifted the lid. He pulled out the first bag, and then began examining the contents with the pocket light he carried so he didn't have to walk back and forth to the alley lamp to read what he was finding.

At the auction, Anna nervously signed in with her name and home address. She was given a paddle for bidding. She slipped into a seat at the front of the room so most of the bidders would not have a view of her face. She was tempted to call the gallery and tell them everything was going fine, but Claire had warned her that the phone wasn't fully charged, and only had so much battery time. The last thing Anna wanted was the battery to run out during the middle of the sale.

There were four hundred lots in the auction, and the painting was number eighty-five. The first fifty lots seemed to fly past in a matter of seconds, and Anna began to sweat. She had never heard anyone talk as fast as that auctioneer! Lot sixty, lot sixty-one... Anna told herself to take deep breaths and stay calm. Lot seventy-five... Anna dialed the gallery.

Trevor picked it up on the first ring. "Anna? What lot are they on?"

"Seventy-seven," she whispered. "Trevor, you guys never told me how fast this was!"

"Just stay calm. I'll be with you the whole time."

There were a few moments of silence. Then Anna said, "Here it comes...."

Back in the alley, James thought he saw something interesting at the bottom of the trash can. It was a large notebook that had been shoved down inside, but it had rained during the week, and the moisture had expanded the fabric-covered binder. The notebook was now firmly stuck. James began to pull.

In the auction room the bidding started off slowly. But as the painting passed its estimate of $5,000, Anna could feel the interest in the room grow rapidly. She knew there was someone bidding against her, not just the house trying to reach the low estimate. She was too frightened to turn around and try to see who else was bidding, and besides, Waldo had stressed the need for her to be as anonymous as possible. She could feel people straining to see her face, and she knew the portable phone was generating extra interest in her actions. She began to feel hot, but she forced herself to concentrate on Trevor's voice. Calmly he told her to keep bidding and not to worry about anyone else in the room.

The price edged up past twenty thousand, and the auctioneer started taking bids in larger increments. "Twenty-two thousand; twenty-five thousand; twenty-eight thousand..." Anna kept bidding against her unknown competition.

At fifty thousand the auctioneer made a jump to ten thousand-dollar increments. At one hundred thousand he made twenty-five thousand-dollar jumps. The noise level in the room increased as the audience started cheering for each new bid. Nothing had ever been sold for this much at Toppers.

"Stay calm," Trevor's voice reassured Anna over the phone. "Just hang in there. You're doing great."

Back in the alley James was tugging and tugging, but the notebook wouldn't budge. Finally James threw down his pocket light, took off his shirt and grabbed the notebook with both hands. He pushed his foot against the trash can for leverage and gave the notebook one mighty pull. It didn't move, but James refused to let go. Sweat poured down his face. He felt that if he didn't let up, sheer force of will would eventually make the notebook move. Suddenly, he started to slip. "Oh, shit!" he exclaimed as he began to fall over backwards.

"Four hundred thousand; four hundred and twenty-five thousand; four hundred and fifty thousand..." Anna was poised to make the five hundred thousand bid. Just as she heard Trevor saying to Charles in the background, "Should we go one more after five hundred?" the phone went dead.

At the last moment of James' fall in the alley, he had grabbed onto something he'd hoped might arrest his downward tumble. It was the telephone cable running along the outside wall.

Inside the gallery, Trevor heard a click, then nothing. "Anna? Anna!" he said frantically, but the line was dead. "What the hell!" he exclaimed. "What's going on here?"

"I think I heard something outside," Charles said, and he dashed for the back door, with Waldo right behind him.

Back at the auction Anna sat frozen, completely terrified. She didn't know why the phone had disconnected, but she didn't have time to re-dial the number. She had just bid five hundred thousand, and after a few moments of hesitation her opponent had made the next bid. The auctioneer was looking at her expectantly. "The bid is five hundred and fifty thousand. Your bid, young lady. Say five hundred and fifty thousand. Last chance. Going once, twice...."

Anna closed her eyes and lifted the paddle.

The other bidder, whoever he'd been, must have shaken his head, for suddenly the auctioneer was crying out, "Sold! To the young lady in the front row, for five hundred and fifty thousand dollars! Congratulations!"

The room erupted. Strangers began patting Anna on the back and asking her questions. Alarmed, Anna jumped up and ran to the administration desk.

"I have to go," she stammered. "Here's a cashier's check for $100,000 to hold the painting until I can transfer the rest of the funds to my account tomorrow." The gallery had supplied her with this check, just in case. The cashier took it as collateral and excitedly flashed it to her co-workers.

146

Anna fled the auction and hailed a cab. All the way back to the gallery she kept repeating to herself, "I hope they're not mad at me for spending so much! Oh, I hope Charles agreed to go that extra bid!"

To Anna's surprise, she arrived at the gallery at the same time as a police car. Anna walked into the gallery with the policeman and encountered a strange scene.

James Hardwick, the manager from the gallery across the street, was tied to a chair in the middle of the room. Charles and Waldo appeared to be standing guard over him. James was shirtless, and filthy, as if he'd rolled around in garbage. Charles and Trevor were interrogating him, alternately asking him "What in the world were you doing in the alley?" and "Do you realize it's a crime to cut the phone lines?"

But as soon as Anna walked in Trevor rushed up to her. "Please tell me you got the painting," he whispered in her ear.

Anna nodded. "But I had to pay five hundred and fifty thousand," she whispered back.

"Good girl!" Trevor exclaimed out loud, giving the rest of his colleagues a "thumbs-up." Charles' and Waldo's stern expressions left their faces long enough to smile at Anna and compliment her on a "job well done," and Claire rushed over and gave her a hug.

Charles began explaining to the policeman why they had James Hardwick tied to a chair, and Claire began explaining it as well to Anna.

"We found him in the alley," she told her friend. "He was going through our trash, would you believe! He fell over and accidentally cut the phone line. Anyway, now we can guess who's been behind the leaks all these months."

"Gosh, what a sleazeball!" Anna said.

"My sentiments exactly," said Claire, and raising her voice so James would overhear her, she added, "and I hope they put him away for life!"

TWENTY

Anna returned to Topper's the next day to make the rest of the payment for the Tarbell painting. To her alarm, a reporter was waiting by the cashier's office. Anna would have slipped away and returned later, but the cashier recognized her before she had a chance.

"There's the young lady who bought the painting! Miss Lipski, this is a reporter from the *New York Post*. He'd like to interview you."

Anna took a deep breath and told herself not to panic. She walked over to the reporter and quietly said, "You'll understand, I hope, but my employer doesn't allow me to talk to reporters."

"So this painting isn't going to belong to you personally?" the reporter asked. "Is your employer the person you were on the telephone with during the bidding?"

"I can't say any more, I'm sorry." Anna turned to the cashier. "Here," she said, "Here is the rest of the payment."

The cashier took the second cashier's check from Anna, while the reporter tried to get a good look at the document. Annoyed, Anna nudged the reporter away from the cashier's window. "I've arranged for Grosso Moving and Packing to come get the painting later today," she told the cashier. "You have my phone number — give me a call if there's any problem."

Anna turned to leave but the reporter started following her. "Hey," he demanded, "why all the mystery?" Anna began walking very quickly, and to her relief the reporter didn't persist in trailing her. She thanked God the man did not have a photographer with him.

When Anna returned to the gallery, she found Lewis and Bernard there. They had been let in on the whole adventure, and were eagerly awaiting the arrival of the Tarbell. Anna stammered out the story of her encounter with the reporter to her colleagues. At first, even Waldo was rather complacent about the incident.

"At this point, honey, let 'em find out. The painting's ours! I don't see what anyone else can do about it."

"What about that speech you made to me about keeping the Sargent a secret when you brought it here?" Trevor wanted to know. "How is this different?"

"It's a public sale, Trev. Toppers couldn't be expected to keep the biggest windfall of its history a secret. No collector worth his salt is going to care that you're the genius who discovered and bought this painting. This will only add to your illustrious reputation!"

"But there is a problem..." Bernard interjected.

The rest of the group looked at him.

"No collector worth his salt will buy this painting without an authentication. They'll want to know if it's going to be in the catalogue raisonné."

"So we'll get the person compiling the catalogue raisonné to authenticate it. Who's the expert on Tarbell?" Trevor asked.

"Lavinia Worthington," Lewis and Bernard said in unison, and the way they said it let Trevor know this was not a good thing.

"What's wrong with Lavinia?" Trevor asked.

"She hates you!" Lewis exclaimed. "Oh, Trevor, we didn't want to tell you this before, but she absolutely despises you! The woman lives to see you fail! It's completely unjustified, but it's true."

Trevor had turned red during this speech, then pale.

"Trevor," Bernard asked gently, "you don't happen to know why she hates you so much, do you? It would be a good idea to let us in on it, if you do, because maybe we can help you get around it."

"I'm not sure..." Trevor began. "But I met her once, years ago, in Europe. We were introduced at a party." He paused. "I have a feeling I may have offended her somehow."

The men in the group shook their heads in sympathy, as if they completely understood Trevor's meaning. Claire raised her eyebrows

150

and wondered just how Trevor had "offended" Lavinia Worthington.

"Well, can't you apologize or something?" Claire asked, hoping to elicit more information.

But Lewis answered for Trevor. "I believe this is one of those instances when the apology is too long overdue to be of service to us today," he announced.

"So, let me make sure I understand our current situation." Charles offered the group a recap. "We have a reporter who will probably discover our ownership of the Tarbell — a painting we just spent a record amount of money on. In order to sell this painting, we need authentication from Lavinia Worthington, who won't give it to us if she knows we own the painting. I'd say this is a big problem."

"We have to work fast!" The group turned to Anna, who was suddenly animated. "If we get the authentication before the reporter figures us out, we'll be okay!"

"Anna's right!" Claire exclaimed. "We must have at least twenty-four hours to play with, at least until tomorrow's paper comes out. Now, who can bring the painting over there today?"

"Well, it can't be Bernie or me," Lewis said. "Lavinia knows we're tied to you."

"It can't be me," Waldo said, "Lavinia will know I'm not the real player. She won't give me the authentication unless I fork over that information."

"Well, it obviously can't be me, or Charles or Claire," Trevor said. He grinned at his youngest colleague. "Well, Anna, it looks like it will have to be you again."

This time, Anna was not surprised, and she even tried to be enthusiastic. She felt partly responsible for the mess they were in, for she was sure that one of her older colleagues could have found a better way around the reporter. "Okay," she said. "I'm game."

"Good girl!" Bernard exclaimed. "I have an idea. Call Grosso and tell them to bring the painting directly to Lavinia's gallery. That will throw the reporter temporarily off the trail, anyway. Then you go to the pay phone on Madison Avenue, Anna, and call for an appointment. Lavinia will have heard by now that it was a young woman bidding on the painting, so she won't be surprised to hear from you. The tricky part will be when you're in there. You'll have to convince her that it's in her best interests not to push you too much on who you're working for. I have an idea about that too...."

Two hours later, Anna found herself being ushered into the private sanctum of Lavinia Worthington's gallery. Lavinia's office was more a boudoir than workspace. The room was painted and upholstered in shades of pink, except for the owner's mahogany desk and gold-accented desk accessories. Lavinia directed Anna to take a seat on the pink velvet tufted lounge in front of the desk. Anna, who knew all about Lavinia's reputation, couldn't help wondering how often Alfred Cummings had reclined on that same sofa.

"I'm honored that your employer thought to send the painting — the Tarbell — directly to me," Lavinia said sweetly as soon as Anna was seated. "I was so excited to learn about its discovery. It's a painting I've been looking for for quite a few years. I believe it's one that's described in a sales catalogue from the early part of the century, but it was never illustrated."

"My boss, Mr. Ma--, I mean, my employer, said that you were the expert on Tarbell, and I should bring it to you immediately." Anna paused and leaned over conspiratorially, as she'd been coached. "He naturally hopes you will include it in any upcoming exhibitions you might be planning." This simple request was meant to indicate to Lavinia that the painting's owner did not have his own gallery.

Lavinia was thrilled, as expected. "I would be delighted to.

A discovery of this importance — why, it might be worth planning a whole exhibition around it!"

"Of course, shipping would be complicated..." Anna said, as if considering this for the first time. "My employer lives rather far away. And the painting is so large."

"Far away, you say? My dear, let us be open with each other. I have a good idea who your employer must be."

"Do you? Oh, dear. He did so much wish to keep this a secret."

Lavinia laughed. "You can't have been working for him long! Oscar Manning loves to keep secrets, almost as much as he loves to have the world find them out! Now, we are talking about Oscar Manning, aren't we?"

Anna looked down at her lap with feigned embarrassment. Lavinia was satisfied.

"Don't feel badly, dear. My lips are sealed. And to show my good faith, I'll let you in on a secret of my own." Lavinia paused, then continued with a mischievous smile. "I know who was bidding against you last night."

Anna looked up in surprise. Confessions from Lavinia had not been part of the plan. Anna's mind raced, as she tried to assess if this was a good thing, or not. But Lavinia's continuing words allowed her to see the possibilities: "So you see, dear, I happen to know someone who would quite likely buy the painting, should Mr. Manning ever want to sell."

For a second Anna wondered why Lavinia was telling her this. Then she understood. Lavinia was offering her the chance to sell the painting, right now.

Anna swallowed. *Think*, she told herself. What would Trevor and Charles want her to do? Suddenly, she thought she knew.

"My employer was willing to go quite a bit higher last night," Anna began. "He's really fallen in love with the Tarbell. I wonder if your friend would be willing to spend enough to make it worth his while to consider selling."

Lavinia smiled. "I think so. He was quite distraught himself, last night, because he saw that you would never stop bidding. So he asked himself, isn't it better to let the painting go now, and offer a nice profit to the owner later? You see, if your boss had paid too much for the painting last night, you're right — there would be no room for negotiation. But really, you know Mr. Manning got it for a reasonable price. If he could be convinced to part with it, I know my friend would make it worth his while."

Lavinia's friend could only be one person — Alfred Cummings. Claire had told Anna that Alfred Cummings was always competing with Oscar Manning for the best American paintings.

"How much?" Anna asked boldly.

"Why, you tell me!"

Anna saw that she'd made a tactical error. She didn't want to set a price. If she did, and Lavinia accepted it, she'd probably be obligated to sell it. What would Trevor and Charles think of her actions? But then, wasn't the point of buying the painting to sell it, and if so, weren't they better off selling it as quickly as possible, before the whole world knew they owned it?

Anna picked a number so high that Trevor and Charles couldn't possibly be disappointed. "One million two hundred and fifty thousand," Anna said.

Lavinia blinked. "My!" she said. "That's some profit!"

But Anna was afraid to come down on the price. "I'm not authorized to go any lower," Anna said. "I'm sorry," she added, as if apologetic.

"Well," Lavinia said. Then she smiled. "It can't hurt to ask, can it?

Wait here while I make a phone call."

Lavinia left the room. Anna sat staring at a Laura Coombs Hills still life of peonies on the wall, wondering if she'd just done the dumbest or the smartest thing of her life. In a remarkably short time, Lavinia was back. She walked into the room holding out her hand.

"It's done," she announced, to Anna's astonishment. "I'll have a check for you tomorrow."

Tomorrow! Anna knew that by tomorrow the papers could be announcing to the world the painting's real ownership. Anna had to be bold one last time.

"I'm flying out today," she said. "I'm afraid I'll have to take a check with me, if I'm not bringing the painting."

Lavinia frowned at her, as if her request was outrageous. "I'll at least need an hour to transfer the funds," she complained.

But Anna was all sweetness. "Take a few hours," she offered. "But please have the check made out to me. I would prefer it if my employer never knew I'd disclosed his identity."

When Anna returned to The Trevor Whitney Gallery and recounted what had happened, astonishment was followed by hugs and cheers.

"Oh my God... a million two-hundred and fifty! I'm so proud of you, Anna!" Claire grabbed Anna's arms and started jumping up and down.

"What a coup!" Waldo said, with real admiration.

"We couldn't have done better ourselves!" Charles laughed and shook his head in amazement. "We should have anticipated that Alfred Cummings might have been our competition."

Trevor hugged Anna hard and announced, "We're going out tonight to celebrate! Claire, make a reservation for all of us at Tavern on the Green. Anna's never been there, and I can't think of a better place to throw an impromptu party."

Lewis began giggling. "Oh, my," he said, "what I wouldn't give to see Lavinia's face tomorrow morning. Why, I think I'll call the papers myself and make sure they get the correct details!"

Bernard was horrified. "You're joking, please, Lewis. With any luck, Lavinia will never know who really owned the painting. Poor Trevor doesn't need any more reasons for that woman to hate him."

Lewis sobered. "I suppose you're right, Bernie. But it's a shame. Who knows when next we'll have such a delicious joke at that woman's expense!"

"It will have to be our little secret," Trevor said.

"Yes," Lewis sighed. "Our little secret that will bring us hours of pleasure whenever we dwell on it!"

TWENTY-ONE

The celebration dinner went on for hours. The champagne poured freely and there were many toasts to good fortune, so by the end of the evening the whole party was inebriated. Eventually Waldo stumbled off to his hotel, Charles escorted Anna home on his way to the train, and Lewis and Bernard ordered a taxi. Claire and Trevor were left alone.

They couldn't stop smiling at each other. They both shared the most delightful viewpoint on the whole experience. It was a dream come true. Discovering an unknown masterpiece, selling it for a tremendous price — this was what one lived for in the art world. And they had both experienced it for the first time, together.

"You know, Claire," Trevor said, "I can't think of anyone else I'd rather be celebrating with right now. You really love this as much as I do."

"It's the best! I don't think it's possible for another career to be this much fun, do you?"

"Definitely not. We have it all — art, money, intrigue and fun!"

Claire nodded. "What an amazing two days. I'm so proud of Anna, aren't you? She was wonderful."

Trevor smiled at her. "I've been watching her these past weeks. She's learned a lot from you. She idolizes you, you know."

Claire blushed. "Really?"

"Sure. You're very talented, Claire. I know we butt heads sometimes over things, but you're incredibly talented. I really respect your opinion about things."

"You do?" Claire was overwhelmed. "Thank you for telling me that. It means a lot to me." She looked down at her hands for a moment, then added, "I really respect you too, Trevor."

To her surprise Trevor laughed. "That's a relief! I wasn't sure."

"You weren't?"

"No. Honestly."

"How can you say that? You're so brilliant! Everyone knows it."

"They do?"

"Of course! Gosh, Trevor, I thought you knew how great you were." She giggled. "I mean, I thought you had all this self-confidence."

Trevor said quietly, "I'm not self-confident at all, Claire. I really don't know what anybody thinks of me."

Claire was amazed. "We all admire you! You have such a great eye, and enthusiasm, and great knowledge — and you're daring. It was daring to start the gallery like you did. The odds were completely against you and you've been this amazing success!"

"I had to rely a tremendous amount on Charles. I still do."

"Well, of course you do. He's got fifty years of experience. You'd be crazy not to take advantage of that, but you'd also be too hard on yourself if you thought that in just a few years you should know as much as he does."

Trevor looked at Claire gratefully. "Yeah, you're right." He smiled. "I am too hard on myself."

"Who would have guessed it?" Claire put a finger up to her lips. "I won't tell a soul! Scout's honor. No one would believe me anyway," she added.

Trevor laughed, then stood up and stretched. "Come on. Let's go; I'll get us a taxi."

Claire felt lightheaded when she rose from her seat. "Wow. I guess I drank more than I thought."

"Hold on to me," Trevor offered. He put his arm around her. In the cab, Claire leaned her head on Trevor's shoulder, and Trevor smiled.

When they got to the door of Claire's apartment, Claire suddenly leaned up and gave Trevor a quick kiss on the lips. "That's for self-confidence," she said. "Don't ever doubt yourself."

Claire was referring to their earlier conversation. But Trevor took her words to refer to the immediate moment. He pulled her close and kissed her, hard.

They kissed for a long time. Finally Claire pulled away. "We've had a lot to drink," she said. "Maybe we should think about this."

"I don't want to think about it," Trevor said.

Claire sighed. "Neither do I." But neither one made another move toward the other. They stood there, deep in thought.

"Maybe you're right," Trevor said after a moment.

"I think it's best," Claire said.

"I'll see you tomorrow, then."

"Right. Tomorrow."

They parted in a fog of confusion.

And neither one had the slightest idea what the other was really thinking.

TWENTY-TWO

Lavinia Worthington did, unfortunately, discover who the real owner of the Tarbell painting had been. It wasn't the intrepid reporter who spilled the beans; Lavinia put it together herself when Anna accompanied Claire to the American Painting auction in May. Lavinia spied Anna in the back of the room at Christie's, but as she made her way back there to say hello she saw Claire walk over, hand Anna the auction catalogue and say, "Keep tabs on the bids for me for a moment, Anna. I'm just going to run to the ladies room." Something in the way she said it left no doubt that Anna was an employee of The Trevor Whitney Gallery.

Lavinia stood stock still for a minute. She felt the blood drain out of her face, but in an instant her feelings had rebounded to rage. That bastard Trevor Whitney had pulled one over on her. Well, she'd get her revenge.

Continuing over to the back of the room, Lavinia tapped an unsuspecting Anna on the shoulder. Anna turned and went pale. There was a hard glint in Lavinia Worthington's eyes.

She leaned over and whispered in Anna's ear. "Listen, you little bitch, you'd better never leave that gallery of yours, because I'll make sure you never work in this town again. And tell your boss that Alfred Cummings may sue for misrepresentation."

Lavinia leaned back again. "Lovely to see you," she said cheerfully for the benefit of their neighbors. Then she walked back to her seat.

When Claire returned to the auction room she found a pale and shaking Anna, who tearfully explained what had happened.

"Oh, pooh," Claire said, trying to sound reassuring, "she can't do anything to you! And Alfred Cummings isn't going to sue us, because if Lavinia is as smart as I know she is, she'll never tell him the truth. She'd just look like an idiot."

"But she won't authenticate any Tarbells for us."

"Oh, that. We're unlikely to come across any more that need authenticating anyway! Don't worry, Anna, it will be all right. I'm sorry she was so horrid to you, though. She's really a witch."

But Anna was no longer comfortable at the sale. She wanted to go back to the gallery to tell Trevor and Charles what had happened. Claire put her in a cab and was sorry Anna's first auction experience had been ruined.

Normally, Claire and Trevor would have been at the auction together. But Trevor had suggested that she take Anna, and Claire felt it was a sure sign that Trevor was avoiding her. Ever since the night of the celebration, they were awkward together. She had no idea what Trevor was thinking, but as time went on and he didn't say anything to her, she sadly concluded that Trevor must have decided that any relationship between them was a bad idea. She tried to be her usual cheerful self at the gallery, but after work she found herself feeling blue. She'd never realized how much she liked Trevor until it became obvious that nothing was ever going to happen between them. And she still could taste the memory of that kiss, which had been incredible.

Trevor, for his part, was walking around in a funk too. He was sorry he'd ever kissed Claire in the first place, because it was all he could think about. He was certain Claire hadn't given it a second thought — otherwise, how could she act as if nothing had happened? There was no sign at all from her that could be interpreted as encouraging. Apparently she thought any relationship between them was a bad idea.

It never occurred to him that she could be waiting for a sign from him.

The tension between Trevor and Claire wasn't obvious to anyone else in the gallery, but the moment Lewis saw the two of them together he knew something was wrong.

"What happened with Trevor and Claire?" he demanded of a

surprised Charles. "They're hardly speaking to each other."

"They aren't?" Charles asked in real bewilderment. "I hadn't noticed anything."

"Oh, the tortuous paths of love! How will these two ever get together if you don't pay attention?"

"Lewis, I'm not sure there's anything to pay attention to. As far as I know, nothing's happened."

Lewis put his arm around Charles' shoulders. "They both think of you as a mentor, Charles. It's up to you to step in and take charge. Talk to them. Show them the way to each other's hearts!"

But Charles, of course, would do nothing of the kind. He'd never intruded in their personal lives before, and he couldn't imagine anything more awkward than starting now. But he promised Lewis he'd keep an eye open, just to appease him.

A few days later Charles received some news that completely eclipsed the supposed romantic troubles between Claire and Trevor. Mary, his wife, was sick.

Something about this illness was different. It started as a cold, then worsened into pneumonia. When Mary finally allowed Charles to admit her to the hospital, the illness' resistance to antibiotics confounded the doctors. Finally they began to wonder: could Mary somehow have contracted the HIV virus? A blood test confirmed the worst. Mary had AIDS.

Five years previously a needle had slipped when Mary was taking blood from a patient. Although the patient was a street kid known to be a heroin user, Mary hadn't worried. It was 1981 and the medical community was unaware how pervasive AIDS could be. Mary didn't even bother getting tested when an HIV test eventually became available. Why should she? She was a sixty-year-old heterosexual grandmother. But now she knew that needle had infected her.

Mary's greatest fear was not about dying. She was afraid she and Charles would be ostracized.

"Don't tell anyone what's wrong with me," she begged Charles. "Make up a story."

"Why, Mary?"

"People won't want to be near you. They'll think they can catch it."

"Well, then, we'll educate them."

"Charles, people can be so ignorant. I don't want you to suffer for my illness."

"How can you talk about my suffering, when you're the one who's sick, Mary?" Charles cried.

"Promise me! I don't want anyone to know."

"Okay, okay honey. I promise." He thought Mary was being irrational, but now was not the time to argue. Still, Charles had to ask her for one exception. "I have to tell Trevor, Mary. I want to retire so I can be with you; it's not fair not to tell him. You know Trevor. He can be trusted."

"Okay. Only Trevor. But ask him not to tell anyone else."

Charles called Trevor from the hospital. He hadn't been in the gallery for over a week, and hadn't even called to check in. That was so unlike Charles that Trevor already suspected Mary must be very sick. Still, he was unprepared for what Charles had to tell him.

"Trevor, I have some bad news. But I need to ask you, are you alone?"

"I'm in the back office. Claire and Anna are out front. What's wrong?"

"I'm going to tell you something, but first I need to ask you a favor. I want you to promise you won't share what I'm about to say with the girls."

"Well, if that's what you want, of course I won't. What is it, Charles?"

"You know Mary's been in the hospital with pneumonia. Well, it hasn't been responding to the regular treatment. A few days ago we found out why. Mary has AIDS."

"AIDS?" Trevor was astounded. "How is that possible?"

"We think she was exposed about five years ago, when she was taking blood from a heroin user. But we can't be sure."

"Oh my God. Poor Mary. What can I do?"

To Trevor's alarm, he heard Charles begin to sob. "That's the worst part about it. There isn't much anyone can do. Just pray."

"Well, do they... do they think she'll be able to go back home?"

Charles seemed to recover himself. "They've come up with a more aggressive treatment that seems to be working. We won't know for a few more days, but if all goes well she'll come home. And of course I want to be with her."

"Of course you do." Trevor took a deep breath before he said, "You won't be coming back. Will you, Charles?"

"No. I can't. I want to be with Mary."

"That's where you should be, Charles. We'll be all right," Trevor said, although he doubted this was true.

"Listen, Trevor. Mary doesn't want anyone else to know. You'll have to make up something to tell the girls — I don't trust myself to face them. I'll come by one evening and get my things."

"Okay. I'll think of something." Trevor was reeling. How would he get along without Charles? Charles was more than his partner — he was his mentor, a father figure, his best friend.

"What about Lewis and Bernard?" Trevor asked.

"I'll ask Mary. Maybe she'll be OK with them knowing since they've had friends with AIDS."

"I'll miss you like crazy, Charles, but I don't want you to worry about a thing. I'll take care of everything. You just be there for Mary."

"Thanks, Trevor. I knew I could count on you."

"Call me, Charles. Call me anytime. Just to talk; or whenever you want to hear about the gallery."

"I will."

Something in Charles' voice sounded amused, and Trevor couldn't imagine what he'd said to elicit that reaction, until Charles said:

"You know, Trevor, when Sid got sick I stopped by every day to tell him the gallery news. I never realized till now why Sid didn't care. He enjoyed seeing me, but he really didn't care. Now I know. What is art compared to love and life?"

"You're right," Trevor said. "It's nothing compared to what you have with Mary. Please give her my best wishes. Tell her I'll be praying for her."

"God bless you, Son. And Trevor, don't worry. You're going to be fine without me."

As Trevor hung up the phone he wished he felt as confident in himself as Charles did. He didn't even know what in the world he was going to say to Claire and Anna.

Claire. He'd hardly spoken to her in weeks, but now he would give anything to confide in her. She'd understand. She'd say the right thing. But he'd promised Charles. There was no way he could break that promise.

Trevor walked out to the main gallery. Anna was sitting at the reception desk. "Where's Claire?" he asked.

"She went to the framer's."

"Oh. Well, that was Charles on the phone."

"Is Mary okay?" Anna and Claire knew that Mary was in the hospital.

"Yeah, she's fine. Charles just called to make an announcement." Trevor forced a big smile. "He's retiring."

"Retiring? So suddenly?"

166

"He seems to feel that after our big coup last month, the time is right. He says we'll be fine without him. He wants to spend more time with Mary."

"Oh. I guess when she was sick he realized how much he missed her."

"Yes. I think that's it. Anyway, he won't be coming back."

"Not at all?"

Trevor shook his head, trying to look amused.

"Just like that? Don't we get to throw him a party or something?"

"No, he doesn't want any fuss."

"Gosh. It's so sudden!"

"He doesn't want us to make a big deal out of it. After all, it's really the second time he's retired."

"It is?

"Sure. Didn't you know? He used to work at the Steinman Gallery. I hired him out of retirement."

"Oh. I didn't realize. Well, I guess it makes sense, then."

The puzzled look on Anna's face belied that statement, but Trevor took advantage of it to say cheerily, "Well, let Claire know when she gets back. I'm going out for a while."

It was a cheap trick, making Anna give Claire the news. But Trevor didn't trust himself to tell her. He knew she'd ask a lot more questions than Anna had, and he was afraid she'd know he was lying. Trevor hoped if Anna broke the news Claire might actually accept it.

If Trevor wasn't reeling, himself, he would have recognized the absurdity of that hope.

When Claire returned, Anna was still trying to understand what was going on.

"Trevor says Charles is retiring!" she blurted out as soon as Claire walked in the door.

167

"What? What in the world are you talking about?"

"Charles called this morning and told Trevor he's retiring. He doesn't want any fuss about it. He just thinks it's time."

The news didn't make any sense to Claire. "Is Mary okay?"

"Oh, sure. She's great. He just wants to spend more time with her."

"Well... I don't get it. Is he coming back at all?"

"Apparently not."

"Not even to say goodbye?"

Anna shrugged. "I guess that phone call was goodbye. Maybe he would have talked to you, but you were out."

Claire was stupefied. "Gosh, Anna, doesn't the whole thing strike you as strange?"

"Well, yes, it did. But Trevor seemed so jovial about it that I couldn't see any point in worrying. Charles must be happy."

Claire frowned. Why would Trevor be in such a good mood? He depended on Charles! Unless... Claire was struck with a terrible thought. Could it be that Trevor *wanted* Charles to retire?

"What exactly did Trevor say, Anna?"

"Let's see. He said that after the big thing last month, the time was right, and we'd be fine without him. And that we shouldn't make a big deal out of it because it was Charles' second retirement. Oh, and that he had to go run an errand but I should tell you as soon as I saw you. I think that's all."

Claire was furious.

Trevor clearly wasn't upset at all. He didn't even think it was important for her to hear the news from him, much less Charles. All her frustrations of the past few weeks came to a head. *Perhaps it's true after all*, she fumed to herself. *Trevor's ego is unbelievable!*

This was the gist of what had always held Claire back from admitting her feelings for Trevor: she suspected him of being incredibly conceited. That cocksure smile of his, the women who fawned all over him, the way he always got whatever he wanted — the man *had* to be utterly full of himself. That night they'd kissed, when he'd said he was insecure — that was what made her fall in love with him. But it was apparently just a line if he thought he'd be fine without Charles. And he obviously did, if Charles' retirement required no more than a word passed on to her through Anna!

Then, in her frustration and disappointment, Claire latched onto another thought. Perhaps Trevor really did think that Charles' presence had kept the gallery out of the NYHADA, so now he was glad because he could finally join that stupid organization!

This view of things flew in the face of everything Claire really did know about Trevor. But it often happens that rejection, real or imagined, leads one to conclude things about the other person that may be unfair, but make life infinitely easier for one's own ego.

Claire made a sudden decision.

"When Trevor returns, give him a message for me. Tell him I had to leave early because I'm going to Dallas for the weekend."

Claire was not running off after a man she didn't want just to annoy the man she did. Actually, she had been postponing the trip for ages. She needed to see The Colonel in person to break it off. She'd tried drafting "Dear John" letters, but each one had seemed a cheap way of getting out of the relationship. He'd been sending her flowers and calling her religiously for almost a year; he deserved to be let down in person.

But she knew Trevor would get the wrong idea. And as far as Claire was concerned, it served him right.

Again, poor Anna was the unwitting bearer of bad news. Trevor returned to the gallery expecting to face a barrage of questions from Claire. But instead he found Anna cheerfully saying,

"Claire said to say goodbye. She had to leave early to catch a plane for Dallas. She's going to visit her boyfriend this weekend!"

Trevor was taken aback. First of all, he'd come to believe The Colonel was no real competition. After all, Claire hardly mentioned the man, and then only unwillingly. But here she was flying to his side and quite obviously indicating her devotion. Second, why the devil did she have to go right now, when they were in the middle of this crisis? Didn't she understand that Charles' leaving was a catastrophe? How could she desert him at a time like this!

Well, if she was going to run off and leave them now, she could just get a taste of her own medicine, and see how *she* liked it.

Trevor made sure his voice sounded even. Then he said to Anna, "When Claire calls in for messages, find out exactly when she'll be back in the gallery. I'm going to schedule that trip to Europe I've been putting off. I'll leave as soon as I know she's back to run the gallery while I'm gone."

TWENTY-THREE

"...So Trevor went to Europe, and that's where he met Louise,"
Bernard said.

"He was clearly devastated about Charles and Claire," added Lewis.
"So that's how she got her hooks into him. The poor boy had lost his
*senses. She was a **man-eater.**"*

"Well, I don't know about that," Bernard said. "But he certainly
was smitten."

Ten days later, Trevor sat at a little outside table at a corner café
in Paris, sipping coffee. His companion suddenly lifted a perfect
round arm and, gently leaning over, took a soft napkin and wiped a
crumb away from the side of his mouth. "You have a little croissant
crumb, *mon chéri*," she said. Trevor grinned stupidly at her.

Her name was Louise Ceinture, and she was a woman the French
referred to as *magnifique*. She was beautiful to be sure — tall but
small boned, with a petite nose and ripe red mouth, deep green eyes
and thick black hair she always wore swept elegantly back. Except
when she was being successfully seduced. Then the hair would come
undone, spilling about her naked shoulders in a way that said she was
completely and utterly beyond control and wanted to be taken. It was
a gesture, once seen, that was impossible to forget or resist. Many men
claimed to have seen it. They were all telling the truth.

This, then, explains her reputation as "magnificent." Louise had
amazing sexual power, and an uncanny knack for using her sensuality
to control. She surrounded herself with men who found her
irresistible; men who thought everything she did was perfect. Any
scheme, any whim, any design on any person — there were always
a dozen willing accomplices to help her achieve her desire. And her
desires were often illegal and always involved acquiring more wealth.

Louise belonged to a class of women who might have been powerful royal courtesans in another century, but were fated to only be sources of heartache to rich men in the twentieth. She was completely unscrupulous, but so charming, so bewitching, so devoted that by the time the poor mark realized it, he'd been totally plundered.

Trevor was the latest man to fall under her spell.

He had met her in the Louvre. Or rather, he had seen her there. She'd been standing in the room with the great Fragonards, and he'd found his eyes wandering far more often to her than to the paintings. She was wearing a long raincoat and a scarf over her head, yet something about her face was entrancing. At one point she'd smiled — a smile so mysterious yet full of promise, that Trevor told himself he would never forget it.

So imagine his surprise when she'd shown up at the home of Victor Martre. Victor was a wealthy Frenchman who dug up American paintings in European collections and peddled them to American dealers. He'd been begging Trevor Whitney to come visit him for months, for he knew Trevor was one of the most successful, and wealthiest, New York dealers. He'd also heard he was one of the handsomest. So when Trevor called and said he was finally in town, it made perfect sense for Victor to invite his dear friend Louise to meet this rich and handsome American dealer. She'd been complaining again that she was short of money. Victor liked to be generous.

Trevor, for his part, was in the mood for a distraction. The loss of Charles and his believed rejection by Claire had put him in a funk. And, perhaps it was a desire to get even with Claire, but he was, for once, not unaware of his effect on women and literally waiting for a chance to ply his charms.

Trevor arrived at Victor Martre's townhouse and was immediately enveloped in a warm hug by the large Frenchman.

"Monsieur Whitney! How glad I am that we finally meet. I have been eagerly awaiting this opportunity to get acquainted. Ah, allow me to introduce you to my friend, Louise Ceinture."

She turned her luminous face to him, and Trevor instantly recognized her as the woman from the Louvre. Trevor actually felt himself tremble.

"I've seen you before," he said. "You were at the Louvre the other day. In the Fragonard room."

"Ah, *oui*! You were the young man who kept staring at me. Do you know that in France it is not polite to stare?"

Trevor reddened. "I apologize if I offended you."

Louise laughed — a tinkling little laugh like the wind blowing through glass beads. "You take me literally! How charming. No, Monsieur Whitney, I was not offended. I am a woman, and women love to be appreciated! Your stare had much of appreciation in it."

Trevor stammered out, "Yes... yes, I'm glad it did. Please call me Trevor." Then, remembering his host he added, "Both of you."

Victor was beaming. "Ah, we shall all get along famously. Come into the dining room, Trevor. We shall have lunch, and we shall have wine, and when we are completely comfortable with each other, we shall do business."

The rest of the afternoon was a blur to Trevor. He bought two paintings from Victor Martre — an insignificant Daniel Ridgway Knight of a milkmaid in a Poissy garden, and a moody Charles Sprague Pearce landscape of Auvers-sur-Oises — and later could not remember what price he'd agreed upon. Somehow he managed to make a date to take Louise out to dinner that night, but when he showed up at her apartment she was wearing only a sheer blue negligee. "You are early!" she cried, but didn't protest when he took her in his arms. And when she let her hair down, he picked her up and carried her over to the bed.

She was an astounding lover. Her delight in pleasing Trevor was unbounded; she swore he was the best lover of her life and made her feel things no man had ever inspired before. Trevor never wanted to leave her arms.

"Ah, my love," Louise sighed with pleasure, "you see it was destiny. We have crossed paths twice, and must never lose sight of each other again."

For the next two weeks they were inseparable. Trevor took her with him on business visits to galleries, and was delighted with her taste and eye. She seemed to know everyone in Paris, and to know almost as much about the European art world as an actual dealer. "But I am just a novice!" she would cry with delight when Trevor praised her eye. "I love nice things, oui. But I am an admirer, just. In my circle are many who own, but *moi* — I love from afar."

Trevor promised to buy her anything she wanted.

Two weeks passed and Trevor put off returning to the States. He made dutiful phone calls to Claire to make sure nothing that required his attention was happening, but Claire's responses were so business-like and impersonal, they only increased his desire to stay with Louise.

Finally it was Louise herself who encouraged him to leave.

"You must go back to work, my love," she announced one morning over coffee. "I know how much your gallery means to you, and now is not the time to stay away. Those two little girls cannot run the business for long. You must go back and keep the gallery strong for Charles."

"Yes, I know," Trevor said miserably. Trevor had told Louise everything about his life in New York; except, of course, anything of significance about Claire. "But Louise, I can't bear to leave you! Now that you are in my life the thought of being without you again is..."

"It is a tragedy, *oui*. I don't know how I will exist without you!

Who will I be? I will be nothing again...."

"You could never be nothing." Trevor looked deep in Louise's eyes. "Come with me," he begged.

And that was how it happened. Louise promised she would make arrangements to join Trevor in New York in another month.

Trevor was the happiest man on earth. And Louise may have been equally as happy, only for a different reason.

Twenty-Four

Louise Ceinture was born in Algiers in 1953. Her parents, having fled Algeria during the revolution, were blue-collar, lower middle class people who owned a bakery in Paris and worked from early morning until late at night. Louise grew up in the bakery, surrounded by flour and butter, and at an early age learned to roll out dough and make frosting flowers. But Louise was her parents' only child, and when they realized how beautiful she was they determined to make a better life for her. They scratched and saved every franc they could to send her to finishing school. Unfortunately, by the time she was "finished" she'd learned to completely disdain her parents' lives. She set out to make her own way in the world, invented a more glamorous past for herself, and never, thereafter, let common bread or cake pass through her mouth. She claimed this affectation helped keep her slim.

Trevor Whitney had come along at just the right time. Louise's last lover, a wealthy, married financier, had dumped her after realizing she'd been the cause of another man's bankruptcy. She had then blackmailed him for a bit more money, just to make sure she had a little nest egg squirreled away — but the threat to tell his wife had seemed low, even to her. She didn't like to work that way. She liked to think of herself as never needing to expose herself, but rather letting her victims believe their losses were all their own fault.

Trevor was the perfect mark. He was inexperienced, extremely rich, and obviously suffering from a broken heart. He'd never said so, but to a woman like her it was obvious. The heartbroken ones always fell so hard.

She knew just what she would do to him. She would get what she could out of him for a few months, and then she would pull the scam — with Victor Martre's help. It was a simple scam — the simplest, really — and had been done many, many times before. Still, he would fall for it. She might have been uncertain if Charles Brightman were still in the picture, but the situation was ideal without him. Certainly no one else in the gallery was wise enough to see through her. And if they turned out to be smarter than she expected, why she'd just get rid of them. She had only to ask and Trevor would follow her every whim, she was certain.

She had to do one thing for all the pieces to fall into place. In a few months she had to make herself such an indispensable part of the gallery that Trevor would wonder how he'd ever gotten by without her.

Back in the States, Claire awaited Trevor's return with mixed emotions. She'd come home from Texas exhausted. As she'd feared, it had not been easy getting The Colonel to understand their relationship was over. As far as Claire was concerned it had not been much of a relationship to begin with — she'd never even slept with the man. But Edward Halverson had invested their romance with his entire future, and had been patiently waiting for her to see it the same way. Even as she carefully tried to explain that she didn't feel the way he did, he refused to believe it. He challenged her on everything, especially the fact that she'd actually flown to Dallas to leave him — that, he claimed, flew in the face of her desire to be rid of him. An exasperated Claire could only say she'd thought it was the right thing to do, but that if he wouldn't listen to her than she already regretted doing so. She begged him to forget about her; he begged her to reconsider. After two days of discussion she convinced him she was sincere. Still, she couldn't help being grateful that when he asked her — in a final wounded plea — if there was someone else, she could truthfully answer, "No." It was one thing she could spare him.

She'd been greatly dismayed to discover that Trevor had arranged his own absence upon learning of hers. It filled her with a sense of guilt. Not that she believed he'd left because he'd been hurt by her relationship with The Colonel — that would mean he cared for her in a romantic way and there was no evidence of that. But she thought that her cavalier attitude toward the crisis in the gallery had encouraged him to act irresponsibly. This was a time when he should be at the business to assure friends and clients that all was well, but instead he'd gone running off on a jaunt to Europe. Yet she couldn't chastise him for running away when it was something she'd done herself.

Claire determined to make up for Trevor's absence by taking the gallery firmly in hand. She moved out of the upstairs office and down into Charles'. She fielded concerned calls from friends and associates with calm reassurance. She put as positive a spin on the retirement as Charles could have desired, all the while still fuming inside that Trevor appeared so uncaring. She rehung the exhibition hall; sold three paintings; sent transparencies to potential clients; even arranged first right of refusal for Trevor on a small collection of Hudson River School landscapes. Her conversations with Trevor were short, concise and businesslike. It irked her that his "thank yous" for all she was doing sounded equally concise and businesslike.

She did not tell him about Lewis and Bernard.

Before Trevor had left he'd had Anna draft a simple statement about Charles' retirement. The press release went out and appeared in print just days after Claire's return.

Claire had assumed that Trevor, or Charles, had personally informed Lewis and Bernard of Charles' retirement. But to her mortification, the couple found out the same way as everyone else — through the press release.

A very distressed Lewis and Bernard came rushing into the gallery the day the news hit the papers. In an instant it was clear to Claire that they were more hurt than worried.

"What's this about Charles?" Bernard demanded as soon as he was in the door.

"He's decided to retire. It was all very sudden." Claire looked at them in honest amazement. "Didn't you know?"

Bernard waved around the newspaper. "This is the first we've heard of it!" Claire had never heard Bernard growl before. "Why didn't Trevor call?"

"He had to leave town. It was very sudden." Claire wasn't sure why she was protecting Trevor, but she couldn't bear to let Lewis and Bernard think badly of him.

"How could Charles not tell us!" Lewis moaned. "After all we've been through together!"

Claire's hopeless look softened Bernard. "There, there, Lewis," he said, "I'm sure there's a logical explanation. What's the real scoop, Claire? Why did Charles leave?"

"I honestly don't know," Claire answered. "Trevor said he wanted to spend more time with Mary. Anna thinks it's because he realized how much he missed her when she was in the hospital."

"You mean, Charles didn't talk to you, either?"

"No, I heard from Trevor. Well, actually from Anna because Trevor had to leave town...." Claire looked down at her shoes, suddenly miserable again.

"You poor child." Lewis walked over and hugged her, no longer as hurt but now quite flabbergasted by the whole thing. "Bernie, this makes no sense."

"You're right. Something's wrong. Where is Trevor, and when is he coming home?"

"He's in Paris. He's expected home at the end of the week."

"Paris! What is he doing there?"

"I'm not sure," Claire said truthfully. "He's seeing some clients, I guess, and buying some things at auction."

"Well, at least it's a compliment to you, Claire. Trevor obviously thought the gallery was in competent hands."

"Thanks, Bernard. I'm holding down the fort so far. I'll have Trevor call you as soon as he returns. I'm sure he'll want to!" she added.

"You really haven't talked to Charles at all?" Lewis asked, still incredulous.

Claire shook her head. "I wanted to call him," she said quietly, "but I felt a little funny. I mean, if he'd wanted to talk to me...."

"Nonsense!" cried Bernard. "We'll go home and give him a call. And then we'll call you as soon as we know what's really happening."

But when Bernard and Lewis called Charles at home they got the answering machine. They left a message, and, since they didn't know he was sleeping at the hospital, wondered indignantly why Charles was taking so long to return the call.

In the meantime another week went by and the tone of Trevor's conversations changed. He sounded lighthearted, and remarkably unconcerned about the business. Claire wondered what it meant; but it worried her that Trevor could seem so nonchalant about the gallery.

And yet, despite everything, despite all that remained unsaid and unclear, despite a hefty dose of anger and her confirmed distrust of Trevor Whitney's personality, Claire had one overwhelming sentiment that she tried to ignore: she missed him.

She missed him every day he was gone, every minute, all the time.

Trevor got off the plane and found, to his surprise, that he'd missed New York. In the cab on the way downtown he allowed himself the idle pleasure of imagining the city with the added charm of Louise, but soon discovered that the two thoughts were somehow incongruous, and gave up the pastime. By the time he actually arrived on 70th Street he realized that what he wanted most of all was to walk in the gallery to a warm welcome from Claire and Anna. Especially from Claire. If he could make all the bad feelings between them from the past few weeks disappear he would do so. He would apologize, he would be contrite - he would even beg her for forgiveness if that was necessary. And so he entered the gallery with a look on his face that said all of that, and to his complete relief Claire took one look at him and seemed to understand.

She ran over and looked into his eyes for a minute, and in that minute everything that had happened during the past weeks seemed to disappear. And then she hugged him, and they both murmured "I'm sorry" at the same moment. And Claire giggled.

Claire's giggle was her girl-next-door laugh that was as familiar to Trevor as his favorite painting, and felt like home. For a brief instant it flashed through Trevor's mind how completely unlike Louise that giggle was, but because that thought was inconvenient he brushed it away. Instead he just allowed himself the luxury of feeling good about being back at the gallery.

"I missed you!" he said to both Claire and Anna.

"We missed you, too," Claire said while Anna gave Trevor a hug.

But as Claire stepped back and took a good look at Trevor she suddenly felt wary. There was something about the way Trevor looked — something new. He looked excited, breathless, maybe a touch guilty. There was something sexual about it.

Claire's initial feeling of relief and happiness began fading. She recalled that Trevor's latest phone calls from Paris had been very distracted. Now Claire began to imagine why.

"So fill me in on everything," Trevor was saying, but Claire had an agenda of her own.

"We want to hear all about *your* trip! You didn't say much on the phone. Did you buy some wonderful things? Is there a whole crate of new paintings waiting for us at customs?"

Trevor sounded sheepish. "Mostly I just made new contacts," he said. "I did buy a couple of things from that Victor Martre. He's quite a character! Oh, and I found someone to help us in the gallery. You know, to provide an extra hand while we get used to life without Charles."

His words hung in the air. It was the too casual manner with which he said them that instantly gave them away to Claire. She turned away to hide her expression, but Anna was all curiosity.

"Who?"

"A real Parisian lady. Her name is Louise Ceinture. She'll be here in a month. You'll love her!" he added with enthusiasm but not much conviction.

"Is she an art dealer?" Claire had composed herself enough to ask a question.

"No, but she's an art lover. A connoisseur. She has a great eye."

Claire put on a determined smile. "I'm sure she's wonderful," she said. "When is she coming?"

Trevor was visibly relieved by her reaction. "Next month," he said. "She's terribly French — you know, very charming and assured at the same time. The clients will love her."

Charming and *assured*. If Claire had any doubts, the way Trevor said those words confirmed that Louise was more than a friend.

Claire sighed. There it was, she told herself, her last hopes of a relationship with Trevor down the drain. And now she'd have to stay and watch him be in love with someone else. It served her right for running away.

And in her disappointment, Claire forgot that Trevor thought she was happily coupled with The Colonel.

"Louise can use the upstairs office," Claire offered generously. "I'll clear it out for her."

But Trevor's response indicated that Claire would be at a disadvantage not only romantically, but also professionally:

"Why don't you move back upstairs for now, Claire? I think Louise would be more comfortable close to me."

TWENTY-FIVE

Charles arrived home from the hospital. He was exhausted, but happy. Mary was coming home tomorrow. The pneumonia was gone, she was gaining weight and strength, and if all went well they would be able to enjoy the summer together. Hard to believe it was early July, and Mary had been hospitalized for over a month.

The answering machine was blinking. He knew there must be a dozen calls he'd never returned, but today was the day to tackle them. He wanted to get all of that out of the way before Mary came home.

Beep! *Charles, this is Bernard. We saw the notice in the paper that you decided to retire. I hope congratulations are in order! Please give us a call.*

Ouch! He'd intended to call them, of course. But then Mary had taken a turn for the worse and all other plans had gone out the window. Well, by now Trevor must have talked to them.

Beep! *Charles, this is Bernard again. We hope everything is all right. If you get this message give us a call.*

That was from three days later. Uh-oh. Why didn't they talk to Trevor?

Beep! *Charles, this is Bernard. We don't know where you're hiding, but I must say in all honesty that we're getting concerned. Claire hasn't heard from you, and Trevor is still in Paris. A word from you would put a lot of minds at rest here. Please call us.*

That call was only a week ago. What the hell was Trevor doing in Paris? Well, at least he could put Lewis and Bernard's minds at ease. He would never have left them ignorant this long if he'd had any idea that Trevor wasn't in town.

He dialed their number.

"Bernard! It's Charles. I'm so sorry. I know I owe you an explanation."

"No, Charles, we know everything now. Trevor just got back and called us. We can't tell you how sorry we are."

"I had every intention of calling you, but Mary was so sick for a while that by the time I thought of it again I figured you must have talked to Trevor. What was he doing in Paris? Is Claire all right?"

"She's fine, but she's hurt. Whatever you told Trevor to say, he didn't do a very good job. She has no idea why you left and she can't understand why you didn't tell her yourself."

Charles sighed. "I promised Mary that as few people would know as possible. I know it's unfair to Claire, but I couldn't lie to her, so I left the job for Trevor. Believe me, Bernard, I couldn't think straight at the time."

"Of course. That's perfectly understandable; but what about now?"

"I don't know, Bernard. I don't want to talk to Mary about it just yet. She's coming home tomorrow. Let her get her strength back and then I'll talk with her again about how we're going to handle this whole thing."

"How is Mary? You know, we've had some experience with AIDS. Two of our friends...."

"I know. That's why Mary said it was okay to tell you. She's doing much better right now. We're trying to stay hopeful."

"A positive attitude helps. Give her our love, Charles, and let us know if there's anything at all we can do."

"I will. So how is the gallery doing? And you didn't answer my question about Trevor; why did he go to Paris?"

"I'm not sure why he went, only that he came home with a surprise."

"What surprise?"

"He's invited a woman to come over and work in the gallery."

"He what?"

"He invited some woman he met over there to come to the States and work with him. Apparently he's fallen in love."

"You're kidding. Our Trevor?" Charles was astounded. "I don't even know what to say. Who is she? What's she like?"

186

"She hasn't arrived yet; she'll be here any day now. But Trevor told Lewis that she's stunning. He's like an infatuated schoolboy about the whole thing. Poor Lewis had to listen to him jabber on about her for ten minutes."

Charles laughed. "Lewis must be beside himself. How's he taking it?"

"He's taken to bed with a sick headache. His whole concern is for Claire, though — he's convinced she's destroyed."

"I wonder if she is," Charles said quietly. "Do you think she was in love with him, Bernard? I hate to think of Claire having her heart broken. I have to admit, I thought Lewis was a little nuts over the two of them, but I did think they'd eventually get together."

"It's hard to know what Claire's thinking. But she's doing her best to be gracious."

"Ah, Bernard, I wish I could talk with her. Listen, would you do me a favor? Give her a message for me. Tell her you spoke with me and that I specifically asked after her, and that I miss her and wish her all the best. Would you do that?"

"Of course, Charles."

"And tell her I'll call her soon. Just give me some time to talk with Mary about telling Claire the truth."

TWENTY-SIX

Claire nervously paced the gallery, waiting for Trevor to return from the airport with Louise Ceinture. She walked about the exhibition hall, straightening paintings and plucking dead flowers out of the bouquet centerpiece on the mahogany pedestal. Finally she stopped in front of Anna's desk.

"Are you all right? You look pale," Anna said.

"I'm just nervous. Silly, isn't it?"

"I think it's exciting! Trevor's been so happy lately. I can't wait to meet Louise!"

Anna was painfully ignorant of Claire's discomfort, and Claire had no intention of disillusioning her. She told herself to buck up — if she could just get through the initial meeting, certainly things would be easier after that.

The gallery door flew open and a whirlwind of color and perfume blew in. It could only be Louise Ceinture. Behind her, Trevor struggled with luggage, attempting to keep pace with his paramour.

"Ah!" Louise said, as she spun around and surveyed the room, "It is so beautiful, Trevor! I am so happy to be here!" She turned and threw her arms around him, then kissed him long and hard on the lips. Claire felt that display was meant for her.

Claire and Anna stood watching stupidly until Trevor finally ended the embrace and, beaming, brought Louise over to meet them.

"Louise Ceinture," he said, "allow me to introduce Miss Claire MacKenzie and Miss Anna Lipski."

Louise purred. "I am delighted to meet you. Trevor has told me all about you. He thinks you are both so, so terribly capable! You will have to teach me to be so, so...." She paused as if searching for an English word.

"Capable?" Anna offered.

"Oui! There is so much to do, now that I am finally here. I will want to make some changes, of course — little European touches. Trevor will tell you all about them, won't you, darling? But you two will show me — how do you say? — the ropes! We will get along famously!"

Claire smiled weakly.

"Would you care for some coffee or tea?" Anna offered.

"Do you have espresso? No? That is one change we must make immediately!"

"I could run down to the corner for some," Anna said.

Louise smiled sweetly. "You are an angel. I will see my office then, while you go. Claire can show me."

Claire blanched.

"I'll show you," Trevor quickly offered. "It's right through here."

As Trevor pushed Louise into the back hallway she could be heard protesting, "But, you have such important things to do! You should let the young ladies make me comfortable."

"Claire has important things to do, too," Trevor replied, and Claire was momentarily grateful. But then she heard him add, "Besides, it's your first day here — I want to fuss over you. I can leave you to the girls tomorrow." Blissfully, Louise's office door closed then and Claire could hear no more.

Claire marched upstairs, deciding to hide out in her office for as long as possible.

Anna found her up there a few hours later. She plopped into Claire's guest chair and sighed. Claire made a face and they both laughed.

"She's very demanding...." Anna suggested in an encouraging tone — as if she hoped Claire would tell her something comforting.

"Come on, Anna, you can say it. You hate her. I know I do."

"I'm trying to withhold judgment for a few days," Anna replied.

Claire smiled wistfully at her. "You're so nice, Anna. And you're right. I shouldn't prejudge her."

"You're lucky to have an upstairs office, though. I'm always right within her reach. Do you think she'll calm down after she's been here a while?"

Claire laughed. "If it gets too bad I'll trade places with you for a few days. Honest. You shouldn't have to put up with her by yourself."

"Thanks, but that's okay, Claire. After all, it's my job. You're supposed to be above being a gopher."

"I wonder if Trevor would agree with you," Claire said sadly. "I don't know what he thinks of me anymore."

"He thinks the world of you! He always has!" Anna was animated again. "Don't let today get you down, Claire. It's just a little blip in his life. Men always go batty when they fall in love. He'll be normal again, soon — mark my words!"

Claire sighed. "I hope you're right. Thanks, anyway."

Anna got up to leave.

"Hey, Anna," Claire said as she reached the door, "tell me something. If she didn't work here... I mean, in a vacuum, do you think she's the right woman for Trevor?"

"God! I hope not! I'm praying she's a passing phase, and Trevor comes to his senses before long."

Claire laughed, and hoped with all her heart that Anna was right.

The next few months were miserable for Claire.

Luckily, it was summer. Business was slow, so Louise's "little European changes" were not as disruptive as they might have been. First Louise redecorated the upstairs gallery — to the tune of forty thousand dollars. Everything had to be the finest quality: silk fabric, antique furniture, silly, expensive designer accents. The new espresso bar alone cost a fortune.

When Trevor finally became alarmed at the cost, Louise was all accommodation. "*Oui*, you are right! But it is not the renovation that is worrying you, *mon chéri*. Costs in the gallery are high — that I can see. Let me look at the books and see where we can cut costs."

Trevor asked Claire to hand the books over to Louise. Claire was reluctant. "Does she know what she's doing?" she inquired in as objective a tone of voice as she could muster.

"She must," was Trevor's reply. "If you only saw, in Paris, how she lives so well on so little money, you'd know she must be good at watching costs."

Claire could only look at him incredulously.

Louise's method of cutting costs was to fire most of the vendors the gallery had worked with for years. The photographers, caterers, electricians, art handlers and restorers were all replaced. Louise seemed to always know a recent immigrant from Europe who was "down on his luck" and had just the right skill. It didn't seem to matter to her whether they were good. They were cheaper, and the money saved on their talents increased the amount Louise had to spend on her own desires.

Claire was astounded at the lengths to which Trevor let Louise control the purse strings of the gallery. But she couldn't think of an appropriate way to voice her concern. So she turned to Lewis and Bernard for advice. She stopped off at their apartment one evening on the way home from work, and gave vent to all her worries.

"It's just crazy," she concluded. "He lets her do whatever she wants. And these people she's hiring — their work is second-rate. But they all seem to be old friends of hers or something."

Bernard shook his head and handed Claire a glass of wine. "Drink this," he said, "you need it."

"But what do you think?" Claire asked. "Am I being paranoid? Does it matter if we have all these strange people running around? I mean, they're not criminals or anything. At least, I don't think so," she added glumly.

Lewis, who'd been waiting for a chance to put in his two cents, suddenly exclaimed, "The man has lost his mind! Giving the books over to her — what in the world is he thinking? It goes against every bit of business sense. He can't be that trusting."

"Ah, Lewis," Bernard said, "he can and undoubtedly is. He's in love! He doesn't see any danger in it at all."

"That's what's really worrying me," Claire confided. "Do you think it's dangerous to trust Louise that much? We don't know anything about her. But now that he's letting her handle the books, she sure knows everything about us. I mean, I don't want to sound petty or mean-spirited...."

"Or jealous?" Lewis piped in hopefully.

"I'm not jealous!" Claire said hotly. "I'm just worried. She could be an embezzler, for all we know."

"Well, I doubt it's as serious as all that," Bernard said. Bernard had met Louise at the gallery and thought she was very dramatic and overly enthusiastic, but no other alarm bells had registered. "Still, it's just plain bad business to let Louise handle all the money," Bernard added. "I think you should make a point of checking the books every month yourself, Claire."

"I'm afraid Trevor will be hurt if I suggest it. I tried once to bring it up and he assured me that he looks at the books himself all the time."

"Can't you couch it in terms of 'regular business practices' or some such official-sounding reason?"

"I could try, I guess."

"And if he blanches, then do it behind his back," Lewis said.

Claire and Bernard looked at him.

"He deserves it!" Lewis insisted.

Claire's eyes appealed to Bernard.

"Well," Bernard said, "I don't like the thought of Louise having that much control of the money, but I can't countenance Claire going behind Trevor's back. Trevor's a big boy. We can only do so much to protect him."

"I don't want to do anything to deceive Trevor," Claire said quietly. "Someday he might need a friend, and I want him to know he can trust me."

Lewis became all soft and protective. "You're right Claire. I'm sorry. You should just be the angel that you are: a friend, a shoulder to cry on, a little piece of heaven in his warped little world. Someday Trevor will realize his mistake, and then...."

"Lewis!" Bernard interrupted.

Lewis smiled at him and at Claire. "I can dream, can't I?"

TWENTY-SEVEN

Louise unlocked the door to Trevor's apartment with her key, dropped numerous shopping bags on the floor, kicked off her heels and draped herself over the new white leather couch. She sank back and sighed with delight. How she loved living off Trevor's money!

Today she'd purchased a lovely new Chanel suit and Via Spago shoes in a matching taupe. Then she'd wandered over to Saks to pick up her evening gown for tonight's reception at the Met. Then there was a long stop at the beauty salon for hair, nail and face treatments — and the additional purchase of the latest face creams and eye colors. What a marvelous day! And it was only two o'clock.

Trevor would be expecting her back in the gallery for a few hours. But she couldn't be bothered. Why work today when it was so much more appealing to take a nice long nap? She'd come up with some excuse; Trevor would indulge her.

Besides, it was the end of August and the gallery was technically closed. Louise would never understand this American notion of closing for vacation but working anyway.

The phone rang. Oh bother; if that was Trevor she didn't want to be home yet. She let the phone peal until its persistence let her know it couldn't be him. Trevor would have given up after four rings.

"Hello?"

"Louise? Is that you?"

"Victor! Where are you calling from?"

Victor Martre sounded annoyed at the question. "I'm in Zurich. As we planned. Is someone else there?"

"No! You have caught me perfectly."

"I want to know how things are progressing at your end. I'm ready to set things up over here."

Louise frowned. She was having such a good time; she really didn't want it to end so soon. "These things take time, Victor. I'm still learning how Trevor works."

"What's to learn? You set up the bait and the rest is simple."

"But I was thinking, my dear...." Louise started to purr. "The longer we go on, the better my alibi. If I stay too short a time it looks suspicious. A few more months, and we'll be — what is the phrase? — home free."

"You are playing a dangerous game, Louise. What if he gets tired of you before then? All our work will be for naught."

"You offend me, Victor! No man has *ever* tired of me first! How dare you suggest such a thing?"

Victor sighed. "I'm just looking out for you, my dear."

"You are not forgiven!" Louise pouted, and used Victor's faux pas to her advantage. "Do not call me again until you hear from me! When I am ready to do it, then we will go. Until then — I will do what I think best!"

"I'm not waiting in Zurich."

"Then go about your business. I will find you."

Victor's voice became plaintive. "Louise, dearest, do not be angry with me. I only think of you and your future happiness. You know you are precious to me, like the daughter I never had."

"Really, Victor? But you hurt my feelings."

"No, my dear, I meant no insult. No woman is more entrancing than you. A man would lay down his life for you."

Louise was appeased. She leaned back and smiled like a cat with a belly full of cream. "Ah, my Victor, we have shared so many adventures. I can never be angry with you. Tell me again how Monsieur Roseau came to you and cried when I left him. It was such an amusing little story. Tell me again how he begged you to help him!"

While Louise was on the phone with Victor, Claire and Trevor found themselves alone at the gallery for the first time in months.

Anna had gone on a week's vacation to Nantucket with her family. Claire came downstairs to fill Trevor in on some potential sales she was pursuing, and found Trevor standing in the exhibition hall, admiring a large George Bellows portrait he'd recently acquired.

"She's wonderful," Claire said, joining him in front of the painting. "I love her clothing. Just look at that purple and green fabric."

"It's the first chance I've had to really look at it. What would you think about doing an Ashcan school exhibition this fall? I know we're a bit behind the eight ball, but I think we could pull a show together by early December."

"I'd love it! I know where a George Luks is in a private collection that I think we could borrow. It's a street scene of a bunch of urchins having a snowball fight! It's incredible."

"I know a couple of Sloans are for sale over at Kraushaar Galleries. Who knows — maybe they're one of the few galleries that doesn't hate us!"

"That's one way to find out!" Claire concurred.

Trevor and Claire stood smiling at each other. "It will be fun to have a new project," Claire said.

"Yeah. I think this show could be really exciting." Trevor paused. "I've been a bit distracted since Louise came, you know? It will be nice to focus back on the gallery again." He playfully nudged Claire on the arm. "This will give you an excuse to invite The Colonel to visit, huh?"

Claire blinked. "Oh," she said. "Oh, I guess you didn't know. We broke up."

"You did?"

"Yeah. It's no big deal. I mean, I'm all right and everything."

"Gee Claire, I'm sorry. I never dreamed the guy would give you up. He was so crazy about you."

"He didn't. I broke up with him." Claire smiled wearily. "He wasn't right for me. I always knew it; it just took me a long time to do something definite about it." She shrugged. "Really, I'm fine. In fact, I'm going upstairs and get my Rolodex and start working on this show."

As she turned to leave, Trevor felt compelled to ask, "When did all this happen?"

Claire didn't turn around. She made her voice light as she answered, "That weekend, when Charles left. That's what I went to Texas to tell him."

Trevor felt a sinking feeling in his stomach, and stared at the archway where Claire had exited long after she'd left the room.

Eventually Claire came bounding back downstairs, bubbling over with excitement. She'd secured the Luks painting for the show, and had reserved two fabulous Glackens beach scenes from Keny Galleries in Columbus, Ohio. She had a wish list of paintings in her head: a couple of great Robert Henri portraits, at least one Maurice Prendergast oil and a couple of good watercolors, an Ernest Lawson of New York City, a couple of theatrical Everett Shinn paintings. Along with some Sloans from Kraushaar, she declared, this was the minimum they would need to mount a great exhibition.

Trevor was delighted, and decided to reward her enthusiasm. "I think we can pull this off if I put you in charge. How would you like to curate this show yourself?"

"Really? And write the catalogue and everything?"

"Of course! I'll help you every step of the way, but you deserve a show where you get to take the credit. Think you're up to it?"

"Oh, Trevor — I'd love it! You know that! Yes, I'm up to it."

"Great. I'll go check out some leads I have — I think I know where to get those Shinns you want."

Trevor turned to leave and Claire reached out and touched him on the arm.

"Thanks," she said.

198

"Hey, you earned it," Trevor replied.

They stood looking at each other, and Trevor suddenly felt a tremendous desire to kiss Claire. Claire felt equally convinced that he was about to. Before either had time to react to this moment, there was a pounding at the front door.

Waldo was standing there, glaring at them through the glass.

Trevor hurried to let him in. Waldo began complaining the minute his voice could be heard.

"So there I am, taking my first August off in years, hanging out with the kids and missus in Wildwood, swimming and sunning and thinking to myself, 'Waldo, old boy, this is your golden time. You can relax! You've had your best year ever, and your favorite gallery — the one you've given your heart and soul to, the one that will always be your best friend — your trusted harbor in an insincere world, the one business you would stake your life savings on — that gallery is stable, and secure, and nothing will ever change.' And then I run into Howard Godel and his family, and he tells me that it's all gone to hell in a hand-bag. All gone to hell! Charles has left for no apparent reason and you, Trevor, have taken up with some foreign lady." (Trevor frowned at this point and even Claire winced, but Waldo was in a tirade and tirades have to run themselves out.) "So I says to myself, 'Waldo, get yourself up there and find out what the hell is going on.' So I kiss the wife and kids and promise I'll only stay away as long as it takes to fix things. And I hop on the first train, and here I am, so I want you to tell me: Where the hell is Charles? Who the hell is this French lady?"

Claire ran over and put her arms around Waldo and gently maneuvered him toward a chair. "Please calm down, Waldo. I assure you, we can explain everything. Everything's fine! There's a perfectly logical explanation for Charles' retirement, and Louise is Trevor's girl-friend. He met her in Paris and I'm sure you'll like her." Claire was barely aware of what she was saying; she just wanted Waldo to calm down before he gave himself a stroke.

"His girlfriend? But I thought you and Trevor...." Even Waldo suddenly realized this was not the most diplomatic thing to say.

"No. We've always been just friends." Claire looked at Trevor helplessly. "Trevor, help me out here."

Waldo spun around in the chair to address him. "Then what's up with Charles?"

"Well you see, Charles had to... well, Mary was sick, and then... well, he just needed to spend more time with her, and the time was right, so he decided to retire. It was entirely his decision."

"And the old boy didn't tell anyone?"

"He didn't want a fuss made," Claire piped in. "Isn't that right, Trevor?"

"Right. He wanted to bow out gracefully."

"So everything's OK? You guys are all right? I mean, after Godel got through talking to me I thought you guys had all had some big fight or something."

Claire and Trevor looked away from each other, but Trevor murmured, "No, it was nothing that dramatic. Just normal business evolution."

Waldo looked at Claire. "And this woman, Louise — you like her, Claire?"

Claire looked alarmed at the question, but answered, "Sure. She's very... energetic."

An awkward silence filled the room. Then Trevor suddenly rallied.

"Hey, why don't you stop by my apartment after work and meet her yourself? We're going to the Met tonight — you're welcome to join us — but we could have a few drinks together before the opening. What do you say? You'll love her, Waldo, she's wonderful."

"Well, I guess I could," Waldo replied. "I'm not really dressed for a soirée at the Met, but I suppose I could meet you for an *apéritif.*" Waldo could not help a bit of sarcasm creeping into his voice. He was still feeling wounded.

"Great! You know the address — come by around six o'clock. That will give us plenty of time for you to get to know her."

Claire began telling Waldo her plans for the December Ashcan School exhibition, and Waldo became calmer with the knowledge that there were things for him to do — paintings for him to find. A reluctant Waldo was finally convinced to leave the building and go off to scour other galleries for possible loans. He promised to meet up with Trevor promptly at six. Trevor and Claire breathed a sigh of relief when he was gone, then exchanged slightly sheepish smiles and went on about their business.

But the next morning, Claire received a private phone call from Waldo.

"Claire," he said, "After meeting Louise last night I got one thing to say to you. 'Get the hell out of Dodge,' babe. You know I love you, so I'm telling you straight. Get the hell out of there while you still can."

And he refused to elaborate. Not then, and not until it was way too late.

TWENTY-EIGHT

"...When Charles retired, hardly anyone noticed. I always thought that was sad," Lewis said.

"Well, if they'd acknowledged that his absence was a loss, they'd have had to admit he'd been a big reason for the gallery's success in the first place. The art world wasn't that evolved in 1986; I'm not sure they even are today."

"Touché, Bernie, touché. They might not have thought anything about Louise joining the gallery either, if not for Waldo."

Bernard laughed. "God bless him, he wasn't about to let anyone ignore that! Too bad none of us believed him...."

It was only after Waldo began his search for Ashcan paintings for the new Trevor Whitney exhibition that people began paying serious attention to events at the gallery. It wasn't that Waldo actually said anything, it was the way he had of shaking his head and sighing whenever he brought up the gallery name. Then he would look around, make the gesture of "zipping his lip," and say, "But you didn't hear it from me."

Naturally, dealers began wondering *what* they weren't hearing from him.

It made for delightful gossip. And for most people, it ended right there — in frivolous gossip and speculation. But Sonny Kaufmann, always on the lookout for a way to eliminate the competition, decided to dig a little deeper and see if there was anything he could use to his advantage.

First Sonny tried to pry more details out of Waldo. He pounced on him one day when Waldo stopped by Kaufmann-Kramer Gallery to check out some new inventory.

"Waldo! Long time no see! Well, actually, you've been getting around a bit more now, haven't you? Since events across the street took a turn for the worse."

Waldo eyed Sonny suspiciously. Sonny didn't usually condescend to speak with him when he was in the gallery. Of course, Waldo had to stop by on a regular basis to keep up with things — to keep his finger on the pulse of the art world. But he didn't come by more than he had to, which wasn't often, as he'd never much liked Sonny and was quite sure the feeling was mutual.

"Seems to me I get around just the same as I always have," he answered. "Doesn't seem to me anything in particular has changed."

"Come now, old boy. We've been in this business together a long time. We both recognize a sinking ship when we see one, eh?"

"Do we now?" Waldo shook his head with amusement.

"Of course, your loyalties are well known. Can't blame you for that. The Trevor Whitney Gallery has been a boon to you, a real boon. But you know, Waldo, with the changing landscape, a man's got to make sure he's got other places to butter his bread."

"Well, I'm not starving yet." Waldo grinned at Sonny. "You're just dying to know something, aren't you?"

"Know something? What is there I don't know?"

"Good. I like doing business with informed men. There may be some business we could do together, yet." Waldo looked deliberately at his watch. "Seems I've got to run to another appointment. I'll see you around, Sonny."

Waldo made his escape out the door, and paused to chastise himself a bit. "Better keep your mouth shut, Waldo old boy. You do know where your bread is buttered!"

Back inside, Sonny was disappointed but in no way discouraged. He went to the phone book and looked up Lewis and Bernard's telephone number.

Lewis answered the phone. Sonny decided the direct approach was best.

"Lewis, what's this I hear about The Trevor Whitney Gallery?"

"Have you heard something?" Lewis asked, caught off guard and momentarily confused.

"Well of course. It's all over town about Charles, and now this French woman."

Lewis sighed. "I'm sorry word got out about Charles. I don't think it's anybody's business about poor Mary."

"Oh, well that," Sonny said, not knowing what Lewis was referring to, but seeing immediately that if Mary was the cause of Charles' sudden retirement, it wasn't the type of information he could profit by. "I was referring more to Trevor and that woman."

"Yes, it's all very frustrating. Who can explain the human heart?"

Lewis suddenly realized whom he was speaking to. "But why should you care, Sonny? Hoping to try for Claire yourself now that James is out of the way?"

Sonny, exasperated, said, "Very amusing, Lewis. I'm not the least bit interested in her."

"Then why did you call?" Lewis wanted to know.

"Just trying to extend my condolences to those who care!" Sonny barked. Then he hung up.

So it was all much ado about nothing. Charles had retired because of something having to do with Mary, and everyone was in a snit because Trevor had dumped Claire.

Sonny might never have found out anything more, if not for a chance event. He had a cousin, Len Berger, still in the garment industry, who regularly went to Paris on buying trips. One Friday evening Sonny's wife invited Len to their home for Shabbat dinner.

Over coffee, it suddenly occurred to Sonny to ask, "Hey, in your travels, ever come across a woman named Louise Ceinture?"

"Louise Ceinture! Sure. She's infamous."

"Really? How do you mean?"

Len glanced over to the kitchen, where Sonny's wife was doing the dishes, as if what he was about to say was not meant for delicate ears. "She's a professional user, if you know what I mean. Beautiful, *real* sexy — the kind rich men always go for. But she's ruthless. She's never left a relationship yet without gaining something financial out of it."

"How interesting!"

"How is it you've heard about her? She hasn't been after you, has she?" Len looked positively alarmed.

Sonny chuckled. "No, another dealer. She's here in New York now, living with him."

Len whistled. "Whoever he is, if he's a friend of yours you'd better warn him. If she's bothered to come all the way overseas for this guy, he must be a pretty big fish she's planning to land."

Sonny smiled to himself. He was fairly certain he was the only person with this information.

"Thanks, Len — I think you've just done my friend a great service. I'll let you know what happens."

It was too good to be true! Trevor was going to be taken down by his own girlfriend, and all Sonny had to do was sit back and watch — and make sure no one who might want to warn Trevor looked too deeply into Louise Ceinture's reputation.

There was one person, though, he simply had to share this information with. He picked up the phone and dialed Lavinia Worthington.

"Lavinia," Sonny said, "do I have news for you!"

Ten minutes later the two had agreed that neither was to breathe a word of this, and that Sonny should do his best to deflect further interest in the doings of The Trevor Whitney Gallery.

Sonny made a point after that of saying with a knowing air to anyone who asked about the goings on across the street, "It's all a tempest in a teapot. The old man retires and Trevor takes up with a new woman, and Waldo Picker goes into histrionics. Trust me, The Trevor Whitney Gallery's in no more danger of going under than I am."

And since Sonny was generally considered the voice of ill-gained wisdom, speculation about the gallery soon ceased to be a topic of interest.

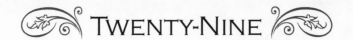

TWENTY-NINE

The phone call from Waldo the morning after he'd met Louise had been distressing, but Waldo's reluctance to pin down his concerns, and Claire's knowledge that Waldo could be a bit dramatic, combined to help her put the whole conversation out of her mind. Besides, she was too excited about the chance to curate her own exhibition to be in a funk. This was a wonderful opportunity for her to shine. And if in the back of her mind she knew that the show would look good on her résumé in case she ended up having to leave the gallery — well, that only contributed to the dedication with which she pursued the whole thing.

Louise, on the other hand, was not happy about the exhibition. She didn't like the authority it gave Claire, nor the message it sent about her importance to the business. She was not unaware that Claire was probably the person responsible for Trevor's initial broken heart, and although she had total confidence in her control over his current emotions, she nevertheless didn't trust the gallery assistant. She was also aware of Claire's loyalty to the business — the type of loyalty that could later undermine Louise's schemes. She'd been hoping to convince Trevor to get rid of her, but she now saw this was an impractical plan. Trevor, for all his infatuation with Louise, would not countenance a bad word said about Claire. So Louise would have to try a different tactic: making life so uncomfortable for Claire that she would choose to leave of her own volition.

This had to be done very carefully. Any direct attack on Claire ran the risk of backfiring. Louise ruminated on her options for quite some time before hitting upon a brilliant idea.

Anna could go. Anna could be replaced with a person of Louise's own choosing.

If Anna left, not only would Claire resent the loss of her friend, but she'd lose her best asset for managing the Ashcan show. Anna was efficient, organized and a whiz at taking care of details. Claire would end up struggling to manage the exhibition alone, or having to rely on the person Louise hired.

And Louise knew a person to hire who would appear — at her command — all eagerness and efficiency, but in reality wouldn't lift a finger unless Louise asked him to.

This mysterious person was none other than Victor Martre's no-account son.

This boy, Victor's youngest, was a constant source of annoyance to his father. He was lazy and whiney, ran with a fast and apathetic crowd, and expected his papa to provide him with the financial means to continue this lifestyle indefinitely. Now twenty-five, Elliot Martre had recently deposited himself in America in order to pursue some obscure record deal as agent for a friend of his who had neither talent, nor connections. The project was doomed to fail, and Victor was already making noises about forcing his son to stay abroad and work for a living.

Hiring Elliot would secure her bond with Victor, put the hapless Elliot under her control, and could be made to look like a coup to Trevor — if she invented a more appropriate history for the youth. It was all a matter of presenting the "facts" in just the right manner.

She began her plot with the simplest of statements. She waltzed into Trevor's office one October morning and said, "I have the most marvelous news! Victor Martre's son has just become available!"

Trevor smiled indulgently. "Available for what, sweetheart?"

"Why, to work here of course! Oh, Trevor, you don't know what a fantastic opportunity has just arisen. This boy is wanted by all the galleries in Europe. He is — how do you say? — highly in demand!"

"Really? I didn't know anyone else in Victor's family was in the business."

"Ah, *oui*, he is the boy-genius of the family. Victor doesn't like to speak of him for fear he'll sound too bragging. But he is very talented!"

"What experience does he have?"

"Oh, all the usual — he has curated exhibits at galleries, he has guest lectured at the Musée Moderne, he knows many collectors and artists." She sighed. "But he has always desired to work with historical paintings instead of contemporary. That's why he only took the job at that Paris gallery for two years. He said he did not want to... ah, yes, *pigeonhole* himself to contemporary art. He wants to pursue new horizons."

Trevor was amused, and even intrigued. "So I gather you want us to hire him here?"

"Why not! Such a great opportunity doesn't come along every day."

"Yes, but Louise, a new employee — especially one with that much experience — is probably beyond our budget right now."

Louise sighed again. "What a pity. Another man about the gallery would be so beneficial to Claire, too, for unpacking and hanging the show. It's especially a pity because Anna, of course, wishes to leave."

"She what?"

"She wishes to leave. Surely you have noticed, or is it just woman's intuition? She is not happy here; she is a PR person at heart, and this is not a PR job."

"Are you sure?"

"But of course! She is very dear. She spends a lot of time with me and I see things."

"I had no idea!" Trevor said. "I'll admit, things have been a bit strained with all the changes, but I never dreamed that Anna was unhappy."

Louise shook her head sympathetically at her lover. "She would never want you to know. She adores you, of course. And she would never want to leave you at a time like this. But if she knew some-one else was coming — someone who could replace her and do a wonderful job — I think she'd be relieved."

Trevor was thoughtful. "What makes you think that Elliot Martre would take the job? Would he — as a European — be interested in American art?"

"We would have to see. But all young men love the chance to come to New York City, *n'est pas*? If he came here there would be more to attract him than just the art." She made her voice into her signature purr. "Besides, this could be a chance for us, *non*? We talked about moving into European paintings — Cezanne, Picasso, Monet! Elliot knows where such paintings are... and who wants them."

Trevor considered Louise's proposition. "I know that's something you would love, Louise. And it would be fun to handle some of those works, but I'd be afraid to touch them without having a client list."

"See! Elliot has a list. He would be good for us in so many ways!"

"I don't know, though. Anna's been so wonderful. I'll have to have a talk with her...."

"Oh, no, *mon chéri*, that is a job for me. She has been open with me already; she will be more comfortable if I bring it up." She smiled. "I know just how to approach it, so she will be happy to leave!"

"Don't do anything without securing Elliot Martre first," Trevor said. "We don't want to get left empty-handed."

"But of course! I will call him today." Louise threw her arms around Trevor and kissed him. "It is all going so well, is it not? You will soon have the biggest and most important gallery in New York — in the world! I am so proud to be with you."

Trevor glowed. Louise left the room humming, already plotting how to make Elliot look presentable and how to ease Anna out.

That afternoon, Louise slipped over to Elliot Martre's hotel — he was staying at the Waldorf on credit he'd already used up. It was two o'clock and yet when her pounding on the door finally brought him to the threshold, it was obvious she'd woken him. Louise cut right to the chase.

"You are a disgrace," she announced.

"Mademoiselle Ceinture!" Elliot exclaimed. He knew her well — every young man in Paris with active hormones did — and he'd often bragged that she was a friend of his father's. But until that moment she'd never spoken directly to him. He was instantly suspicious.

"My father sent you to check up on me?" he asked indignantly.

Louise narrowed her eyes and regarded the young man with distaste. "Of course not. He already knows all about you."

Elliot blanched, and Louise took advantage of the moment to strike.

"I've come to make you an offer. This is not an offer I'd advise you to turn down. Not if you want to make your father happy."

Elliot was quite aware of his father's desire to cut him off completely, so he looked appropriately alarmed. Louise continued. "Your father and I have been having a conversation about you. And we've both decided that you can be useful to us. If you are good, and do what we say, we will reward you." Louise flashed a brilliant smile. "I will move you into a nice apartment. You will have all the money you need, new clothes, access to all the best people. You will be remade into a new man, and as long as you obey me I believe you will find your new life quite appealing."

Then Louise frowned. "But if you are bad, and do not do what we ask, your father will cut off all relations, and you will be on your own from now on."

Elliot gulped. He was terrified of what Louise was about to require of him, being aware that some of his father's dealings were on the shady side. Flashing through his mind were thoughts of "hit man" or "art thief" or even worse, "working stiff." "What do I have to do?" he asked.

His worst fears were realized. "You have to come work for me," was the answer.

Elliot's eyes panicked, but Louise laughed her silvery laugh at him. "You will find me a delightful employer," she assured him. "You have heard that I have joined with a gallery here. Your father and I have plans for this business, and I need an employee that I can trust. Someone who will do exactly what I say — no more, no less. Someone who understands that they may appear to work for the gallery, but they work only for me." She lowered her voice. "You understand, *non*? It is simple, what I ask of you. In fact, I want you for something you will no doubt find amusing — I want you to appear to be industrious, but to do very little work. I want you to convince the others that you are *très laborieux*, but do only the things I want you to!"

Elliot was by now staring at Louise in disbelief. "You want me to come work for you, pretend to work hard, but do pretty much no work? And in exchange you will pay me well?"

"*Exactement!*"

Elliot began grinning. Why, his father was a veritable genius, and Louise was a wonderful, wonderful woman. "I'm your man!" he exclaimed happily. "When do I start?"

"First," Louise said, regarding her young friend critically, "we must make you presentable. You will go to Barney's and see Monsieur White in the men's department. He will be prepared for you; do not argue with what he suggests. It will take a few days for the alterations. In the meantime you will see my hairdresser and manicurist. And every day you will spend at least five hours in the library, studying art. Focus particularly on the Americans, and the European realists and modernists. I have made you a list of the artists you must know, and I will quiz you at the end of the week."

Elliot's face fell. Louise's voice became hard. "You did not think it would be just a game of pretending, did you? *Non*, this role requires preparation." Louise softened her voice and began purring. "But don't worry, my little lazybones. If you do well, you will find I am very grateful." She suddenly reached out and ran a finger lightly down Elliot's face, then down his side, ending with a gentle squeeze on his buttocks — just to show the kind of gratitude he might possibly look forward to.

Besides, when he was cleaned up, Victor's son was very attractive, and young men were always so enthusiastic.

Elliot's eyes grew wide, then lit up. "I am an excellent student," he announced.

"*Bon*! Then we shall have many a memorable lesson," Louise promised. "We will have to find time alone to study, *n'est pas*? Ah, I look forward to this partnership already."

Louise turned to leave. But she turned back to say, "if there are to be more, how do you say — private? — aspects of our arrangement — they must remain between us, agreed? My partner at the gallery is, of course, in love with me, and your father — well, your father can be so...."

"Say no more," Elliot grinned. "I am always a gentleman in matters of the heart." This was getting better and better — he'd not only pull one over on the old man, he'd even be making a cuckold of his new boss!

"Ah, the father's son!" Louise said affectionately as she departed.

Elliot was on board. Now all Louise needed to do was get rid of Anna.

It took about five weeks to bring Elliot up to speed as a credible art expert. When he was ready, Louise asked Anna to join her for lunch at Three Guys on Madison Avenue.

Anna loved to eat at Three Guys because so many gallery employees lunched there. She always ran into people she knew. Of course, Louise knew this.

Anna wondered why Louise had invited her to lunch, but the older woman had been making noises about thanking her for all her hard work, so Anna assumed this was Louise's little show of gratitude. As they entered the restaurant Anna called out hellos to a number of people. They sat down at a table in the middle, and both women perused the menu. Anna was surprised when the waiter came over that she was the only one who ordered lunch. Louise suddenly expressed no desire to eat, and asked for a cup of coffee.

"So," Louise began, "you have worked at the gallery for how long?"

"Oh, about six months," Anna said. "It seems like longer, though. I mean, so many things have happened."

"And, Claire tells me that you are trained in marketing and public relations?"

"Yes, I got my degree in January. But the market was really tight, so I jumped at the chance to get this job."

"But it is not really what you are trained to do, *non*?"

Anna shrugged. "I guess not. But I really love it. The gallery is so much fun!"

To Anna's surprise Louise sighed. "You are not making this easy for me, Anna."

Anna blinked. "What do you mean?"

"I am looking for a way...." Louise shook her head and began again. "You know, I believe, that most galleries cannot afford to have PR people on staff. They hire consultants."

Anna nodded. She was suddenly afraid to speak.

"The best galleries, they keep a staff only of experts. Experts in art," Louise added pointedly.

"So," she continued, "we want Trevor's gallery to be the best, do we not? Trevor needs another expert in the gallery. I am a big help, but not..." she waved her hand dismissively, "an expert either. With

216

Charles' absence Trevor needs more help." Louise paused to let her words sink in, then added, "He cannot, of course, afford to add another person without letting someone go."

Anna turned pale. Louise looked at her sympathetically.

"I know you want to do what's best for the gallery, Anna. Trevor would never have the heart to let you go. But it must be done. I know you can see that."

Anna felt ready to burst into tears, but remembering her surroundings, she fought to hold them back. "Am I fired?" she asked softly.

"But of course not!" Louise replied. "I only want you to do what's right. You must make the decision that is best for the gallery yourself! I know you will do the right thing."

Anna stared at Louise. She felt completely trapped — if she didn't quit she was ungrateful; if she did she would be completely miserable.

"Can I at least look for another job before I leave?" she asked unhappily. In the back of her mind Anna hoped she could talk to Claire, or even Trevor, and see if she might work out some way to still do consulting work for the gallery.

Louise's look turned from sympathy to impatience. "You can have three days," she said. And with that, Anna knew she had no real choice at all. Louise was determined to get rid of her.

At that moment the food arrived. "But look at the time!" Louise exclaimed. "I must get back to the gallery."

Anna rose to leave too, but Louise stopped her. "You have not touched your food! Stay as long as you like and eat your lunch. I'll make up some excuse for your absence."

Louise exited the restaurant with a great deal of flair, causing most of the other patrons to look at her, and then to look toward Anna. As soon as Louise was gone Anna, to her horror, began silently crying. Aware that all eyes were upon her, she clumsily dug some money out

217

of her purse, dropped it on the table, and fled.

The next morning Anna went to the gallery and, after making sure Louise was not in, called Trevor and Claire into her presence.

"I'm very sorry to tell you this," she began, looking down at the floor, "but I've found another job — a job in my field. It's an opportunity too good to pass up." She started stammering, "I feel really bad about it, and I hope you guys can forgive me" (here she began sobbing) "but I really need to take this other job."

Claire was stunned. Trevor, of course, had been expecting this.

"It's all right, Anna," he said. "You have to do what's best for you. We understand that! Don't we, Claire?"

"Well, I guess if it's what you want. It's just kind of sudden. Oh, Anna, why are you crying? We're not angry!"

"I feel so bad," Anna said helplessly.

"Don't feel bad about it!" Trevor insisted. "It's not the end of the world. In fact, I'll tell you a secret if it makes you feel better — we've been thinking of hiring this young man from Paris — Victor Martre's son, remember I told you about Victor? His son has tons of experience in the art business, and apparently wants very badly to come work for us. Of course, there was no question of taking him on while you were here, but now that you're leaving it will all work out just fine!"

Anna began crying louder. Trevor, alarmed and confused, looked at Claire for help.

Claire had heard nothing about Victor Martre's son, and immediately had a bad feeling about the whole thing. But she put on a good show for Anna's sake. "It's okay, Anna, really. It will all be just fine. Now, you mustn't be so upset. You said yourself this was a great opportunity — we're happy for you! Really we are!"

Anna struggled to dry her eyes.

"Tell us all about the job," Claire said.

Anna swallowed hard. She'd practiced to make sure it sounded plausible. "It's with a PR firm in midtown. I'll have two or three small clients, to start out, but if I do well I'll be able to bid for bigger accounts in a few months. Oh, and the salary is really good."

"That's great!" Claire said. "We'll sure miss you, though. When do you have to start?"

"Umm... tomorrow. I know it's rather sudden, but they just lost the person who had the job before me, and they need me right away. A friend recommended me."

"Oh." Trevor and Claire looked sadly at her. "Can we take you out to lunch today to celebrate?" Trevor asked.

"Sure," Anna said. "No, wait... I have to run a bunch of errands and stuff during lunch. How about if I call you next week and we do lunch then?" In truth, Anna knew she'd never get through a good-bye lunch without giving herself away.

"Okay," Trevor said, "but make sure you do. I think we've had enough around here of sudden good-byes." Claire looked at him curiously — it was the first time Trevor had admitted, even subtly, that Charles' manner of departure had bothered him.

"Can I do anything for you today, Anna? And I guess we should go over where we are on this Ashcan show." Claire said.

"Yes, if you could spend some time with me, that would be great," Anna replied.

"I'll leave you two to get everything in order, then," Trevor said. "But I just want to say, before I go, that we've loved having you here Anna, and we wish you the best of luck in all your future endeavors." He gave Anna a hug and kissed her lightly on the forehead before leaving the room.

Anna and Claire spent the next few hours upstairs going over business details. Claire couldn't help herself from saying over and over how much she would miss Anna, always adding that Anna, of course, shouldn't worry about them. "Oh, Anna," she finally exclaimed, "I'm a really rotten friend! I should just be happy for you and all I keep thinking about is how I'll miss seeing your smiling face everyday!"

Anna fought back tears again, but said, "It really is best for the gallery, though, isn't it Claire? I mean, this guy who's coming to work here sounds really great. He'll be a lot better to have around; I mean, he has a lot more experience than I do, so he'll be a real asset, won't he?"

"I guess," Claire said. "I wish he wasn't *French* though." Then she clapped a hand over her mouth. "Gosh, Anna, Louise has turned me into a bigot!" she sputtered. Anna laughed.

Later, when Anna had cleaned out her desk and climbed into a taxi with her box of belongings, it occurred to Claire that when Anna had told them she was leaving, Trevor had never said a word about telling Louise. She wondered if that was because Louise already knew. But if she did, it could not be because Anna had told her first; it could only be because Louise had something to do with it, and Trevor knew it.

And although that scenario opened up all sorts of unpleasant possibilities, Claire could not quite see what it meant.

THIRTY

I felt myself tearing up a little at the story about Anna's departure from the gallery. Lewis and Bernard looked like they might cry too, just from the memory. "That was rotten, what Louise did to Anna," Lewis said.

"Of course, we didn't know at the time. Thanks goodness we were able to help later."

"Where's Anna today?" I asked.

"Oh, she's a hotshot PR person now! She works for NBC. She was too talented to stay down long," Bernard said. "But it was touch and go there for her for a while."

Elliot Martre started work at the gallery two days after Anna's departure.

He walked in as if he owned the place. He was dressed impeccably in an Alexander Julian suit, silk tie and gold cufflinks. He shook hands with Trevor and called him "Sir," air-kissed Louise in the French fashion, and solemnly kissed Claire's hand — adding a salacious wink as he rose up. The wink, unseen by the others, made Claire uneasy.

Elliot then proceeded to walk around the gallery making favorable comments on the paintings. He was particularly praiseful of Trevor's personal favorites. Claire thought his actions seemed rehearsed — but couldn't see why the young man was trying so hard. After all, he had already been promoted as God's gift to the gallery.

A problem immediately arose as to where to place Elliot's desk. He couldn't just take over Anna's position because he was above-and-beyond the receptionist role. Besides, he explained, he needed relative quiet when he worked, and the main floor was the busiest part of the gallery. He suggested moving into the upstairs exhibition space and using it as a combination office/viewing room.

Yet to have no one sitting at the front desk to answer phones and greet visitors was not an option. Trevor suggested they take turns, each spending two hours a day out front.

Claire was grateful for Trevor's attempt at even-handedness, but knew this plan would never work. Louise hated to be "on display" (as she called the front spot) and was a disaster at taking messages, and Elliot, it was clear, resented any work deemed beneath him. Claire assumed neither would willingly hold up his end of the bargain. So through gritted teeth she volunteered for what she figured would be the inevitable result anyway — she said she'd move back downstairs at least through the end of the Ashcan exhibition, since she'd be spending so much time down there anyway. Trevor promised to find a way to hire a receptionist as soon as possible.

That settled, Elliot wanted to know what his title would be. Trevor raised his eyebrows in surprise. "To tell you the truth," he said, "we've never really used them. Claire's business card just has her name. I'm not big on putting people into categories."

But Elliot insisted. "When I deal with friends overseas they wish to know what my position is. It gives them a sense of trust. They don't know you," he reminded Trevor, "so they have to believe in me."

"Oh, darling, do let him have a title," Louise said. "It's only words on a card; in truth it is meaningless, but it will help Elliot fulfil our expectations."

"What were you thinking of?" Trevor asked.

"Perhaps, 'Director' or 'Vice-President of Paintings?'" Elliot answered.

Trevor frowned. "I suppose 'Director of Paintings' is all right. Would you like a title too, Claire?" Again, Trevor attempted to be equitable. Claire felt like screaming.

"I'm fine, Trevor. Everyone knows who I am by now."

Trevor looked grateful. "Okay, then. Why don't we all help Elliot get settled upstairs."

As the group moved toward the back stairway Trevor pulled Claire aside and said, "Thanks. You're being an angel and I want you to know I know it."

Claire just had time to smile back appreciatively before Louise called Trevor up to ask him another question about Elliot's role in the gallery.

Elliot set himself up in a princely style in the upstairs office. He ordered a substantial desk, fancy desk accouterments, all sorts of office supplies, and even his own Macintosh computer. He looked to all the world like a man ready to do business.

But Claire soon discovered that Elliot had a remarkable ability to appear to be working, but really did just enough to seem occupied. The gallery's phone bill to Europe rose substantially under Elliot's attempts to buy and sell overseas, but whenever Claire caught a stream of the conversation, the foreign collectors sounded suspiciously like young buddies. Trevor's requests to Elliott for this or that job to be done inevitably ended up in Claire's hands under the excuse of "Louise has me booked up already." And indeed, Louise did often seem to need Elliot for herself — especially if Claire was already overwhelmed with work. Claire could sense the undertones of a plan to make her life miserable, but there was nothing she could point directly to that would support such an allegation.

In the meantime, Trevor was swamped with his own business and could barely keep up with running his end of the gallery. There were four employees, but only two were working productively.

Perhaps over time this state of affairs would have driven Trevor to distraction. But Louise knew how to keep it from impacting her grander schemes. She had only one job that mattered — to continue to fan the flames of Trevor's passion for her.

She was a continuous flirt whenever they were alone. She was always whispering in his ear, promising all sorts of carnal adventures, leaving Trevor in a state of almost constant sexual excitement. This feeling also imparted a certain adrenaline to Trevor's actions, making him feel that no amount of work was too much to handle. His super powers, he believed, extended beyond the bedroom to his workday.

And so the gallery struggled along. The bright spot on the horizon was Claire's exhibition. Despite the immense effort it had taken to get it organized all by herself, it was coming together nicely. The only thing left to worry about was the catalogue. Claire had insisted on hiring her favorite printer, and although the photographs had been taken and separated by one of Louise's "friends," they were ready on time. The catalogue essay was written and on a diskette. All that was needed was for the two items to go in an envelope to the printer.

To Claire's surprise, Elliot offered to hand-deliver it for her. "I have to run an errand in that direction anyway," he said, "so it's no trouble."

Claire, swamped with work, was grateful for his offer. "Make sure you get the name of the person who receives it," she told him, "just in case. They're very busy over there."

Later that day Elliot reported that the envelope had been safely deposited at its destination, and Claire thought no more about it.

Four days later, Claire received a phone call from the printer.

"Where are your transparencies?" Ray, the owner, wanted to know.

"They were in the envelope with the diskette. Don't you have them?"

"No. All I have here is the disc."

"Wait a minute. Let me put you on hold and I'll ask Elliot who he gave the envelope to."

Claire buzzed Elliot's office. "Do you remember who took the envelope at the printer's?" she asked. "They have the diskette but they can't find the transparencies."

224

"I knew it the day I delivered it, but you didn't ask me and now I've forgotten."

"Well, do you remember anything about the person? Was it a man or a woman?"

"I'm not sure."

"Elliot, this is important! Think!"

"You don't have to get all snotty about it. I was doing you a favor, if I recall."

"Elliot, please. Those transparencies will take days to be separated again if they're lost. The catalogue won't be ready in time for the exhibition!"

"Well, then you should have allowed time for that possibility. Anyway, it's not really my problem, is it?"

Claire was stunned. It was the first openly hostile statement Elliot had made to her. She suddenly knew that Elliot had purposely sabotaged her catalogue.

Claire hung up on him and talked to the printer. "I can't find out who Elliot gave them to, Ray. Please search the shop one more time, and in the meantime I'll call our photographer and get another set made."

"You know this will set back the job, don't you?"

"Yes, I know. Is there anything you can do to speed it up, anything at all?"

"I'll tell you what, Claire. You get me those transparencies as fast as possible, and I'll do my damnedest. You know I have a soft spot for you."

"Thanks, Ray. I appreciate that. I know you guys are swamped."

But the photographer was less accommodating. "Two weeks!" he insisted in belligerent tones. "Two more weeks — that's as fast as I can get to them."

225

"But that's not acceptable!" Claire cried. "It didn't take you that long in the first place. Why is it taking so long now?"

"Now I'm busy. Next month, maybe not so busy. But now — two weeks!"

Claire hung up the phone and began sobbing. There were only two weeks until the exhibition opened. The catalogue would not be ready.

With a tear-stained face Claire went to tell Trevor the bad news. She found Louise also in Trevor's office — sitting on his lap.

"Claire!" Trevor jumped up as soon as she entered, almost dumping Louise on the floor. Claire would have had to laugh if she weren't so miserable.

"I have bad news. The catalogue is going to be late. Somehow the transparencies were lost between here and the printer's."

Louise expressed concern. "But, Claire! You have worked so hard. It is too, too bad."

"Can't we get another set of transparencies over there in time to make the deadline?" Trevor asked.

Claire looked at Louise. "The photographer says he's too busy and needs two weeks. Could you talk to him, Louise? Maybe he'll listen to you."

Claire had to swallow her pride to beg a favor of Louise, but she was too desperate to care.

Louise smiled sweetly. "But of course! I'll go right now." She stopped at the door to remark, "I have a way with them, do I not? It is good for you that they listen to me!"

Claire looked at Trevor for reaction to this statement, but Trevor — still a bit pink around the ears from being caught in an embrace with Louise — looked down at his desk and avoided Claire's eye.

In a few moments Louise had returned with her results. "He says that, for me, he will do it in ten days!" She was triumphant, but Claire only sighed.

"That's still not enough time," she said.

Louise shrugged. "It is better than you did," she noted. "Anyway, so the catalogue is late. Pooh-pooh. No one will miss it at the opening; you can ship them all copies later."

Claire gaped at her. The idea was not only unprofessional, but added a huge burden of work. Trevor finally got involved.

"Listen, Claire, I'll do anything I can to help. If you need me to stay and put labels on envelopes for you one night, I'll be happy to do it. If you want me to personally go around town and hand-deliver them, I'll do it. I know this is a really bad break."

"Trevor," Claire said, her lower lip trembling at his kind words, "I worked so hard for everything to be perfect! It's my first exhibition, and now it's all ruined."

"It's not ruined, Claire! It's going to be great. These things happen all the time. Don't be so hard on yourself; it isn't your fault."

Louise didn't like the amount of consolation and understanding emanating from Trevor. "Don't we have a lunch date?" she interrupted. "I think we'd better leave now or we're going to be late."

"Would you like to join us, Claire?" Trevor offered. "We're just having lunch with a collector from Missouri."

Claire declined. "Thanks anyway, but I still have a lot to do."

That was the moment Louise began worrying that her hold on Trevor might not be as airtight as she'd assumed.

Ray the printer kept his presses going for thirty-six hours straight in order to accommodate Claire's exhibition. The catalogues arrived on the gallery doorstep the morning of the opening.

Claire was so grateful she sent Ray a gigantic bouquet of flowers, with a card that said, "For my hero." He kept the card pinned to his bulletin board for years, and when asked about it would always say, "That Claire MacKenzie was a real sweetheart. It's really too bad what happened to The Trevor Whitney Gallery."

THIRTY-ONE

Just before the opening of Claire's exhibition, an unexpected visitor reappeared at the gallery.

After months of negotiation between lawyers, James Hardwick had agreed to plead guilty to trespassing and pay a twenty-five hundred dollar fine. The gallery settled for this misdemeanor charge of trespassing rather than something more serious when it became clear that Sonny Kaufmann was determined to disavow any knowledge of James' actions. He claimed publicly and vehemently that James had acted on his own, and that he, for one, was horrified. No one believed him, but nevertheless James did not return to work at Kaufmann-Kramer. Sonny was rather sorry to let him go, but not sorry enough to stick his neck out for the young man.

Six months after the incident James set himself up as a private dealer. The whole escapade had been a great source of humor in the art world, and James knew his reputation was shot. He decided to do some damage control. He thought he should start by apologizing to Trevor and Claire.

This idea was honorable — if a bit naïve, but James had turned over a new leaf during his months of expulsion. He was glad to wash his hands of Sonny Kaufmann; he would now be his own boss and conduct himself admirably. He would show the art world that without Sonny's influence he really was a trustworthy guy.

Besides, James still had a crush on Claire MacKenzie.

So two days before Claire's opening James trotted down to The Trevor Whitney Gallery. He arrived just after a crate of paintings from Keny Galleries that Claire was borrowing for the Ashcan show.

As soon as the crate arrived Elliot took off on a sudden errand for Louise. Trevor was on an important phone call, and Louise was allergic to physical labor, so once again Claire faced the chore of unpacking the crate all by herself. The last person she was in the mood to deal with was James Hardwick.

But James saw the crate, saw Claire's difficulty, and saw an ideal opportunity to make amends.

"Hey, let me help you with that," he offered, taking off his coat as Claire struggled to move the crate into the center of the room.

Claire saw only a spy, not a do-gooder. She didn't want him knowing what paintings were inside the crate.

"I'm fine. I can do it myself," she said.

"It's heavy! I can help," James replied.

"I don't want any help!" Claire exclaimed. "I can handle it." But her words belied her actions, because the crate was barely moving.

"It's stupid not to let me help you!" James said. "Here, let me just take off my shirt." He removed his Oxford button-down to keep it clean, but was not uninfluenced by the fact that he believed his mesh undershirt flattered his male physique.

A thoroughly disgusted Claire began yelling, "Are you crazy? I said 'No!' and I meant 'No!' and I want you out of here right now!"

In his office in the back, Trevor heard Claire yelling "No!" and became alarmed. "Listen," he said to his telephone caller, "can I phone you right back? I think something's wrong with Claire...."

Trevor came flying out of the back hallway, found Claire yelling "No!" and "Stop it!" to a partially dressed James Hardwick, and jumped to his own conclusions.

"You get out of here!" he cried out. He threw himself between Claire and James and shoved the latter towards the door. "How dare you come here and make advances to my gallery assistant!"

Trevor picked James up by the collar and threw him outside. Then he sent his coat and Oxford shirt sailing out behind him. A terrified James did not attempt a defense. The last Trevor saw of him he was running for his life down 70th Street.

In the minute it took to recover from the shock of Trevor's actions, Claire began to laugh. She laughed so hard she couldn't stand up. She held her sides and slid down the wall until she was sitting on the floor, looking up at an indignant Trevor, trying to sputter out the truth. "He wasn't assaulting me! He wanted to help me open the crate!"

Trevor looked foolish for a split-second. Then he began laughing too. "Oh my God!" he cried. "Did you see the look on his face?" And the two of them, howling with laughter, began rolling around on the floor, clutching each other, unable to breathe.

Louise came out of her office to see what all the fuss was about. When she saw the two of them rolling around together, trying to recount their story, she became furious. "I don't see what's so funny," she said, "but you are making spectacles of yourselves!" She turned on her heels and flounced back to her office.

Louise sat down at her desk and rubbed her temples. She knew Trevor's lust for her was the only thing holding them together, and he was getting closer, every day, to realizing it. It was quite obvious that as soon as she was out of the picture Trevor would realize he was still in love with Claire.

Louise was only marginally jealous. Trevor, she'd decided, was a bore — almost annoyingly naïve, and definitely too pedestrian for her tastes. Claire, with her brave attempts to hide her true feelings, was equally pathetic. They deserved each other.

Louise was ready to pack up and move on, but Christmas season was just around the corner, and Trevor was taking her to Aspen to ski. And there were all those presents to think about too. No, it was still too soon. Besides, if she could just hold out until the spring sales, her take might be so much better. A Renoir had just made $3.5 million at auction; a fever for Impressionist paintings was building. Who knew what could happen in the spring?

Louise told herself to hang in there. Financial freedom was just around the corner. All she had to do was play the game for a few more months.

Louise consoled herself with the thought of all the lovely little baubles she would buy herself when it was over.

THIRTY-TWO

Claire's Ashcan show opened the first week of December, 1986. She had refined the theme to "Ashcan Paintings of New York City Life," and it was an expansive and beautiful exhibition. With the help of Trevor and Waldo, Claire had managed to get prime examples of works by Robert Henri, John Sloan, William Glackens, Ernest Lawson and George Luks, and had unearthed a few surprises by herself, too. She'd discovered a small boxing scene by George Bellows that was a finished study for the Cleveland Museum's *Stag at Sharkeys*, she had borrowed a rarely-seen 1909 Edward Redfield painting of New York City at night titled *Between Daylight and Darkness*, and had tracked down some Bowery pastels by Everett Shinn. To add weight to her catalogue essay, she'd supplemented her painting images with vintage photographs by Lewis Hines of turn-of-the-century city life. It was an excellent job, and Claire was justifiably proud of her efforts.

At Claire's insistence, Anna attended the opening. Anna had been strangely unresponsive to Claire's phone calls, but Claire had managed to catch her on the phone late one evening, and had extracted a promise that the younger woman would come to the opening and stay for a drink afterwards.

The opening was well attended. Claire had hoped that Charles might make a surprise appearance, but Lewis and Bernard did say he sent regards. There wasn't any good press about the exhibition — not without Anna pushing hard for it — but the other dealers expressed words of encouragement, which Claire knew were only bones thrown to someone too unimportant to be any threat. Still, she was flattered.

Trevor stood in the gallery beaming the whole evening, graciously making sure every visitor knew the entire exhibition had been Claire's doing. Louise, at his side, was forced to appear equally proud of Claire.

Lewis avoided Louise as much as possible, and when Waldo arrived Lewis grabbed his arm and led him to a corner where the two of them could drink champagne and complain about Trevor's choice in women. Bernard finally had to come and tell them to break it up before Trevor got wind of their conversation.

For Claire, the highlight of the evening was seeing Anna, although she didn't arrive until the very end of the opening. Anna entered the building, ducked her head, and made her way over to Claire as covertly as possible. She seemed even more shy than usual — which Claire thought was odd considering almost everyone still at the opening was very fond of her.

"You made it!" Claire exclaimed, hugging Anna.

"Well, I knew it meant a lot to you. The show is really beautiful, Claire. You must be so proud!"

"You deserve some of the credit too, Anna," Claire said. "I couldn't have done it without all of your help at the beginning."

"So where's the new guy, Elliot?" Anna asked.

"Over there." Claire pointed across the room to where Elliot was flirting outrageously with a young woman who worked at Ira Spanierman's gallery. "He's not quite the boy genius he was billed to be," she whispered.

Just then Trevor spotted Anna and came rushing over. "Anna!" He gave her a hug. "We've missed you!"

Anna flushed. "I missed you too," she stammered.

"You look a little pale. Are you eating enough?" Trevor stepped back to scrutinize his young friend, who looked alarmingly thin.

"They work me really hard," Anna said quickly. "I'm probably just a bit run down."

"I can't wait to go out with you afterwards and hear all about your new job!" Claire said. "You never did make up that lunch date with us like you were supposed to."

Anna started making excuses, but Lewis, Bernard and Waldo all came over and began hugging and exclaiming over her. Finally Louise arrived too, dragging along Elliot.

"Little Anna! Is it really you?" Louise expressed the deepest happiness at seeing her. "You remember we told you about Elliot Martre? Here he is!"

"Nice to meet you," Elliot mumbled. He was eager to get back to the girl from Spanierman's.

"Here we all are, all together again!" Louise exclaimed with apparent delight. "One big happy family, *non*? Oh, there goes someone very important... I must have a word. Excuse me! Anna, do come back and see us again...."

Elliot made his excuses and left too.

"Anna," Claire said, "give me a minute to put some things in order and then we can go. You don't mind closing up, do you Trevor?"

"Of course not. But where are you two going? We've hardly had a chance to talk to Anna ourselves! Maybe we'll join you."

Claire would have invited the whole gang, but she caught a look of panic on Anna's face. She put her arm around her. "I've decided to monopolize her company tonight. I'll make her promise to keep in better touch, but tonight it's 'girls night out.' You guys understand, don't you?"

Bernard took Anna's hand in his. "Now, Anna, you must come by our apartment one evening and have some of Lewis' famous lemon cake. I'm not letting go until you promise."

Anna smiled. "I promise."

"And don't let this young lady keep you out too late," Bernard added, gesturing toward Claire. "You do look tired."

Bernard gave Claire a hug for doing such a splendid job with the exhibition, and then he led Lewis and Waldo away. Trevor went to begin closing the gallery, so Claire and Anna were finally alone.

235

"Where do you want to go?" Claire asked. "How about the bar at The Mark hotel? It's pretty quiet there."

"That sounds great."

The two young women headed up Madison Avenue. They found a private corner at The Mark and ordered drinks.

"So, tell me about your job!" Claire said. "It must be so exciting!"

To her shock, Anna burst into tears. "Oh, Claire," she said when she finally found her voice, "there isn't any job!"

"What! What happened?"

"There *never* was any job! I thought I'd find one by now, and I wasn't going to tell you, but everyone was so nice to me tonight, and I'm so unhappy!"

"But Anna, I don't understand. Why did you leave if you didn't have a new job?"

"Louise told me it would be best for the gallery."

"Louise? When?"

Anna blew her nose and told the story of her lunch with Louise.

"That's unbelievable! How dare she!" Claire said.

"But she was right, Claire. At least, I thought she was. But now that you say Elliot's not so great, I wish I hadn't done it."

"Anna, I'm so sorry! And you haven't been working all this time! How are you getting by?"

"My parents sent me some money to tide me over. It's not all that bleak, Claire. I've got some interviews next week and perhaps one of them...." Her voice trailed off into a sigh.

"You should never have left the gallery. I wish you'd told me! I would have marched right into Trevor's office and told him what a snake his girlfriend was."

"That's just what I didn't want you to do! If Elliot had been what Louise had said he was, then it would have been right for me to leave.

I can't hold Trevor back like that! He deserves to have the best gallery in the city."

"Oh, Anna, you are much too good for this business." Claire sat there shaking her head, trying to digest it all. "What I still don't get is why Louise did it? I mean, she must have known that Elliot wasn't really all that wonderful. I wonder if she owed Victor Martre a favor." Claire looked Anna in the face. "She probably sleeps with him too," she declared.

Anna grinned for the first time. "Which one? Elliot or Victor?"

Claire laughed. "I wouldn't be surprised if she sleeps with both Elliot *and* his father!"

"Claire," Anna said, laughing too, "she can't be that bad. Trevor couldn't be that crazy about her if she was really that bad."

"I guess you're right. He really seems to love her." Claire sighed. "I've just got an evil mind."

Anna shook her head earnestly. "Claire, you're the best thing going for that gallery right now. That's why I didn't tell you. I was afraid you'd quit in protest."

"I probably would have."

"I know."

They sipped their drinks quietly for a few minutes, each deep in thought. Finally Claire said, "Anna, you can't go on without a job. I want you to do something for me."

"What?"

"You have to promise first. Promise you'll do whatever I say."

"What if I can't?"

"You can. So promise."

"All right, I promise."

"I want you to go see Lewis and Bernard and let them help you get another job."

237

Anna shook her head with alarm. "I can't do that! They hardly know me!"

"They do too, and they love you, Anna — like we all do. I know they can help you. Please - you *promised.*"

"Well, maybe." Anna was quiet for a moment, thinking. "But should I tell them the truth about what happened?"

Claire thought about it. "Yes. They've been supporters of Trevor's since the beginning. They deserve to know what goes on."

"Won't they be mad at him?"

"Not at him, Anna. They know Louise has him under a spell. I don't know what's up with her, but sometimes I think... Well, never mind. But if Trevor ever got in any real trouble, he'd need to turn to Lewis and Bernard."

"All right, I'll tell them. But I'll have to emphasize that if Elliot had been what he was advertised to be, it would have been all right for Louise to ask me to leave. I really believe that."

"Okay." Claire reached over and brushed a piece of Anna's hair away from her face. "You're the nicest person I know, Anna."

"I'm glad you're my friend, Claire. You're so brilliant and talented! Your exhibition is just wonderful."

"Let's propose a toast," Claire said as she raised her glass. "To good friends — who from now on will tell each other when they need help!

"To good friends!"

THIRTY-THREE

Lewis was completely worked up by the time Anna left their apartment the next day. "How *could* Louise fire that sweet child?" he exclaimed. "And for that little twerp Elliot!"

"Anna wasn't technically fired," Bernard reminded his partner. "She quit."

"She was coerced! It's the same thing."

Bernard didn't reply; he was thinking the matter over. Finally Lewis couldn't stand his silence any more.

"Don't you want to run down there and tell Trevor the truth about his girlfriend?" he demanded.

"That's just it, Lewis. What truth? That she thought it would be best for the gallery if an impressive employee with a wonderful pedigree joined the firm? There's no crime in that."

"It was all a ruse to get rid of Anna."

"We don't know that. Even Anna doesn't really think so. And anyway, why would Louise? I mean, what was it about Anna that was so disagreeable to her?"

Lewis suddenly snapped his fingers. "I've got it! She did it to hurt Claire. She's jealous."

"That seems a bit of a stretch, my love."

Lewis threw his arms open wide and said, "Not if you look at the big picture!"

Bernard chuckled. "The big picture seems to be getting foggier and foggier. I wish Charles were here. He'd have a scorecard we could follow."

"Charles never did believe me that Trevor was in love with Claire," Lewis pointed out petulantly.

"I didn't either, and I'm still not convinced. Anyway, the real question is, what can we do for Anna?"

"Let's call around," Lewis suggested. "Someone we know must have a connection at a good PR firm."

By the next week Anna had three job interviews lined up, and all resulted in job offers. Anna picked the one she liked best, and excitedly telephoned Claire to tell her the good news.

"And they really seem to think I'm talented!" she said. "I don't think it's only because of Bernard and Lewis that they offered me the job."

"Of course not, Anna. You *are* talented!"

"But you should have seen Lewis and Bernard's faces when I told them about Louise asking me to leave. Lewis turned so purple I thought he was going to have apoplexy."

"Really? I don't think they've said anything to Trevor."

"I hope they don't."

"I don't care if they do or not," Claire said, "as long as they're there to help Trevor out if he needs it."

The next three months flew by. Christmas season 1986 came and went. Trevor and Louise spent two weeks in Aspen and returned looking more attached than ever — Louise sporting a new diamond bracelet and matching earrings. Trevor began planning an exhibition of Maurice Prendergast watercolors to open in May, and Claire followed up on leads earned from her Ashcan exhibition. Business was bustling and the art market was booming. Claire noticed that even Louise seemed a bit more energetic about the gallery.

And then one day at the beginning of April, just after an extraordinarily successful sale of Impressionist paintings at auction in London, Elliot called everyone to his office and made a surprise announcement.

"I've done it!" he declared triumphantly. "I've convinced Helena von Savant to sell her Cezanne to us!"

They knew exactly which painting he was talking about.

A few months before, renowned art historian John Rewald had published a definitive biography of the artist Paul Cezanne. Trevor had purchased a copy and the whole gallery had pored over it. Illustrated in the book were many paintings that had not been exhibited publicly for decades. Among those was a striking still life owned by the Austrian heiress Helena von Savant, *Apples and Pears on a Table*. When Trevor had seen it he'd said, "I love that one! It might be the best still life in his whole oeuvre."

Apples and Pears on a Table is the simplest of paintings, yet the image is moving and powerful. On a plain wooden table, a crisp white cloth has been tossed and cascades over the edge. On the left side of this tablecloth rests a basket of apples, its contents spilling out onto the table toward the viewer. On the right is a small plate holding three ripe pears, and beneath this an ivory-handled knife hangs off the edge of the table, suspended impossibly in space. The background is a mottled slate blue that suggests sky. At twenty by twenty-eight inches the painting's size invests the image with monumentality, yet the modesty of the plate of pears compared with the raucousness of the tumbling apples is somehow poignant. The whole design has the solidity of a mountain landscape, while at the same time the multiple viewpoints and the position of the objects — impossible to recreate in real life — make the painting a tour-de-force of illusion.

Louise clapped her hands with delight at Elliot's announcement. Trevor was flabbergasted. "How did you manage that? When?"

"Oh, she's an old friend of the family. I've been talking with her for weeks — ever since you said how much you liked the painting, really. It took a while to convince her that you were the man to handle it, but now she says she's ready to trust you. I promised her you'd conduct the whole thing professionally — you know, wire the money before the painting was sent, that sort of thing."

"Wait a minute; we're getting ahead of ourselves. You don't think I can actually buy it, do you? Without a buyer? I don't even know if I can afford it. How much does she want?"

Elliot smiled innocently. "I talked her down to ten million."

Louise gasped. "Oh, but you are marvelous! A mere ten million! It is a steal!"

Trevor was incredulous. "Ten million! That's a steal?"

"But darling, look at the London sale! Just last week the van Gogh "Sunflowers" made almost forty million! The whole post-Impressionist market just tripled!"

"It's that sale," Elliot said, "that convinced her to sell. She knows she may not get another chance to cash in on all the fever for the Post-Impressionists."

"The van Gogh may be only a fluke," Trevor said. "Besides, it was a Japanese buyer. They seem to have unlimited money."

"Then we will find a Japanese buyer and offer him the Cezanne!"

"It's not that easy, sweetheart. The Japanese have their own consultants and networks. We're not hooked into that. We don't even know if the Japanese are interested in Cezanne's paintings."

"But my love," Louise purred, "do you agree that if the van Gogh is worth almost forty million, then if we could find a buyer the Cezanne could be worth twenty million?"

"Perhaps." Trevor thought about it for a minute. "Maybe. Yes, I'd say it would be."

"Then this is our chance! We must buy it!"

Claire, who'd been following the conversation with growing skepticism, decided it was time to put in her two cents. "We don't *have* ten million. Even if it was the greatest buy of the century we couldn't actually purchase it."

Louise ignored her. "Trevor, we must be serious. If you wish to enter this market you must go in — how do you say? — with guns blazing! No holds barred! You must prove you are a player! That is what the market respects. Elliot was telling me that only the other day, weren't you, Elliot?"

Elliot nodded. "It's been my experience, Trevor, that most of the art sales on this level are made by pure guts. People put themselves out on a limb to prove they're sincere enough to risk their own money. But if you don't think you're ready to play with the big boys" (here Elliot shrugged) "I can call Helena back and tell her I was mistaken about you."

Trevor contemplated the situation for a moment, then he turned toward Claire. "I do, actually, have a way to get the money. I just wasn't planning on doing it. But I could."

Claire stared at him. "You're not serious. You can't risk that much money on the chance that you can sell this painting. Come on, Trevor, this is crazy!"

"I think Elliot has a point. If we want to deal at this level we have to take some risks."

"Why do we have to deal at this level?" Claire asked, but Trevor brushed aside the question and turned back to the others.

"I want this painting," he said. "Tell Mrs. von Savant she has a deal."

Louise squealed with happiness. "It is too, too wonderful! The Cezanne of the decade — the Cezanne of your dreams! You will find a buyer in no time."

"I'm planning on it," Trevor said. "How long do you think Mrs. von Savant will give us to get the money together?" he asked Elliot.

"Ten days, maybe two weeks. She'll set up an escrow account with us in Switzerland, and when the money's deposited she'll ship the painting."

Elliot, Louise and Trevor continued talking excitedly about the details in securing the painting, but Claire stepped back and felt as if the room were spinning away beneath her.

Claire knew that the retail value of the entire inventory and all the cash on hand added together probably equaled less than fifteen million. Almost all of that was tied up in art works and couldn't be immediately liquidated. If they bought no other paintings and put everything they made from sales into the Cezanne for the next year, they might barely pay for it.

But Trevor had said he had the money. Claire wondered if he still had some family money left over. But ten million? He couldn't have that much — he'd once told her that his whole future was wrapped up in the business.

Suddenly a terrible feeling came over Claire. She knew what he would do. He would mortgage the gallery — the business itself. He'd put the whole thing up for collateral.

Think! She said to herself. *You've got to try to stop him.*

Claire cleared her throat, and the others looked at her. "You should probably get a condition report, Trevor, before you seal the deal. I mean, the painting's been out of the public eye for so long, who knows what kind of condition it could be in?"

Elliot and Louise glared at her, but Trevor said, "Good idea. Elliot, have a restorer go into the house and do a thorough exam. If he sends me a favorable report, I'll proceed. You don't think Mrs. von Savant will mind, do you?"

"No, of course not," Elliot replied. "I'll have someone get on it right away."

Good. Claire had bought some time. Now if she could only use it to convince Trevor he was out of his mind.

THIRTY-FOUR

The condition report — stating in glowing terms that the painting was in perfect condition except for a layer of old varnish — arrived in only three days. Claire was alarmed by the speed. In the United States these things never happened that quickly: restorers would be too busy to rush out to do the report; owners would be too busy to schedule the restorer's visit. The restorer — whose unfamiliar name on the letterhead gave no indication of his qualifications for the job — seemed to have a lot of free time, and Mrs. von Savant was surprisingly under-occupied. It passed through Claire's mind that the report might be a fake.

She expressed her concerns about the speed to Trevor, but he only smiled knowingly. "I asked Louise about that and she suggested that I check it out," he said. "I called Victor Martre and he assured me the restorer is well-known and reliable."

"So you are really going to proceed?"

"Sure! I've been thinking about it and I think it's a golden opportunity for us. Come on, Claire, admit it — aren't you the least bit excited? It's a Cezanne for Christ's sake!"

"I'm happy for you, Trevor. It's just that I worry that we're overextending ourselves so much. It's such a risk!"

"Sure it's a risk. Our whole existence is a risk, Claire! The art market is built on it. We're just moving into a higher level, that's all. Once we get used to it, it will seem like old hat in no time."

"Do you have any ideas for a buyer?"

"I'm working on it. I got this great lead from an old law school friend who works in international trade. He's putting me in touch with a guy who has direct access to some Japanese buyers. And then there's the Getty Museum — I've got a call in to them right now. Don't worry, Claire. This Cezanne is magnificent, and it will be fairly priced. It should fly out of here!"

245

That night, Claire sneaked the Rewald book out of the gallery and stopped at Lewis and Bernard's apartment on her way home. She placed it on the coffee table in their living room, opened to the page for *Apples and Pears on a Table* and asked, "What do you think of this Cezanne?"

Bernard gave out a long, low whistle of appreciation. "It's a beauty. Outstanding. Why do you ask?"

"I'll tell you in a minute. First tell me what you think it's worth."

Bernard considered for a moment. "Hard to say in this market," he finally answered. "Maybe, ten or fifteen million? What do you think, Lewis?"

"Oh, more than that!" Lewis said with a casual wave of his hand. "Everything in this book is worth twice what it was before the van Gogh sale!"

"But it's Cezanne, not van Gogh. And the Japanese are driving the market," said Claire.

"Well, there's no indication that they plan on dropping out of the market any time soon!"

"Okay. Here's the deal. Trevor is going to buy it for ten million."

"Ooh!" Lewis exclaimed with delight. "The old boy's hitting the big time! I had no idea he was doing that well!"

Bernard cut off his exuberant chatter. "What's wrong, Claire? Why do you look so glum?"

"I don't think we have the money," Claire said. "I can't be sure because I've been out of the loop for a while, but I really don't think we do. I'm afraid that Trevor is going to mortgage the business to buy it."

Lewis frowned. "Oh, he shouldn't do that!" he said. "I've seen a lot of businesses over the years go under from doing that. Just poof! Anything goes wrong, the bank forecloses and they're gone. We'd better have a talk with him, Bernie."

246

"I don't know, Lewis. It's none of our business."

"None of our business! We nurtured that gallery! We planted the seed that made it grow. We watered the foundation to keep it strong, praised the flowers when they finally bloomed! We've tended garden over that gallery for years. Of course it's our business!"

"We've never told Trevor what to buy or not buy. That's his domain."

"Oh, but I'm sure this whole thing is just youthful indiscretion! If Charles were here he'd never be doing this. The young man just needs a word to the wise! How could he know what a dangerous idea it is, if no one tells him?"

"What does Louise say about all this?" Bernard asked Claire.

"Elliot arranged the deal, so it's the pinnacle of all her hopes for him. She's thrilled. She's always wanted the gallery to be dealing at this level."

Bernard turned to Lewis and shook his head. "We're not getting involved," he said. "I'm not interfering with him and Louise. It's up to Trevor to run his own business. He's not a babe-in-the-woods — he's been at this game for four years."

Lewis looked askance, and Claire asked, "But what if the gallery really does go under?"

Bernard put his arm around Claire. "That would be a great shame. But I don't think it will. Louise will probably move heaven and earth to keep that from happening! Trevor's her meal ticket - I can't believe she'd let the gallery go down without a fight. All that steel charm has to be good for something."

Lewis brightened at Bernard's words. "Bernie's probably right, though I hate to admit it. Louise is barracuda enough to keep the gallery floating just on will power."

Claire didn't have any faith in Louise, but she didn't know what else to do. She couldn't bring herself to speak of her own secret notion — that Louise might actually be planning the gallery's downfall. She knew she was jealous of Louise, and that made her question her judgment.

The next day Trevor pulled Claire aside to inform her with excitement, "I talked to that guy — Mr. Osaka, the one recommended by my friend — for two hours last night. He has three or four potential buyers he's shopping the painting to. He says we should know in a week if he has a buyer! And then early this morning the European Paintings Curator of the Getty called. They're definitely interested. We may even be able to have our own little private auction, with all this competition!"

"Wow!" Claire breathed a sigh of relief. She even allowed herself a bit of excitement. "I guess you really are going to pull this off! I'm sorry I seemed so unenthusiastic. I guess I'm just much more conservative about money than you are. I guess that's why you're the boss," she added with a smile.

"I don't mind your wariness, Claire. It keeps me on track. I know you have the gallery's best interests at heart, and I appreciate that. Even when I ignore your advice."

"So when are you wiring the money?" Claire asked.

"I should get clearance from the bank today. And we don't have to worry about the shipping of the painting. Louise and Elliot are flying to Austria themselves to pick it up and hand-deliver it back here. Louise wants to visit her relatives since she didn't go home for the holidays, and Elliot feels he owes Mrs. von Savant a personal visit."

Trevor was actually whistling when he hung up the phone after arranging the wire transfer. Louise threw her arms around him and covered his face with kisses. Elliot opened a bottle of champagne, and everyone drank to the gallery's success.

Then Louise and Elliot left early to pack for the trip. Trevor savored his imminent ownership of the Cezanne.

"Did you ever dream, Claire, when you came to work here, that within four years we'd be handling multi-million dollar paintings?"

Claire smiled and shook her head. "Back then there hardly were any multi-million dollar paintings. The market has grown so much it's almost unbelievable. I wonder when we'll start seeing American paintings reach that level?"

Trevor took another sip of champagne. "Oh, not for a long time," he said. "It's not the same. The great European artists have an international appeal. American art still has only a native audience."

"That's true. But plenty of Americans have millions of dollars to spend on art. I could see a few artists, if the subjects are right — like a Shinnecock Chase or Isle of Shoals Hassam, or maybe a South American Church — breaking the ten million mark before too long."

Trevor shrugged. "I hope you're right! But in the meantime, it will be nice to make five or ten million dollars on one deal, won't it? You have to admit, Claire, it hasn't been that bad for business to have Louise and Elliot around, has it?"

Claire was gracious. "No. I guess after today I have to admit they have their benefits."

Louise called from the airport to say goodbye.

"I'll be home soon, darling," she promised. "We'll make love all night with the Cezanne hanging on the wall in front of us!"

That evening, when Trevor went home to his apartment, he opened the bedroom closet and discovered that Louise had packed every item of clothing she owned. He smiled to himself. It was so like her to worry about what to wear on such a short trip.

Then it hit him. A wave of nausea crept into his stomach. Maybe Louise wasn't planning on coming back.

Trevor remembered Louise's final words on the phone: "We'll make love all night." He swept the panic out of his mind. Of course she was coming back. Of course.

THIRTY-FIVE

Trevor realized by the end of the next day that he had no way to reach Louise or Elliot. He didn't even know where they were staying. It hadn't seemed necessary because Louise had promised to call as soon as she arrived and give him that information. But she hadn't.

Trevor tried her old apartment; the phone had been disconnected. He left a message with Victor Martre — who was apparently out of town — asking him to call Trevor if he heard from Louise.

Claire couldn't help noticing Trevor's agitation. He was pacing the gallery. "I'm worried about Louise," he finally admitted. "I hope she's all right. She was supposed to call."

"Well, you know if the plane had crashed it would be all over the news. She's probably just tied up with friends and relatives. I bet she'll call you tonight."

Louise did not call that night, but Trevor lied to Claire the next day about it. "She's arrived safely and she's meeting Elliot at the end of the week," he reported.

"Great! Did she mention if the wire arrived?"

"No. But I checked with the bank this morning. Everything went smoothly. The money's in escrow until the painting arrives."

Three more days went by. Trevor didn't hear from Louise, and Claire realized he was in a state of constant anxiety. "What's wrong?" she finally demanded. "You're walking around the gallery like a caged tiger."

"I have to tell you something," Trevor said. "Louise hasn't called. I lied the other day when I said she had. I didn't want you to worry."

"You're kidding. I don't get it."

"And Claire, she took everything. I mean, when she left. She packed up everything she owned."

Claire stared at him. "Oh my God! You don't think? I mean, the money's safe in escrow, right? So if we don't get the painting, it's no big deal."

"Claire, I've got buyers lined up. I'll look like a fool."

"Better to look like a fool than be one. Thank God for that escrow account. I mean, Louise may have left you, but at least she didn't get the money."

Trevor looked down at the floor.

"Oh, Trevor, I'm sorry. That was a terrible thing to say." Claire walked over and put her arm on his shoulder. "I don't know what's come over me. I'm really sorry. Anyway, I'm sure we're worried about nothing. Louise is crazy about you! I bet we're making a mountain out of a molehill! Why don't you just call Helena von Savant and ask to speak to Elliot? He'll be able to clear the whole thing up, I'm sure."

"I don't have the number, do you? Elliot handled everything with her."

"I'm sure we can get it from directory assistance. There can't be that many Helena von Savants in Austria!"

But directory assistance informed them that the von Savant phone number was unlisted.

"Don't worry," Claire said. "I'll call John Rewald. He'll have her number, I bet."

Claire left a message with the publisher of the Cezanne book, asking them to forward a message to author John Rewald. Then she called some of the museum scholars she knew, trying to get Rewald's home phone number. The curator of European art at the Met said she thought he was holed up somewhere working on his new book, *Cezanne and America.*

"Dead end," she reported. "But someone's bound to call us back with the information soon."

* * * *

252

Meanwhile, a man walked into a bank in Switzerland and handed the manager a card.

"Ah, Mr. von Savant! We've been expecting you. Follow me."

The bank manager and this gentleman retired to a discreet back office. "We received the fax this morning," the bank manager said. "The painting arrived in the States quite safely. Now, we just need your signature on a few forms, and we can release the money to you. Will a cashier's check suffice?"

"Actually," the man said, "I was wondering if you'd mind wiring the money for me, to my account in the Bahamas."

"Of course. I'll just need the account and routing numbers."

The man handed the manager the account information, and thought to himself with great satisfaction, "My dear, today we are not only rich, we are inextricably bound together. I will have you for my own after all."

Another day went by. And still Trevor did not hear from Louise.

The publisher called Claire to report that they'd passed on her message, and that she should be hearing from John Rewald soon. By the end of the day he hadn't called. Claire walked into Trevor's office to check on him, and found him staring at a pile of Prendergast transparencies as if he had no idea what to do with them.

"When was the last time you ate a decent meal?" Claire asked. "I'm going to order in some sandwiches."

But Trevor raised blank eyes to Claire and said, "Claire, I checked with the bank. The money left the escrow account. It went to an account in the Bahamas."

Claire stared at Trevor with a stupefied expression, then sat down, stunned. "I don't understand. How could it? Only you could release that money!"

"They said they received a fax from me authorizing them to release it."

"But that's impossible!"

"I told them that. But they insist it's legitimate. They're faxing a copy of the letter to my lawyer."

Claire blinked her eyes hard, as of she could shut out the obvious. "It can't be. I don't believe it. How could the bank be that stupid?"

"Claire, do you understand what this means? I don't have the money and I don't have the painting!"

"This is crazy! There must be something we can do. Call the FBI or something! Maybe they can catch them."

"No." Trevor rubbed his temples. "Give it another day. Elliot and Louise could still show up with the painting."

"Of course. Maybe it's all a big misunderstanding. Maybe they picked up the painting today, so they arranged for the money to be released. That would make sense."

"Yes, it could be." Trevor looked at Claire with misery in his eyes. "But you don't really think so, do you Claire?"

Claire's eyes filled with tears. "No," she whispered. "Oh, I don't know what to think! I'm scared."

"So am I," Trevor said softly. "I really loved her, Claire," he suddenly moaned. "How could I be so stupid?"

Claire stood up and began pacing to avoid the pain in Trevor's eyes. "This is insane! We need action! We're both going crazy because we don't have any way to get in touch with anyone. I'm going to call that publishing house back and leave a detailed message for John Rewald, so he knows how important it is to call us."

Claire did leave the message. She said they had purchased the

Cezanne from Helena von Savant, but that a colleague who'd arrange the deal was unreachable, and they had to check on the arrival of the painting. Within an hour the publisher called back.

"Mr. Rewald said to give you a message. He said you couldn't have purchased the Cezanne from Mrs. von Savant, because she died eight months ago. The painting in question is sitting in a Sotheby's warehouse. It is scheduled to be sold for the benefit of the von Savant heirs at a Sotheby's sale in November."

THIRTY-SIX

Louise sat at a little table at the side of a model's runway in an exclusive Paris showroom, while women too thin and too young pranced around in front of her wearing the latest in haute fashion. It was the fall preview, and Louise had wrangled an invitation to this exclusive designer's collection because he was the hottest name in wedding dresses. Wedding dresses were of particular interest to Louise right now. She was going to marry Victor Martre.

She wasn't really paying attention, though. It was too much fun to relive the past months, and contemplate the reaction her little escapade was causing back in New York City.

It had gone so well, and so easily! First, of course, there was Victor's brilliant impersonation of one of Helena von Savant's sons. A slight disguise, a fake passport — why, he had handled his end of the escrow account beautifully. And now that the money was safely tucked away under an assumed name in an account in the Bahamas, it was almost impossible that anyone would tie the money back to them.

And there was Elliot, too. He'd been the perfect student. His performance as a seasoned art dealer was worthy of an Oscar. The way he'd handled the paperwork for Trevor's side of the deal had been flawless. Trevor had never realized he'd signed an extra paper authorizing the release of the painting. Really, Elliot was a natural-born actor. He said he was planning to open a recording studio with his share of the money, but perhaps once that little enterprise had failed Louise would encourage him to try his luck in the movies.

There was going to be some trouble, undoubtedly. Louise had already hired a lawyer — one of the best — and the way he looked at her left little doubt that he planned to keep her happy as a client in more ways than one. That was all to the good. Victor wouldn't need to know, but he'd be happy with the excellent service.

Louise chose to ignore the fact that her upcoming nuptials were predicated more on blackmail than affection. Victor simply wanted to tie her to him so she couldn't change plans midstream and decide to make him and Elliot the villains. He had threatened her with exposure if she refused to marry him, and she had laughed with disdain at his arrogance but nevertheless had agreed to the wedding. He was a good partner. He was dull in bed, but then he wasn't the sexually possessive type. Louise had no doubts she could continue to take lovers after her marriage.

Elliot was sulking about the wedding. He was only a child after all, and had deluded himself that he was all the man she really needed. But he would get over it, and in the meantime she knew he could be trusted to keep his mouth shut. He knew better than to incur Louise's wrath by telling his father about their little tête-à-têtes.

Did she feel sorry for Trevor? Not in the least. He was the most boring man she'd ever met. That someone so handsome, so wealthy and so young should spend almost every waking minute thinking about paintings — what they mean, why they're important, how he can acquire the next great one and who he can sell it to — well, it was all a great waste of time. She felt sometimes as if she'd throw up if she had to pretend interest in another run-of-the-mill American painting.

Yet, ironically, Louise had never intended to dupe Trevor out of so much money. It was just that the art market kept going up and up — could she help it if circumstances conspired to make her an extremely wealthy woman?

And as for the long-suffering Claire, Louise knew just what she'd do. She'd run around in a rage, blaming everyone including Trevor. And then she'd try to fix things — unable to resist throwing in any number of 'I told you so's' at Trevor. After thoroughly humiliating both of them, Claire would never get her man. When it was all said and done Trevor would want nothing more than to escape the woman whose very presence was a reminder of his public denouement.

And any legal battles — should Trevor attempt to connect her to the theft — would take years to unravel. The whole overseas aspect of the lawsuit alone would tie up the courts for ages. And Louise was fairly certain, anyway, that her plan was flawless. Perhaps she looked guilty, but the money could never be traced to her.

With millions of dollars tucked away, she and Victor could lead the life she'd always dreamed of. Who knows? Perhaps the two of them would put away their evil ways and become respectable citizens. Perhaps she'd even have a child. Stranger things had happened. It might be nice to reinvent herself one more time.

Louise smiled into space, imagining her future as a beloved dowager of France, doting on children and grandchildren, perhaps owning some wineries or perfume factories, and — when not in her Paris penthouse — pottering around in the garden of her country chateau in the Loire Valley.

THIRTY-SEVEN

The day it became clear that Trevor had been hopelessly swindled — that there was no Cezanne and that the gallery owed the bank ten million dollars and would probably be foreclosed on — Claire went home and cried.

Then she decided to clutch at the only straw she could conceive of. She got on the train and went to see Charles.

What, exactly, she thought Charles might be able to do or say, she had no idea. It was just that Charles was so wise — surely he would offer some advice or words of comfort. Even though he'd left the gallery without giving her an explanation, he'd constantly sent regards to her via Lewis and Bernard, so though they'd been out of touch so long she was confident she still had a place in his heart. It was still unclear why Charles had retired, but she no longer thought it was caused by any actions or words of Trevor's. Apparently Charles had his reasons; and anyway, it no longer mattered. What mattered was figuring out if there was a way to save the gallery.

The first thing Claire noticed as she walked up the walkway toward Charles' front porch was the wheelchair. The front steps had been replaced by a ramp, and the wheelchair, neatly folded, was leaning against the porch rail. Claire suddenly became very worried. Perhaps Charles was sick — perhaps he'd been sick all these months and she'd never known. Claire almost ran up to the front door.

Her fears were not allayed when a nurse, in a starched white uniform, answered the door. But when she asked for Charles the nurse replied, "Oh, I'm sure he'd love some company! Mary's sleeping and he's out back on the dock. I'll just go and get him."

Claire waited a bit nervously for Charles to arrive. When he finally entered the hallway, she saw that he looked perfectly healthy. With a cry of relief she flew into his arms.

"Oh, Charles," she said, "you're all right! I saw the wheelchair out front and for a moment I thought...." Claire stopped talking. Charles looked both embarrassed and alarmed.

"Oh, dear, you weren't expecting me, and I've just shown up out of the blue and I should never have come without calling you but I was afraid you might not let me see you and something has happened, you see, and I need your advice, and I'm sorry I'm rambling on like this, but please, Charles, tell me what's wrong!" Claire said.

In response Charles gave her a big hug. "Oh, Claire, I've missed you!" and when Claire pulled back she saw he had tears in his eyes.

"Is it Mary?" Claire asked.

Charles nodded, too emotional to speak for a moment. "Yes, yes, it's Mary," he said when he found his voice again. "She has AIDS, Claire."

It took Claire a moment to process the news. "What? Charles, no! I'm so sorry."

Charles told the story of Mary's illness, and the fact that he'd asked Trevor to keep it a secret. "I bet it killed Trevor to keep it from you," he said, "but those were Mary's wishes and I didn't have the heart to argue with her."

Claire now understood why Trevor had made Anna tell her about Charles' retirement, and why he'd avoided her. And why he'd seemed so cavalier about the whole thing at the time — he was trying to put up a good front. But it was sad. That one unfortunate secret had started a chain of events that had led to where they were today.

"Charles, so much has changed at the gallery. Something really bad happened. I don't know what to do, so I just hopped on the train and came out here. I'm hoping you can give me some advice."

Charles' look became all concern. He directed her to the dining room table, and the two of them sat down. "Tell me what happened."

So Claire filled him in. She started with Louise and Elliot and tried to recreate for Charles the past few months, recounting the story until its bitter end when they'd realized they'd been scammed out of ten million dollars. "Is there anything we can do?" she ended, "Anything at all?"

Charles, who'd been interjecting comments throughout the story, was nevertheless taken aback by its conclusion. "Are you sure Louise really stole the money? It just seems incredible. She was with Trevor for months! Lewis didn't like her, but as far as I know, no one thought she was a con artist!"

"I don't think there's really any doubt. Now it's just a matter of what we do about it."

Charles sat back in his chair, wearing an expression of exhaustion and pity. "Poor Trevor! All that work to build up the gallery — it was a great job, too. I was so proud of him. What a shame!"

"He's really shaken up, Charles. He's heartbroken, and embarrassed, and scared — we both are. We don't know if we'll lose the gallery. I hate to see him this way; I'd do anything to help him! Do you have any ideas? Any, at all, that could turn this around?"

Charles gave Claire a penetrating look. "How I answer that depends on you, Claire. I need you to answer a question for me. I need you to tell me the truth. Then I'll tell you what to do."

Claire squirmed uncomfortably. She knew what the question would be before Charles even asked it.

"What's more important to you, Claire — Trevor, or the gallery?"

Claire's voice was barely more than a whisper. "Trevor," she answered.

Charles broke into a big grin. "Good! I can't save the gallery, Claire, but I can save you and Trevor. Ten years from now you'll look back on this whole thing and laugh." Seeing Claire's incredulous look, he adjusted his statement. "Well, maybe not laugh, but it won't seem the huge tragedy that it is today."

"But how? What should I do?"

"You should leave the gallery, immediately."

Claire stared at him. "I can't do that! It would be like deserting a sinking ship! He'll think I'm horrible!"

"You must. If you see him through this whole thing — which, by the way, I must remind you is not in any way your fault nor your financial obligation — you'll be witness to every humiliation he has to face. You'll try to be his friend but he'll only feel embarrassment in front of you. He needs to heal, he needs to handle this on his own like the grownup that he is, and he needs to move on. *Then* he'll turn around and thank his lucky stars that you still care for him."

"But where would I go? And how do I leave without it seeming like a terrible desertion?"

"I think I can get you a job in the American paintings department at the Met."

Claire's eyes opened wide. "You can? How?"

"You know that fellowship they have in American paintings? The one started a few years back by an anonymous donor? That's Steinman Gallery money. Sid endowed the fellowship in his will, and every fellow is approved by a board of just two: me, and whoever is the current head curator of American paintings."

"You never told us!"

"That's what being anonymous is, Claire."

Claire laughed. "But still, is it fair for you to give it to me? I mean, most of the people who get it are so qualified!"

Charles chuckled. "You have no idea how talented you are, do you? That Ashcan exhibition was wonderful. Lewis and Bernard told me that some of the staff from the Met came to see it. I won't have any trouble getting you in once you put your name forward."

"I don't have a Masters degree. Does that matter?"

"No. The fellowship is set up for anyone worthy."

"But doesn't it go from year to year or something? I thought the new fellows started in September."

"We have some extra funds because a few years ago we lost someone early — she took a permanent position at the Terra Museum in Chicago. So in theory we could start you right away. But here's the important part, Claire. If Trevor knows you're going to the Met he won't be upset with you. He'll be happy for you. He knows it's an incredible opportunity."

Claire looked at Charles gratefully. "I don't even know what to say. Wow. The Met! I mean, it's every art history student's dream."

"Then do it!"

"I don't know." But Claire began thinking about the past week, and realized she already knew how awkward it would be if she stayed in the gallery.

"Well, maybe you're right. It's probably best if I stay out of Trevor's way. But who's going to be there for him through all this? He'll need help."

"Between Lewis, Bernard and myself we'll see him through. It's going to be long, and drawn out, and ugly. The hardest part will be making Trevor realize he probably has to let the gallery go."

"Do you really think so? Can't you think of any way he can hold on to it?"

"I could fill you with all kinds of hope. The lawyers undoubtedly will. But Claire, it's unfortunately very simple. He owes the bank ten million dollars. He doesn't have it — can't even afford to make monthly payments at that level. He could try to collect from Louise, but that will take years. The best thing he can do is bite the bullet and liquidate."

Claire looked miserable.

"It's not all that tragic. You'll see. I've learned that there are more important things in life than the art business. Trevor will move on. And I have a feeling that where he's going to end up is really his true calling, anyway. And I'll be beside him, as much as I can, every step of the way."

Claire was amazed that Charles could look so optimistically upon the whole thing. The gallery was Trevor's life! It was pretty much her life, too — although she knew in her heart it was Trevor that was her life, not the business. She could live without the gallery. She couldn't live without Trevor.

"I don't know why everything you're saying sounds so comforting and possible," Claire said. "But I believe you. I sure hope you're right about Trevor and me, though. I haven't allowed myself to think about that for months. I'm afraid I'm hopelessly in love with him, Charles. I think I must always have been."

"Well, that really comes as no surprise — Lewis has been saying so for years! I have a feeling, Claire, that deep down Trevor feels the same way about you, too."

"You wouldn't know it from the way he's been with Louise all these months."

Charles smiled knowingly. "Men don't always think with the right part of their anatomy, Claire. But sooner or later their heads get put on straight. Have faith, Claire. And patience. Give him lots of space and time, and he'll come running."

Claire sighed. "Well, at least the patience part will be easy. I've had lots and lots of practice!"

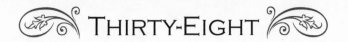

THIRTY-EIGHT

The last months of The Trevor Whitney Gallery can be summed up in a few words. Claire left to work at the Met — and just as Charles had predicted, Trevor was happy for her. He was relieved to have her off the payroll, since he wasn't sure how long he could continue to pay her salary.

Claire loved being at the Met. She kept her communication with Trevor to a minimum, but occasionally sent him goofy cards or little messages just to let him know she was thinking about him. Her usual reticence about matters of the heart returned as soon as she was out of Charles' presence, and despite her almost weekly conversations with the older man, she refrained from asking him if Trevor ever mentioned her, or wondering out loud if he might miss her. Instead she immersed herself in her new life, and hoped for a miracle.

It wasn't hard to follow the actual demise of the gallery, for the press relished its every convolution. First, life became one huge legal tangle for Trevor. He sued the Swiss bank; and then Trevor, in turn, was sued by an irate Japanese businessman who'd been promised first right of refusal on the Cezanne by the go-between. Trevor's lawyer counter-sued the go-between, which tied everything up until the Sotheby's sale in November — at which point the Japanese businessman was the successful bidder, and he finally dropped his suit. To add insult to injury, *Apples and Pears on a Table* sold for $19.2 million dollars, buoyed by another incredible van Gogh sale earlier in the year — *Irises*, which sold for almost fifty-four million in May.

In the meantime, Louise and Elliot were tracked down. Louise's lawyer demanded that Trevor's suit be dropped, saying it was only a personal vendetta on Trevor's part. Louise claimed not to have the money, and not to know anything about the money. She declared that Trevor was only a scorned lover, suing her because he was furious she had ended their romantic relationship. As for the Cezanne, she said it was all a pretense on Trevor's part, and defied him to find any proof that there had ever been any communication between anyone at the gallery and Helena von Savant. Which of course there hadn't been, which, also of course, was the point. The whole thing dissolved into a war of 'he said' 'she said,' while Trevor spent thousands of dollars hiring overseas investigators in a fruitless attempt to tie Louise or Elliot to his money.

Only the lawsuit with the Swiss bank produced a favorable outcome. That venerable institution settled out of court for two million dollars. The money went to pay Trevor's lawyer; so at least, when it was all over, Trevor wasn't left with legal bills.

Trevor's bank started demanding payments on the ten million dollar loan, and ultimately the gallery assets had to be liquidated. A sale was held at Christie's in March of 1988. Everyone who was involved in American art turned out for the preview and the sale. The New York dealers, who'd been gloating for months over Trevor's downfall, were in high spirits.

Sonny Kaufmann and James Hardwick, who'd become thick as thieves again over the course of months, perused the offerings together. "Not a bad group of paintings," Sonny admitted. "I might consider picking up one or two for inventory. Glad to help the old boy out, anyway. Hate to have an ex-art dealer added to the roles of welfare recipients!" he added with a snicker.

Lavinia Worthington came up and joined them, and exchanged a glance of happy significance with Sonny. "Can you believe this turnout?" she said. "Count on art dealers to eat up a scandal!"

"You're not feeling sorry for Trevor Whitney, are you?" James inquired.

"Me? Are you kidding? I just hate to see all this competition. It might mean we actually buy him out of trouble." She shivered. "Ugh.

What an awful thought."

Over in a corner, Waldo Picker held court and recounted to everyone about the first time he'd met Louise Ceinture. "There was a look in her eyes," he told his enthralled audience, "that let you know she was evil. Evil! Oh, she acted like she loved him — hung all over him like a warm towel, but I'm telling you I knew the minute I laid eyes on her that she'd do that poor boy wrong." He stopped and dabbed at his eyes. "Poor Trevor. He was a great friend, a great dealer. Being here today it feels like a funeral. The end of The Trevor Whitney Gallery! I never thought I'd see the day."

Trevor never made an appearance during the preview, and no one saw Claire or Charles, or Lewis and Bernard, either. The New York art world concluded they were too embarrassed to show their faces.

The day of the sale, Christie's was overflowing with spectators. Predictions for the outcome of the sale ranged from dour to overly optimistic — the dour faction being worried about the impact of a stock market crash just five months before. But the actual sale results were more affected by those in the audience who hoped to snatch some of Trevor's great inventory at a fraction of its value. Their fevered bidding eventually caught on in the auction room. After a slow start paintings began selling for their high estimates or more. The Trevor Whitney sale of American paintings made a healthy twelve million dollars.

Trevor's financial worries were over. But The Trevor Whitney Gallery was officially no more.

THIRTY-NINE

Mary Brightman passed away in April of 1988. In May, Claire received a phone call from Charles.

"Claire, I want you to be my guest at opening night of the NYHADA Armory Show next week. I won't take no for an answer."

Claire knew tickets for the private opening were five hundred dollars. "I'd love to go, Charles, but it's so much money...." she protested.

"Indulge me, Claire. I haven't been out to an art function in ages. Besides, there will be a lot of big spenders there, and I plan on bending their ears about the Mary Brightman Foundation." Charles was starting a special fund to help members of the medical community who contracted AIDS in the line of work.

"Well, since you put it that way, I'd love to!"

"Great. I'll send a limo around to pick you up, and you can meet me at the Armory."

A limousine! That was not a typical Charles gesture. Claire wrote off the strange extravagance as stemming from a newfound sense of freedom. After almost two years, Charles had finally emerged from the sick room.

When the limo arrived to bring Claire to the opening, she was startled to find Anna already in it. "Surprise!" the younger woman said. "Charles bought me a ticket, too."

"Anna, it's so great to see you!"

"Well, you've been like a hermit since you took that job at the Met. I told Charles this was probably the only way I could see you. You look wonderful, by the way."

"Thanks, so do you."

Claire was wearing a short, off the shoulder black dress by Donna Karan that emphasized her white skin. Her blond hair was swept up and back down as it had been the night of the Sotheby's preview, and in Claire's ears were two brilliant emerald studs that perfectly matched

271

her eyes. Lewis and Bernard had presented them for her last birthday.

"Do you think Lewis and Bernard will be there?" Anna asked. "What about Trevor — do you think he'll show up?"

"I don't know. I mean, I would think Lewis and Bernard would be there, but Trevor seems to have gone into hiding. No one's seen him for a few months now." Claire carefully turned her head and said this looking out the window. She had never shared her feelings for Trevor with anyone but Charles, and she was afraid Anna would guess them if she saw her face.

If she'd been looking at Anna, however, she might have caught her mischievous grin.

They arrived at the Armory and hurried inside. As they entered the exhibition hall Claire grabbed Anna's arm and gasped. "It's amazing, Anna — it's just like the pictures I've seen of the real thing!"

Indeed, the NYHADA had finally done something significant. The exhibition walls were covered with works by the artists who'd been featured in the original International Exhibition of Modern Art in 1913. Paintings, sculptures and works on paper by Degas, Cezanne, Redon, Brancusi, Matisse, Braque, Duchamp-Villon, Gauguin and Archipenko filled the aisles. Not to mention works by the American artists who'd sponsored the event. If the effect wasn't quite the same — no one was screaming about the degeneration of art or threatening to throw tomatoes at the works — it was still quite impressive. Claire thought wistfully of how much Trevor would have loved to be a participant.

"Come this way," Anna was saying. Claire dutifully followed her along to the exact center of the room, where an elaborate bar had been set up to quench thirsty exhibition goers. There the two of them found Charles, along with Lewis and Bernard.

"It's a mini-reunion!" Anna joyfully exclaimed, as they all

272

exchanged hugs. Claire immediately felt the glaring absence of Trevor, but the others seemed perfectly content.

"Have you seen the whole show yet?" Charles asked.

"No, we just got here."

"Well, go check it out, but make sure you're back here at eight o'clock exactly."

"Why?" Claire asked.

"Oh, that's when they do the special announcements and such. They're going to put in a plug for the Mary Brightman Foundation."

Claire had barely covered a third of the show when Anna began pulling her back towards the bar area. "It's almost eight o'clock!" she said, and Claire laughed at her insistence. "It's just going to be a lot of boring 'thank yous' at the beginning." But Anna dragged her along.

Sure enough, when they returned to the center of the exhibition hall Lavinia Worthington, as president of the NYHADA, was holding forth about all the wonderful donors and guests to a polite, but jaded, audience. Beside Lavinia were many of the other leaders of the NYHADA — Sonny Kaufmann, Leo Maxwell, and Gerald Townsend among them. Bored, Claire allowed her eyes to wander through the audience and discovered Waldo Picker standing a few yards away with Doris Ogilvy and Barney Digglewelder. It suddenly occurred to Claire that between the NYHADA members and the other dealers and collectors in the audience, almost everyone they'd ever dealt with in the art world was there.

Lavinia finished talking and the crowd began to disperse. Claire had just put out her arm to stop Charles and remind him that no one had mentioned the Mary Brightman Foundation, when she suddenly felt every eye in the vicinity turn to look at something behind her. Claire turned around and her knees went weak....

"...and there he was, walking up the aisle towards her," Lewis said. "Oh, you should have seen him! He looked fabulous. He was in a Christian Dior tux, remember, Bernie? We helped him pick it out. And, listen to this — the crowd parted for him. I swear, it parted as if he were some young god."

"He did look awfully good," Bernard said. "Not at all like someone who'd just had his life destroyed."

"Well, of course he didn't look that way. He was in love! Real love, this time; not some cheap version of it. Anyway, he was holding out a red rose to Claire. I was afraid she'd faint before he could give it to her.

"And then he leaned over, and whispered in her ear...." I watched the dreamy look on Lewis' face. "And her face just lit up. I've never seen anyone look so happy in all my life."

"It was an incredible moment, I'll give you that," said Bernard.

"And that was that. Happily ever after. They've never been apart since."

"You forgot the best part," Bernard interrupted. "The crowd."

"Oh!" Lewis jumped up and down with excitement. "Oh, I forgot the crowd. You'll never guess what happened... guess what happened when Trevor kissed Claire!"

I shrugged, bemused and, I'll admit, quite eager to hear.

"The crowd applauded! All these people who hated Trevor's guts actually applauded for them. It was unbelievable!"

"That's the power of true love," Bernard said with authority. "One can't help but get caught up in it."

"It was certainly an epiphany. I've seen anger and jealousy and greed move the New York art world, but that's the only time I've ever seen it overwhelmed by true love."

"So what happened to them after that? I assume they got married," I asked.

"Oh, of course. I was Maid of Honor," Lewis said proudly.

"But where are they now?"

Just then, the doorbell rang. Lewis rushed to open the door.

And suddenly, Trevor Whitney was shaking my hand. He was everything they'd said he was: handsome, charming, boyish grin. He seemed genuinely delighted to meet me, and I felt very strange. It seemed rude to know his entire life story, while he was only just meeting me.

Bernard was quick to fill him in. "We've been telling the young man the story of your gallery," he said.

"I hope you got to the good part," Trevor laughed. "The now."

"We were just about there. How's Claire?"

"She's wonderful. She stayed home with the baby this trip, but she sends her love."

"And how's the Gallery?"

I opened my eyes wide. Trevor Whitney had another gallery?

"Well, except for the part about going up before Congress every year for funding, it's great."

Lewis saw my confusion. "Trevor is head of American Paintings at the National Gallery of Art, in Washington, D.C," he explained.

"Wow," I said. "Is that what Charles meant about finding your true calling?" I asked.

"Boy, you two really gave him the long version of the story, didn't you?" Trevor said. "But to answer your question, yes. It turns out I'm a curator at heart, not a salesman."

"But how did you? I mean, here you were all broken-hearted and all, with this huge lawsuit, and having to sell your business...." I was worried

I'd crossed a line, but Bernard motioned for us all to take a seat around the coffee table, and passed around a tray of wine and cheese. Once settled on the couch, Trevor leaned forward and spoke earnestly to me:

"Well, the broken-hearted part only lasted about forty-eight hours. That's when I realized I didn't miss Louise at all. In fact, instead I missed Claire — I started missing her the moment she walked out the door. That's where these guys come in. If it hadn't been for them, and for Charles, I don't know if I would have believed that Claire missed me too. I couldn't imagine what she'd want with someone who'd made such a spectacle of himself over another woman."

Lewis and Bernard smiled knowingly.

"And as for the business, I don't know. It hadn't been the same since Charles left. I really didn't like being there without him. I never felt ready. Now that I can look back on the whole thing objectively I realize that was Louise's biggest appeal. She wanted to run things for me, and I wanted someone to.

"So it wasn't as hard watching the gallery go down the drain as I thought it would be. And that turned out to be the clue I needed. I had to be in the wrong part of the field if I could watch my own business disintegrate, and not really feel all that bad about it. That's when I knew I was a curator at heart."

"And a damn good one!" Lewis said.

"Hear! Hear!" Bernard raised his glass of wine and toasted Trevor.

"Did you ever get your money back from Louise?" I ventured to ask.

"I dropped the lawsuit after a few years."

I know I looked surprised, because he continued, "I was never going to beat her. It was an emotional and financial drain. The day Claire and I decided to drop it, a huge weight was lifted from our shoulders."

"It was a wise decision," Bernard concurred. "It took a wise man to do it."

Trevor went on. "Claire, in case you're wondering, works for the Art in Embassies program — she arranges loans to American embassies around the world. And we have a son! Six months old this week."

"And your dog," Lewis said. "Don't forget him! They have a Labrador retriever named Digglewelder," he explained for my benefit.

"And Charles? Where's he?"

I felt a sadness descend on the room. "Charles passed away last summer," Trevor said. "My son is named for him: Charles MacKenzie Whitney."

Bernard poured more wine and we all drank to Charles.

"So there you have it," Lewis said. "The rise and fall of The Trevor Whitney Gallery. From beginning to end, an amazing tale. Now that you've heard it, do you still think you want to go into the art business?"

"I don't know," I said. "You've certainly given me a lot to think about."

Then I shyly added, "I was also considering becoming a writer...."

"Oh!" Lewis said. "Do we have a story for you...!"

But that will have to wait for another day.

Author's Note

A short primer on Who's Who in
The Rise and Fall of the Trevor Whitney Gallery

Most of the characters that appear in *The Rise and Fall of the Trevor Whitney Gallery* are fictional, but real people do appear in the story:

Raymond and Margaret Horowitz were well-known art collectors.

Alex Acevedo, Ted Cooper, Stuart Feld, Howard Godel, Jim Hill, Carl Jorgensen, M.P. Naud, Glenn Peck, Ira Spanierman, Hollis Taggart, Bill Vose and Terry Vose are (or were) actual art dealers. Keny Galleries still deals in American art, as does Kraushaar Galleries, but only by appointment.

Ted Stebbins is a significant American art historian, and the premier expert on Martin Johnson Heade. John Rewald was one of the world's experts on Cezanne. Ira Glackens was the son of the artist William Glackens. Adelyn Breeskin was renowned for her work on the Mary Cassatt catalogue raisonné.

Institutions that are mentioned are all real, with the notable exception of Topper's. But the description of Topper's fits many small auction houses in the 1980s.

With one exception all artists are real, and the works described are indicative of actual paintings by these artists. The only fictional artist in the novel is the Connecticut Impressionist, Gerald O'Connor.

Acknowledgements

I wrote the first draft of this novel back in the late 1990s. I was suffering from a bad case of missing my job at Hollis Taggart Galleries, as Hollis has moved the gallery to New York City. I thought I could cure my depression by incorporating a lot of my gallery experiences into a comic novel – what actually happened is that I had terrible writer's block. I found it hard to polish the story to a point I was comfortable publishing it. I put it aside for many years, but luckily, time gave me the distance I needed.

However, one of my earliest readers was Thomas Hoving, former director of the Metropolitan Museum of Art. We exchanged commentary on our works-in-progress; his was on the heiress Doris Duke. He was very helpful, and I wish I'd published this sooner so my thank-you would not be posthumous.

Additional readers were Don and Gail Lively (Don is author of the novel *The Social Event*), and my aunt-by-marriage Ruth Wheeler, whose critical comments were absolutely spot on. The flaws that remain in this book are my fault entirely.

Johanna Skibsrud read the first chapters at a writer's conference and showed me how to overcome a sticky technical problem with the manuscript. I can't thank her enough for her help.

I am grateful to Julie Rustad for her layout of the text; Donna Snyder for her gorgeous cover design; and the artist Jesse Waugh for making that design possible. Even though I hate having my photograph taken, I want to thank Bob Snyder for making it painless.

Finally, I want to thank my husband David, for his ongoing patience with my pursuit of projects that make me happy.

15854487R00175

Made in the USA
Middletown, DE
24 November 2014